ZOMBIE ZOOLOGY

Severed Press

A Severed Press Book
Published by arrangement with the authors

www.severedpress.com

http://davelange.carbonmade.com/

The stories in this anthology are works of fiction. Names, characters, places and incidents are the product of the author's imagination, or are used fictitiously. Any resemblance to actual events, locales or persons,
living or dead, is purely coincidental.

ISBN: 978-0-9806065-9-1

CONTENTS

MONKEY HOUSE

Tim Curran

In late March the army swept through the city putting the living dead back in their graves for a final time. They came with heavy machine guns and .50 caliber sniper rifles, flamethrowers and 7.62mm miniguns mounted on armored personnel carriers which cut the dead down in waves. Mop-up units followed, eliminating the stragglers, and searching house to house for those infected by the Necros-3 virus. The infected were put down; the uninfected were given injections of the experimental antiviral Tetrolysine-B, which inhibited the replication of the virus within the host body.

Necros-3 had put two-thirds of the world's population into the graveyard within seven weeks and nearly all of the dead had returned searching for flesh to eat.

Tetrolysine-B, which had been developed for use against HIV, proved to be the magic bullet. The pestilence was stopped dead in its tracks, but by that time the cities of men were cemeteries.

***

Emma Gillis was ready to leave.

She'd watched her neighbors sicken, die, then return to feed. No one would ever know how many people they slaughtered and Emma tried not to think about it. Gus had fortified their house, turned it into a bunker with gunports, a generator, and a razorwire perimeter that was carefully mined.

The dead had never breached it.

But now the war was over and Emma had had her fill. For the past three months she'd been stuck inside their trim crackerbox house cum-bunker and she was ready to leave.

"It's just time, Gus," she told her husband who watched the streets through one of the gunports, hungry for enemy activity. "Time to move on."

"I'm not leaving," he said.

Good God. He was still in the Marines. He was living some prepubescent G.I. Joe fantasy. The zombies had been vanquished. There was no reason to hole up like this any longer.

When the Army came—and Gus, of course, had warned them off until they trained antitank guns on the house—they said that out at Fort Kendrix there were hundreds of people—men, women, children, all rebuilding their lives. They had fresh meat, fresh fruit and vegetables. Water that didn't taste like metal. And medical care. Real medical care. And the guy in charge, Captain McFree—handsome, dashing really, with his black commando beret and pencil-thin Errol Flynn mustache—said they had electricity and a DVD library.

"Gus, be realistic. It's time to go."

He looked around, pale and paunchy and unshaven, camouflage pants worn and dingy. "I'm not leaving all this. I'm not leaving my home."

Emma sighed. "Home? This isn't a home, Gus, it's a barracks."

There were cases of MREs fighting for space amongst iron crates of ammo and jugs of purified water, the guns and first aid supplies. A survivalist's wet dream, but hardly a home. The walls were tacked with maps, the windows boarded over and criss-crossed by duct tape so they would not shatter. The brass coat tree by the front door was hanging with gas masks and waterproof ponchos and web belts.

Home?

Sure *Good Housekeeping* as seen by *Soldier of Fortune.*

Emma didn't bother arguing. She packed up what she could in a suitcase and a nylon duffel and dumped them before the front door. "I'm going now, Gus. The war is over. Time to put away our guns and pick up shovels and saws and rebuild."

"Fuck that," he said.

Emma felt sad. She had watched a good man degenerate into this paranoid wreck. And as he degenerated, so had her love and respect for him.

She threw the bolts on the door and stepped out onto the porch. Gus slammed it immediately behind her, fumbling locks into place.

"You'll come back," he said.

No, I won't.

"You're making a big mistake, Emma," he told her through the mail slot, using that calm and authoritative voice of his that had been so effective in the past for everything from getting money to getting into her pants. "You won't make it out there. You'll be dead before you reach the Army base. You're not a survivor type and you know it."

She didn't argue with that. "The survivalist thing is you, Gus, it's not me."

"You just don't have what it takes, Emma."

"You're right," she said, leaving the bunker.

If surviving means becoming a rat afraid to leave its den, then I'll be a victim, Gus, and be happier for it.

It was wonderful to be outside again.

The clean-up crews had hauled away the bodies and remains and for the first time in weeks and months the breeze did not smell like it had been blown from a morgue drawer. It was coming from the south and she could smell sweet odors of spring growth, lilacs and honeysuckle. The sun on her pale face was warm, inviting.

She moved down the walk and stopped beneath one of the big oaks out there.

Thank God, thank God, thank G—

The wind shifted direction and soured right away, bringing with it a vile odor of bacterial decay and corpse gas. It was not old, but recent, very moist and organic like rotten meat shoved in her face.

Emma froze up.

She dropped first one bag, then another.

The sun was behind her.

Her shadow was cast over the walk as was that of the oak. She could see its twisting limbs and threading branches...and in them, hunched-over shadows like gargoyles.

Something hit her in the back of the head.

She heard a high chittering sound.

She turned and something hit her in the face.

Something wet and crawling and stinking.

She clawed it away with her fingers...bloody meat that crawled with bloated white grave maggots. Gagging, she tossed it away, the stink of putrescence putting her down to her knees.

With a gore-streaked face she stared up into tree.

She saw a grinning, demonic visage staring down at her. It snapped its teeth at her.

Emma screamed.

***

Through the gunport slit in the living room wall, Gus watched his wife walk away. She was making a big mistake and he was angry that she did not know it. Angry that a bright woman like that did not realize the fix they were in.

And after all he had done for her.

Betrayal.

He didn't need the Army.

He didn't need Fort Kendrix.

Everything he needed was here in the shelter where he was master and commander.

He lit a cigarette. It was stale but he didn't even notice anymore. He blew smoke out through his nose and scratched at the beard stubble at his chin. Automatically, obsessively, his hands roamed his body making a quick inventory: .45 Smith in the holster—check; K-Bar fighting knife in its sheath—check; extra magazine for the—

What the hell is she doing?

Emma had stopped on the walk. She had dropped her bags. She made a gagging sound, digging something from the back of her head that was tangled in her hair.

Gus grabbed his M-14 sniper rifle and ran to the door.

He threw the bolts and was outside in seconds.

Emma was sitting there on her ass as something dropped out of the tree not five feet from her.

The thing saw him, hissed, and charged in his direction.

Gus just stood there, shocked at what he was seeing.

A baboon.

A *baboon* of all crazy fucked-up things: thick-bodied, compact, covered in a down of shaggy brown fur. Its eyes were shining a tarnished silver like dirty nickels, huge jaws wide open, fangs bared. It left a trail of slime in its wake.

There were huge ulcers eaten through its skin.

You could see its bones.

Zombie.

When it was ten feet away, Gus automatically shouldered the M-14 and fired just as he'd been taught at Parris Island so many years before. He popped the ape in the left eye socket with a .308 round that blew its skull apart in a spray of gray-pink mucilage and sent its corpse tumbling through the grass. A jelly of worms bubbled from its ruined head.

"EMMA!" he called out. "EMMA! RUN!"

Two more baboons dropped from the trees, then a third and a fourth. There had to be a dozen more up in the branches. They were shrieking and growling, absolutely enraged.

Gus heard a scratching, scrambling sound and turned. Two more were up on the roof. They were leaping from the trees onto the top of the house.

He dropped one that was five feet from him, pivoted, and knocked another off the roof that had only one arm.

He could hear Emma screaming.

The baboons were coming at him from every direction.

They looked like the remains of test animals that had been slit and bisected, poked and peeled and drained: grave-waste. He saw one lacking legs that swung its torso forward with its arms and others that seemed to be missing sections of flesh as if they'd been biopsied.

They all had huge holes eaten through them, bones jutting from their maggoty hides, meatflies rising from them in clouds. Baboon faces were skinned to pink meat or gray muscle, some were chewed to the bone by carrion beetles.

He dropped two more and then there was no room to shoot as they nipped at him, raking his legs with sharp skeletal fingers. He used his rifle like a club, swinging it, bashing in heads and smashing snarling faces to pulp until he was sprayed with rancid gouts of brown and red fluids.

The baboons circled him, gnashing their teeth.

He waited, the M-14 encrusted with gore and dripping a foul corpse slime.

He knew Emma was out there, but he didn't dare look for her. He couldn't even hear her now over the wailing and yipping sounds of the baboons.

Claws laid his knees open as he smashed the butt of the gun into a baboon face that was threaded with a filigree of mildew.

Then one of them bit into his ankle.

Another vaulted forward and bit into his left hand.

Crying out, he dropped the rifle, pulling the Smith .45 with his good hand.

A big baboon with a reddish-brown pelt and a pronounced white mane charged in at him, scattering the others. It had no eyes and the blind black beetles swarming in the sockets did not count. The flesh was eaten away from its face revealing a cadaverous simian skull, jaws yawned wide to expose gleaming yellow upper and lower canines, each long and sharp enough to lay an artery open.

But what Gus noticed mostly was that its belly and chest had been completely shaven, a Y-shaped incision running from crotch to shoulders.

Autopsied. This thing had been autopsied.

Bleeding and hurting, Gus faced off with it while the others formed a tight and cohesive circle around them.

"EMMA!" he shouted. "GODDAMMIT, EMMA!"

The beast kept snapping its teeth at him, making a shrill staccato whooping noise.

Gus put three bullets into it and all that did was piss it off.

It charged and so did the others. The baboons hit him from every side and he felt himself go down under a sea of maggoty hides.

***

Emma, of course, saw Gus charge out of the house with his rifle, heard him call to her, but she was otherwise occupied.

The baboon in the tree above her was amused.

It was making that weird chittering sound that was chitinous and strident.

Staring up at it, Emma knew instinctively it was a female as were the others in the higher branches. She knew this just as she knew the males had gone after Gus.

Wiping slop from her face, she did not dare move.

The baboon stared at her with glassy, fixed eyes, grinning that toothy clownlike grin that made it look very much like some deranged little pygmy looking for meat to skewer. There was some morbid growth like a grave fungus that consumed most of the left quadrant of if its face and was creeping in on the right. It seemed to be moving.

Emma heard Gus cry out.

She felt his voice slide through her heart like a needle.

He was shooting.

The baboon in the tree showed its teeth, letting out a piercing reverberating cry that was chilling and deranged and sounded very much like wild hysterical laughter.

It threw something at her that splatted on the walk. Meat. Greening meat threaded with corpse worms. It made that laughing sound again when it saw or *sensed* the revulsion coming from Emma. Then it slid its black leathery fingers into a gaping bloodless wound at its belly and pulled out more rotten tissue and threw it at her.

Emma ducked away.

The baboon laughed.

Her heart thumping in her chest, she stared at the horror with its greasy, nappy fur and yellow fangs and carrion eyes. Her terror pleased it, made it grin with an idiotic bestial splendor. And this more than anything not only disgusted her, it offended her.

It pissed her off.

It made Emma get to her feet, the ancestral apex predator within rising for battle.

The baboon in the tree stopped cackling now, it made a threatening almost territorial barking that got all the other females worked up. They all started screeching and baring their fangs, beating and scratching at themselves, pulling out clods of fur and clots of necrotic tissue, throwing it like monkeys throwing shit.

Emma was pelted with the stuff.

She heard shooting, fighting, the constant screeching of the baboons.

"GUS!"

She backed away from the tree, made to turn and go to Gus and a baboon leaped through the air and tackled her, knocking her into the grass where she rolled to a stop, coming up not ten feet from the razorwire enclosure and its perimeter mines.

The baboon that attacked her came forward on all fours.

Its face was a mass of scar tissue and suturing that was bursting open from internal pressure, oyster-gray pus and pink jelly pushing its way through. The skin around its mouth had been surgically incised in an oval patch, leaving its speckled gums and fearsome teeth on display.

Emma knew she was no match physically for the beast, living or undead.

There was only one thing she could do.

As the beast roared and leaped on her, she waited it for it. And when it landed, planning on sinking its fangs in her throat, she kicked out and caught it in the chest, flipping it end over end through the air. It hit the ground on its rump, bounced, and came down inches from the razorwire.

There was a resounding explosion as it triggered a mine.

The creature was vaporized into a rain of blood and meat.

Clots of it fell over Emma and she madly pawed it free, stringy pink meat caught in her hair.

She started to scream.

***

When the baboons hit him from all sides, Gus lost his .45.

He hit the ground and they converged on him.

He never even had time to pull his knife before dozens of sets of teeth bit into him, tearing out chunks of meat and severing arteries and splintering bone.

He screamed.

He thrashed.

But it was no good.

There were too many ravenous baboons seizing him by then and he was laid open in too many places.

A large male went right for his soft white throat and found it, seizing it and tearing it open. Gus's scream became a moist gagging sound as those teeth sank into his neck, sank in deep.

The baboon shook him by the throat like a terrier with a rat, blood spraying in every direction, its muzzle stained red right up to the eyes.

The sound of Gus's vertebrae snapping was loud as a pistol shot and still the beast kept at it, driven mad by the blood and the taste of meat and maybe something more.

When it finally dropped him, Gus's throat was literally torn right out, nothing but a ragged bloody mass of sheared muscle and ligament in its place, a few fingers of shattered white vertebrae showing through.

The others kept biting into him.

Chewing on him.

Pulling strips of skin free, tearing out quilts of muscle and sinewy tendon. A set of teeth pulped his genitals, two sets of blood-dripping jaws yanked out his bowels and pulled them in opposite directions, fighting and snapping over them as others ripped out organs in meaty masses and hopped off with their prizes.

As Gus lost consciousness, he could feel them pulling him apart and gnawing on his internals.

The male that had torn out his throat, sank its long ensanguined fangs into his skull, piercing it, impaling his brain.

It kept at it, applying pressure, until his skull was crushed and its mouth was filled with gushing blood and tissue.

***

Still pawing rancid bits of baboon from her, Emma crawled off.

She got to her feet, stumbling.

As she got clear of the tree, a male baboon came loping in her direction on all fours. It had a silver-gray mane and trailing beard that was fouled with dried blood and curdled marrow.

The females screeched with excitement.

Emma stared at the dead thing coming at her.

The fur and flesh at its back had been peeled to pink muscle, as had the flesh of its face. Jutting from the surrounding orbits, it eyes were like eggs translucent with fresh blood.

It snarled at her.

Emma tensed.

It attacked.

She aimed kicks at it, trying to keep it off her so she could at least make the door. Her defense worked at first—her boots struck it in the mouth, alongside the head, driving it back. The baboon was enraged, spinning in circles, growling and barking while froths of pink saliva rained from its mouth like vomit.

Emma knew how powerful the creature must be, resurrected or not. If it got hold of her, she'd never escape its iron embrace or those gleaming fangs.

She had to keep it off her as she backed towards Gus and the door.

Several females had dropped from the trees and were yipping with delight. They went down on their bellies and offered their hairless, callused, maggot-infested asses to the male.

Emma kept kicking at the baboon.

But it began to second-guess her, began to anticipate her moves. It ducked away from a flurry of kicks and came right in, seizing her right calf in its bloody jaws and putting her down.

Emma was screaming and fighting, kicking out with her left leg while pain threaded through her right in white-hot waves. The baboon wasn't just biting her...it was *chewing,* tearing, rending. Her pantleg was shredded, her calf muscle punctured...as those teeth came down again and again and again.

Screaming, crying, Emma engaged in one last act of defiance.

Instead of trying to kick out, she brought her leg closer to her body, dragging the baboon in with it by its teeth. And by that point it had worked a great flap of meat from her calf and it dangled from the baboon's jaws like a bloody cutlet.

Her mind erupting with blades of white-hot pain, Emma took hold of the animal by the ears and yanked down with everything she had, snapping its head sideways. The agony of its teeth being ripped so crudely from her leg was enough to make black dots parade before her eyes, but something in her—some primal, instinctive barbarism—fought on.

Acting instinctively, she jammed her thumb into its eye.

She buried it right to the second knuckle and the eye went to a soft mush like a rotten grape.

The baboon went wild.

It whimpered and howled, contorting and thrashing, tossing her onto her back and then jumping up on top of her, growling and snapping its jaws.

An inky fluid dripped from the ruined eye and the stench was like rotting fish.

It held her down and she could feel its blunt, stubby penis pressing against her thigh.

On the ground as she was with the beast hovering above her, she could see beneath its shaggy beard. There was a perfectly symmetrical bald patch circling its throat.

She could see the gray flesh beneath and it had been sutured...as if the creature's head had been removed, then sewn back on.

With a scream she grabbed hold of its shaggy head mainly to keep those teeth from her. The baboon was extremely powerful, but she held on. Beneath the dirty fur, the flesh of its skull was spongy and soft. Emma dug her fingers in and they slid through meat and tissue soft with putrid decay.

The baboon cried out.

It trembled spasmodically.

She dug her fingers in deeper, a black sap running down her arms. Her fingertips scraped along the inside of its skull and she squeezed gray matter to mush in her fists, yanking out clods of brain that spurted between her fingers like oatmeal. Gouts of black blood fell into her face.

The baboon dropped away, whining and hissing, the top of its cranium crushed to a globby slush. It crawled in gyrating circles on the ground, leaving a slime trail of mucus behind it, its entire body contorting madly as if every neuron was misfiring and they probably were.

Emma pulled herself away, wet and stinking with the male's drainage.

The females hopped and shrieked and beat the ground with their skeletal fists. One of them had no eyes. In fact, the sockets had been stitched closed.

What the hell is this about?

Bloody, agonized, bile spewing from her mouth, Emma dragged herself towards the doorway. Blood, oh so much blood everywhere. In the grass. On the concrete. Sprayed in loops up the siding.

She looked for Gus.

But he was gone.

Piecemeal, he had been dragged off.

***

Emma crab-crawled up the steps onto the porch, trying to work the doorknob with blood-greased fingers.

The Primate Research Center, that's what this was about.

It stood just outside the city. Animal rights activists were always protesting there. In the chaos of Necros-3, it had been forgotten. But the virus must have jumped species and reanimated these...*things.*

She could hear the yelping and barking of the baboons.

They were coming for her.

Her fingers kept slipping on the knob. She pulled herself to her knees, her damaged calf sending fingers of agony right up into her chest.

She got the door open.

She pushed herself through, leaving a trail of blood behind her that marked her progress from the yard to the porch.

The baboons yammered hungrily behind her.

A gun. There were many and she had to get one.

She slammed the door shut behind her, throwing her weight against it and the baboons hit it from the other side, one after the other. She jerked with each impact, her back against the door, trying to keep it closed with all her strength as her fingers reached shaking for the lock.

The door burst in and she went down.

She scrambled across the floor, nearly blacking out from the pain. She could smell the hot green wave of putrefaction the zombie baboons pushed before them. It was moist and heady and repulsive.

Gnarled fingers scraped against her ankle.

The sound of them squealing and piping was cacophonous echoing through the house.

One of them grabbed her ankle and she kicked back, freeing herself.

More fingers raked her leg.

She grabbed wildly at the rifles in the case and they fell over like dominoes from her searching fingers, a .12 gauge pump coming free, bouncing off her head, and then she had it just as the baboons seized her and began to drag her back to their voracious waiting mouths.

She swung around, the shotgun in her hands.

There were three baboons gripping her legs.

One of them was missing the top of its head, just a gleaming dome of exposed skull that was punctured with holes as if from primitive trepanning. Another's face was pitted from probes and cutting.

They opened their mouths, howling, diving in for the attack and Emma fired, pumped, and fired again.

.12 gauge buckshot at such close range is devastating.

The faces of two of the baboons literally splashed off the skulls beneath, the third riddled with blazing holes that lit its fur on fire. It hobbled away, smoldering.

Emma cut another in half and blew the head off yet another.

The one that was cut in half did not die.

It pulled itself forward, its legs and lower torso forgotten, dragging ribbons of flesh behind it. It made a sharp hissing sound in its throat, its eyes lit with a crimson blaze, mouth open and ready to bite.

"C'mon," Emma panted, tears running down her face. "COME AND GET IT! C'MON, YOU MOTHERFUCKER! LET ME SEE WHAT YOU'RE MADE OF!"

The baboon, of course, needed no prompting.

It slithered forward and Emma blew its head to confetti. That stopped the others. With all that meat sprayed around, they lost interest in her. They began to feed on the remains of the others, slurping up blood and nibbling on brains and gnawing on bloody bones.

They were occupied.

Now was the time.

She looked down at her torn calf, the blood pooling around her leg. God, she needed to do something with it before she got woozy from the loss of blood.

The baboons were ignoring her.

Very slowly, she moved towards the first aid kit near the gun rack. Calmly, she took hold of the plastic box, opened it. With shaking fingers she wrapped her calf and then taped it up.

Now and again, a baboon would look up at her with a blood-stained muzzle and snarl, but that was about it.

Next, she had to get out of there.

But Gus, oh Jesus, what about Gus?

No time for that. She shut her mind down. Went cold. Emotionless. This was survival now, it was war to the teeth. The easiest way out would be through the dining room and into the kitchen. If she could make that, then she could slip out the back door and hobble to the garage. The keys to it and the Jeep inside were in her pocket. Then a quick spin out to Fort Kendrix.

Swallowing, she began to move towards the archway that led into the dining room.

She scooted herself along on her ass.

The baboons still ignored her.

She got to the archway, took one long last look at them to satisfy herself that they had no interest in her. They didn't. There was plenty to eat and that seemed to be the primary motivating force: hunger.

The shortwave radio was in the dining room.

But she didn't dare send a message.

That would mean speaking at full volume.

She pushed herself into the kitchen. Almost there, by God, almost there.

Into the kitchen.

More of a warehouse now with stacked crates of MREs and purified water and flares and radio parts and—

Emma heard a scuttling noise.

A ragged breathing.

She swung around on her ass and an especially large ape was waiting there, puffing out its chest.

A Mandrill.

It was a large shaggy baboon-like beast with an olive pelt, its nose a brilliant bright red, vivid blue spokes fanning out over the cheeks. Emma found herself staring into its eyes. They were a cool, watery scarlet. The top of its head had been cut away, its brain exposed.

She did not want to think about what they had been doing to this animal just like she did not want to think about what it could do to her.

It stepped forward on all fours with an almost swaggering, arrogant stride.

It bared its teeth, yawned its mouth wide and let loose with a high-pitched screaming noise that was instantly answered by a dozen other screeching voices.

Emma licked her lips.

There was a gaping hole in the beast's midsection and you could see right through it, nothing but bones in there. It couldn't possibly be moving, but it was.

She brought up the shotgun.

The Mandrill charged.

She pulled the trigger.

Nothing.

She worked the pump, pulled the trigger again, and in the back of her mind a small voice counted off the five rounds she had already fired.

Five.

Here's what you need to remember about the Mossberg 500, she could hear Gus saying to her. *It has a five-round magazine so if you're going to use it, carry a back-up. It's a devastating weapon, Emma, but not if you run out of shells.*

Shit.

Hopelessly, Emma tried firing it again.

Then the Mandrill was on her.

It took hold of her with great strength, pushing her down and bouncing her head off the floor to take the fight out of her. Then it grabbed her by the hair and swung her like a Barbie doll, smashing her into cupboards, the kitchen table, a green metal cartridge box.

By then she was barely conscious.

The Mandrill seemed pleased.

For alive or dead, it liked its females submissive.

Emma looked up with bleary eyes.

She saw the Mandrill's bright red penis squirt cold urine into her face, marking her. It gushed over her cheeks, burning her eyes, bringing an acidic, nauseating taste to her lips.

The stench more than anything made her pass out.

The Mandrill, grunting happily, dragged her from the room.

***

When Emma came to she was in the cellar.

She was sore, threaded with pain, but the worst part—

What the hell?

She was face-down and something was humping her from behind. Her first instinct was to fight, to scramble free. But she was still dressed so it wasn't like she was being penetrated.

Wait.

There were several baboons gathered around, but keeping a respectful distance and that was because the Mandrill had her. Mandrills were not baboons, she knew, just close relatives, the largest species of monkey in the world and this one was the alpha male of a pack of baboons.

It was humping her to show its dominance.

It screeched.

The baboons yelped and barked.

The females were busy picking maggots from each other's hides and eating them.

Emma knew she could not panic.

A lot depended on what she did now.

She cast an eye around. There was the woodstove, the carefully stacked kindling. The axe. Double-bladed, kept very sharp by Gus. You could slit paper with it.

The Mandrill leaped off her.

The baboons growled at him and he snarled and shrieked, driving them off and up the stairs. He sat back on his haunches. There were insects crawling in his fur. He studied the females.

His harem.

And Emma was now one of them.

She gathered her strength. It was now or never. She had to reach that axe and if she couldn't, that would be it.

The Mandrill was turned away from her.

Now!

Emma dove to her knees, ignoring the pain it brought. She scrambled over to the woodpile. The females made baying sounds. The Mandrill roared and came after her.

Emma grabbed the axe in both hands and swung it with everything she had and such was her state of rage and violation and hate, it was considerable.

The Mandrill came at her with jaws wide.

The axe came down.

It cleaved the beast's exposed brain, slicing deep into the cerebral fissure which separated the right and left hemispheres. The reaction was not one of pain. The Mandrill hopped this way and that, clutching at the axe buried in its head. It shook. It convulsed. It vomited out a bubbling black jelly and then it pitched forward, dead once again.

Two of the females ran.

A third turned to fight.

It dove at Emma.

She never had time to get the axe free from the Mandrill. The female knocked her down and then they were fighting and scratching. The female was powerful, but Emma fought with a manic frenzy. She clambered onto the female's back and did the only thing she could do to win.

She bit into its throat.

Bit deep until blood that was black and tarry filled her mouth.

The female squealed and shook, but finally went down under Emma's weight.

Covered in baboon blood and drainage, she pulled the axe free and chopped off the female's head.

Then she sank to her knees and vomited.

***

When she came upstairs, she braced for battle.

Her shirt and pants were blackened with baboon discharges, blood encrusted over her face and neck. Tissue caught in her nails.

The other baboons did not attack.

They kept well away from her.

They grunted and yelped and whined when she passed them.

Emma stank of decay and corpse slime and baboon piss, maybe this is what drove them back. Maybe they smelled the Mandrill on her and the blood of their own kind.

Outside, there was a rumbling.

Gunfire.

The Army had returned.

Thank God.

Emma moved past the cowering zombie baboons and to the door, still clutching the gore-streaked axe in one hand. She was limping, beaten, scratched, bitten and bruised, but still standing.

You're not a survivor type and you know it.

You just don't have what it takes, Emma.

The hell I don't, she thought as she stepped out onto the porch and saw the dead baboons laying everywhere, several dangling from tree limbs.

She waved the axe to the soldiers in the APC.

One of them put the minigun on her.

"Wait..." Emma started to say.

The minigun could lay down something like 6000 rounds per minute and in the scant few seconds between when Emma was first hit to when she pitched over dead, some two hundreds chewed through her, literally pulverizing her.

What hit the ground were fragments.

Emma was gone.

"Never seen a zombie with an axe before," the soldier on the minigun said.

Captain McFree laughed. "You see it all in this business, son."

The APC rolled up the streets as the mop-up continued.

THE YULE CAT

Ted Wenskus

Jon Haroldsson shifted behind the blind he had built in the narrow alleyway, quietly rested the rifle on a garbage bin lid, and took a long draw of Scotch from his flask. It was cold in Vík that night, even for Iceland. Though Mýrdalsjökull was kilometers away, the arid glacial wind wended its way down through the village like fingers reaching for the sea.

The Scotch warmed him though. Enough so that the cold wouldn't slow his reflexes when the Jólakötturinn came again.

Four hours of daylight had departed quickly, as it always did on Christmas Eve. Now it was moonless and casket black and even the northern lights were absent in the sky.

Perfect. Jon slid his black fleece gloves on again and pocketed the flask in his jacket. He wouldn't be seen.

At least, he eyed down the rifle's night scope to the snowy street again, not until it was too late.

***

Yesterday, twenty-three years.

"But I don't want to wear it!" Arna stomped her foot as punctuation.

"It's polite." Mother continued to dust briskly. Company would be over in just a few hours, relatives from all over the place like Reykjavík and even Akureyri. Vík was a very small village, but it was their family's turn to host this Christmas.

Arna's blond ponytail whipped around as she followed Mother to a pair of wooden picture frames. "The wool she uses scratches my neck!"

Young Jon put a few more ornaments on the tree--figurines of Grýla and Leppalúði, troll parents of the 13 Yule Lads that came down from the mountains every Christmas to give presents if you were good or raw potatoes if you were bad. "Jólakötturinn will do more than scratch you," he said.

She spun to him. "Shut up!"

"One gulp and you'll be gone."

"You!" Arna took off a slipper and threw it at him. He ducked and it hit the tree, knocking tinsel and some low-hanging ornaments to the carpet.

"Jon, Arna, enough." Mother stopped dusting. Never a good sign. "Give your sister her slipper back and, Arna, please go help clean the kitchen."

Jon held out the brown fuzzy slipper and Arna clomped over and snatched it from him. "There's no such thing," she said in a loud mumble. "It's a stupid tradition."

Of course Mother heard that. "Well, if you won't wear the sweater my sister knitted for you, after all the time she spent on it, then I don't need to get you new boots until after Christmas."

"But--"

They continued, and Jon turned back to the tree. He picked up one of the fallen ornaments--Grýla and

Leppalúði's cat, its back arched high, its expression dark, hungry. Jon had his new socks on. That's what kept you safe from the Jólakötturinn. Something new to wear on Christmas Eve. The Yule Cat wouldn't eat him.

***

Jon strained to see the face of his watch. Just after 11:30 p.m. He had been sitting in the alley for hours. But it would come. Especially now the festivities had died down. Unlike New York, where he'd spent the latter half of his childhood, Christmas Eve was very busy with food, presents. Christmas Day, by contrast, was a time to relax, go to church, take walks and--

The scene came rushing back. Even stronger now he was in Vík for the first time since it happened. Bile burned his throat.

He ran his glove across his beard, dislodging ice beads that had formed there from his breath. What if it didn't come? What if all his planning was for nothing? The chasing of a nightmare.

No. He knew what he'd seen. And it was burned into his memory.

***

Christmas Eve went well. Over a dozen aunts, uncles and cousins came to the house and they had a big dinner of smoked lamb and salt potatoes. Afterwards--and only after the dishes were done, which made Young Jon and Arna squirm--it was time for presents.

Jon got a new pair of skis and the latest Batman graphic novel, sent by relatives in America. Arna got a new set of paint brushes, ice skates, and a fancy blank journal.

Their aunt asked about Arna's sweater, but Arna had "spilled" some skyr on it before she could put it on, so it needed to be washed before it could be worn again. Mother was not happy. Arna claimed it was an accident and their aunt took the news well.

The family sat and talked for a few hours more, and then Jon and Arna were sent to bed, already having stayed up well past their normal time.

It was the middle of the night when Arna's poking woke him up.

"What?"

"There's a cat on the roof!" Arna whispered.

"So?" The house was cold and he wasn't getting out of his warm bed.

"It's freezing out there and it's Christmas! We can't leave it out there." She stopped. "Listen!"

Jon actually did hear it. A quiet, pitiful "marou" from somewhere close by.

"It'll be fine." He buried his head under his blankets. "Someone just forgot to let him in. He'll be there in the morning."

"There aren't any cats nearby, because if there were I would know." Arna loved pets, and in a small village, she made it her business to know them all. "Besides, sometimes cats aren't good at getting off things they climb up."

"Fine." He rolled over, but stayed under the covers. So tired. "You explain it to everyone why we have a cat in our room tomorrow morning."

"I will." Then, suddenly, "Jon!"

Jon peeked out. "What?"

Arna stood frozen in her pajamas and socks, staring out the window. Her mouth was open just a bit and she stayed like that for a moment. Then she scurried up and placed her face right on the cold glass and craned left and right as if trying to see something.

"What?" Jon said again.

"I saw a big shadow."

Jon paused. "It was probably a neighbor. Old Erik, maybe."

"Maybe." Her tone indicated she didn't believe that at all. Then they heard the "marou" of the cat again and she unfroze. "Will you help me?"

Jon mumbled. "I'll be with you in a minute."

"Okay. I think it's on the far roof. I'll go open the window down the hall and see."

"Don't wake everyone."

Arna padded off.

Jon closed his eyes for a moment. Just a moment, it seemed. Then he was being jostled again. This time, it turned out to be Mother.

The room was still dark. The sun wouldn't come up until 11:00 a.m. But even so, he guessed it was still early.

"Did one of you leave the hallway window open?"

He yawned. "Arna."

Mother noticed his sister's rumpled, empty bed the same time he did. "Where is your sister?"

"I don't know. She was going to let some cat in from the cold."

Mother frowned. "A cat?"

Jon nodded.

Her face steeled. "Stay here."

Jon rubbed his eyes, ran a hand through his matted hair. Now that he thought of it, he wondered where Arna was, too. Probably has the poor cat trapped somewhere, putting ribbons or bells on it.

He heard Mother calling out for Arna downstairs and then the door outside opened and she called out there, too. She must have walked a distance from the house, as the sound of her walking on the snow grew quieter.

And then the screaming started.

He didn't know what the noise was at first. It didn't sound like any person could make it. He jumped up to the bedroom window and couldn't see anything, so he ran down the hallway to the window that Arna had left open getting the cat. It was closed now, but he could see...

What he saw didn't make sense. The road was all snowy except where it was dark and blotchy. It looked like splashes and for some reason his chest tightened. There was something in the center of the biggest splash and Mother was on her knees next to it. Howling.

Then he noticed there were other smaller somethings in the splashes all around the center. Some of them were stringy like long sausage.

All Jon could do was shake then. Relatives were coming out of their rooms and asking him what was going on. He heard them but the words didn't make sense for some reason. It was just more sound mixed with Mother's screams as she pawed on her knees at the dark snow. He just pointed and they all rushed away.

He watched as more and more people came out and crowded the street and soon he couldn't see the stained snow or Mother anymore. Then he could move and the first thing he did was look away.

But his glance lowered to the roof in front of him, just outside the window. He saw that all of the snow had been disturbed, as if something big had crawled around on it. Did Arna go out and then fall?

He leaned forward and then saw the dark stains in the roof snow. There was a big splotch and then a drizzle trailed off to--

He felt the moan come up his throat. There was a small foot in a yellow sock. Left in the snow with nothing else around it.

And there was something else.

On the edge of the stained snow was the massive imprint of a paw.

***

Everything that followed was a blur. Maybe shock stopped details from imprinting. Maybe he chose not to remember. All he really knew was that the next days were dark and empty and unreal.

The town decided that the attack must have come from a polar bear, although no one had ever heard of an attack like this. Bears weren't native to Iceland, but they occasionally came to shore on ice floes. It had to be, since no big predators normally lived on the island. Of course, the hunting parties they sent out couldn't find one, even after scouring the frozen hills for weeks.

Jon could have told them that. In fact, he did.

"It was the Jólakötturinn!" he insisted. He knew. The print was from a huge cat, a cat he'd heard. That Arna had heard.

"Jon, no." Mother's face was red and wet all the time now.

"It was! Arna heard it and she wasn't wearing her new sweater to keep her safe and it was right here!"

She grabbed him and held him to her chest. "There's no such thing." Then, tighter, with a barely contained whisper. "There's no such thing."

That was the last time she held him. Within the week, Mother began to shut everyone out.

Their family--Mother's sister, especially--helped as best they could. But then Mother began insisting that Jon should live in America with their distant cousins. They tried to talk her out of it, that she and Jon should stay together. But she wouldn't be reasoned with. Even under the medication they started to give her.

When asked why, all she said was: "He'll be safe there. He'll be safe."

Eventually, everyone realized it was probably for the best. Once they agreed, she stopped talking altogether.

Jon went to New York without even hearing her say goodbye.

For the next twenty-two years, she never let him visit. Or the doctors didn't.

Then last year, she died.

***

The wind stilled and the stars hung over the alleyway like daggers.

Jon could feel the cold of the rifle through his gloves as he brushed a touch of snow from the barrel. So many years he'd waited for this. And the U.S. had been a good place to learn how to shoot.

Yes, it would come. It had to eat.

The legend dated back centuries. The news articles, not as far, but the pattern was there if you looked for it. Dead children. Christmas Eve. Almost every year, and explained away as some accident or tragedy. All in this desolate area of the country.

When he inherited Mother's old house--his old house--it all fell into place. He moved back to Iceland. And now he was going to end it. He owed Arna that much.

God, Arna.

He heard a sound.

Something crunching up the ice-crusted snow of the street. Footfalls, soft--too soft for boots. Too many feet.

Then, a plaintive, muffled, all-too-innocent "marou."

Jon swallowed hard and put his eye to the night scope just as the Jólakötturinn prowled into view.

Black lynx ears pointed upward from sharp feline features and impossibly long black whiskers. Its lanky body must have been over four meters from what Jon could see, its tail long and barbed, swishing back and forth in a slow, languorous pattern. From mammoth, powerful paws, bone-white claws curved into the snow with each pace.

Jon's gasp was only the slightest whisper, but it must have been enough for the Jólakötturinn to hear.

It stopped instantly and glared down the alley.

Terror.

Almost half of the Jólakötturinn's skull was devoid of flesh and fur, pale bone exposed in the icy air. Its ribcage was ruined and gaping, scraps of skin clinging to yellow tendons and blackened tissue. Decayed muscle flexed and slid where swaths of hair were missing. But its eyes, jaundiced and narrow, glowed with unearthly animation and bale.

Jon's finger trembled on the trigger. But he had to stop.

The girl dangling by the arm from the creature's mouth must have been about six years old. Unconscious, thank God, as her arm seemed to have dislocated by the way it twisted loosely in the Jólakötturinn's jaw. She was blond. Thin. Bloodied.

Just like...

"You son of a bitch," Jon said and shot.

The bullet slammed into the Jólakötturinn's haunch, spinning the creature's back end to the ground. Just as quick, it righted itself, faced Jon and growled a dark rumble, no longer a luring cry, that shook the very walls of the alley. The girl now hung limp between Jon and the cat. No chance of another shot without hitting her.

Fetid stench rolled up the alley as the Jólakötturinn's dead eyes bore into Jon's. Its claws flexed and pawed and a string of steaming drool cascaded down over the girl's hair.

Suddenly, a shaft of light appeared on the street. A door opening. Someone had heard the shot.

The Jólakötturinn spun and disappeared in an instant.

"Dammit!" Jon knocked over the garbage bin and several boxes in front of him as he scrambled out of the alley.

He slipped in the snow as he spun toward the creature, loping toward the hills with huge bounds. It was so fast.

But it didn't drop the girl.

He couldn't let it get away. God, he couldn't. He knelt, sighted, breathed a prayer, and fired again.

This time the shot hit the Jólakötturinn from behind, knocking it forward into a skid. It lay there for a moment as Jon ran forward. But just as impossible as before, the massive cat righted itself, hissed, picked up something from the ground in its mouth and bounded away.

Jon reached to where the creature had been and found that it hadn't taken the girl. Not all of her, at least.

Amazingly, the girl was still alive. Still unconscious and now shaking with shock, her body trying to come to terms with the fact that her right arm had been ripped off.

He whipped off his scarf and tied it tightly around the jagged stump, and it quickly saturated with blood. There was yelling behind him, so he knew she'd have help. He couldn't wait.

He raced the hundred meters to the small garage outside his house and flung the door open. There would be more snow further up the steep hills but for now the ATV would work.

Jon stopped himself. Think. What happens when you catch up with that thing? It wasn't like bullets seemed to hurt it. Hell, was that thing even alive? How do you kill something like that?

His fury focused him. He'd figure something out. Maybe it just needed to be shot in the right place. But he'd better have some other options.

He grabbed an assortment of equipment and stuffed it all into the storage box on the ATV. The rifle he strapped near the front of the vehicle for easy access. He pocketed a headlamp and some batteries as well. He might have to look for tracks on foot.

Behind him, from the street, he heard his name being called. No doubt the townsfolk wanted to know about the girl, about what happened. Jon shook his head. The monster's tracks should be explanation enough, as they should have been years ago, and there was nothing more he could do here.

He had an idea of where the Jólakötturinn was headed.

He grabbed his helmet, fired up the ATV and aimed for the jagged black hills.

***

The creature's tracks were easy enough to follow for the first few kilometers. Its prints were huge holes in the snow, and while they sometimes climbed out of sight up to bare-rock ridges, they still paralleled the snowed-in sheep path that Jon was able to keep the ATV on.

The tracks eventually wandered down to the path again and even slowed to a trot. Jon steered around an outcrop of black lava rock and braked suddenly. He saw why the creature had slowed.

The small arm had been stripped to bone, the snow around it spotted red in the ATV's headlight. Flesh remained on some of the fingers, but that was all that was left.

Jon killed the engine and the headlight, took out the rifle and flipped up the helmet's face shield. He scanned the area through the night scope. No movement that he could see. But the terrain was getting rougher now and it was much easier for something like that to hide. Still, he had kept up with it for the time being.

And it was still headed north, like he thought it would.

He secured the rifle again, started the ATV, and accelerated.

Another hour or so had passed when he came upon the river. It was frozen, but he doubted it could hold the weight of the vehicle. The creature's tracks led right up to the bank and then disappeared. It wasn't too wide--perhaps four meters--but the cat could have leapt it easily.

He turned off the headlights and was again reaching for the rifle when the weight slammed into him.

He and the ATV crashed over and the Jólakötturinn with them. The creature landed and slid on the snow, losing contact with Jon just long enough for him to scramble away. The cat regained its footing and sprang again, but Jon ducked behind the overturned ATV as it sailed over. But it was so fast. Before it had even landed, it spun and raked Jon's head with a massive claw. The screeching of sharp bone on helmet drowned all other sound.

The blow knocked Jon down again, but he rolled with it and scrambled again to put the ATV between him and the creature. The monster hissed when it saw that Jon was still on his feet and the stench from the creature's skeletal mouth made him gag. Jon steadied himself and shot a look to his left where the rifle had been tossed a couple meters away.

The Jólakötturinn saw where Jon's gaze went and growled. It kept its yellow eyes locked on Jon but began edging toward the firearm.

Jon saw bright orange plastic on the snow near the ATV's storage box which had snapped open on impact. The flare gun he'd packed. He had to do it fast. In a single motion, he bent, grabbed it with one hand, aimed, and fired directly at the black, rotted creature.

His angle was bad and the flare hit the slope in front of the cat, igniting in a flash and bathing the river bank in red glow.

The cat shrieked and stumbled over itself as it sprinted away, huge leaps pounding across the snow, over the river, and toward the far bank.

Jon quickly pawed the ground for another flare. He found one, chambered it, and shot again, this time in a high arc over the Jólakötturinn's retreating form. The glowing fire lit even more of the river area in red.

The cat ran faster, leapt over the crest of the bank and disappeared.

Jon turned to the ATV and righted it, but saw that its wheels were askew. Useless. It didn't matter. He had to cross the river on foot anyway. He took off his helmet and saw that just the one clawing had virtually destroyed its usefulness. He dropped it and rummaged through the spilled contents of the storage box. He found four more flares and pocketed them. Then, he retrieved the rifle, slung it over his shoulder, and set after the creature.

The flares had missed completely. They weren't even close enough for the monster to be burned, and yet it ran. In fear.

Light. It couldn't stand light.

He had it now.

Jon slid across the river ice, scrambled up the snowy incline and looked through the night scope. The creature wasn't even trying to hide now as it headed straight for the mountain of ice that loomed over the barren landscape.

It was headed where he'd expected. Toward the one place where nothing lived--where nothing could live--and where no one would ever hunt for it amid the icy wasteland.

Toward the glacier Mýrdalsjökull and the ice-bound volcano Katla.

***

Millennia of ice and lava had ravaged the earth bordering the glacier, leaving deep gouges in the rock and peaks too steep to climb. Jon slowly navigated around the obstacles, losing valuable time route-finding when it was obvious that the Jólakötturinn had leapt crevasses that he simply couldn't. Worse, snowfall had covered rivers and chasms and he had to be careful with each step lest he punch through and plummet.

When he stepped onto the first pitch of glacier ice, he slipped. He wished he'd brought crampons. But there had been so many other things to think of. So many.

Arna.

He pushed forward and crept up Mýrdalsjökull.

Hours passed and still the creature's tracks hadn't stopped. His one consolation was that this section of the glacier was wide and sloped, so there was nowhere for him to be ambushed.

It gave him time to think.

It made sense now why the Jólakötturinn only appeared around Christmas Eve. It was the darkest time of the year, which gave it the most time to hunt. And with 20 hours of darkness and twilight, it could leave and return to its lair in a day. As it had for centuries.

Jon shivered.

He didn't know what the creature was. Or how it could exist. Or keep existing. It defied nature.

But Jon knew it was past its time to die.

He looked at the gray sky. Christmas dawn. He was so tired. But he'd come this far. And maybe the weak daylight would prevent the creature from attacking him. Maybe.

He jumped over another small crack in the ice and heard a whoosh behind him. He looked back and found that he had just crossed an immense snow-covered crevasse. His small jump had collapsed the snow, leaving behind a gaping canyon.

No way back. That was okay, though. The brown-grey cinder cone of Katla was dead ahead.

And the monstrous paw prints led right into a dark slit at its base.

Plumes of sulfur steam snaked upward from the darkness as Jon approached. He looked around for other cracks, but could see none. If he was lucky, this was the only entrance.

He sidled up close to the darkness and then his chest screamed with agony. He fell head-first backward down the slope, the hard ice scraping his scalp raw as he slid.

The creature's screech was unmistakable and he knew it was over.

But nothing came.

Jon propped himself up and saw blood all around him. He touched his head and his hand came back red. Then he saw the four slashes across his chest, through his shredded jacket and fleece. What they revealed almost made him faint. But he couldn't stop now.

He pounded his fist on the ground and stood up with a scream and advanced again.

He might have seen yellow eyes peering out from the darkness, but Jon wasn't looking that closely. He simply took out the flare gun and fired it at the mouth of the cave. It bounced and didn't go inside, but it sat burning red at the entrance.

The Jólakötturinn yowled as before and he briefly saw its filthy, rotted shape before it disappeared downward.

Jon reloaded the gun and moved closer until he could see into the fissure. And he gasped.

There were maybe nine of them. Huge, decayed, and lynx-eared, hate shooting from their feline eyes, hissing and attacking the lava rock ground in front of them in feints, their black noise making the very ice of the glacier quiver.

Jon shook. It was terror embodied.

And it had to end.

Arna.

He raised the flare gun, aimed into the lair, and fired.

The collective wail was unearthly. The pack of Jólakötturinn leapt and snarled as they tried to escape to the dark recesses of the den. But only one narrow lava tube led away from the brilliant pools of red light and two beasts jammed into the tunnel, unable to move any further, blocking those behind them. The ones in the back began tearing at bodies of the two and snarls turned to shrieks as the rotted creatures ripped apart their kin.

Jon covered his ears, rooted by the sight. The volume of the brutality cascaded over him, through him.

The glacier began to shake.

Jon stumbled from the entrance, fell back, and skidded sideways down the steep pitch as overhanging ice fell onto snow and created a torrent of white that crashed over the mouth of the fissure.

The ice underneath Jon trembled with the impact and echoed down the slope of Mýrdalsjökull. Then, all was silent.

Jon scrambled up the icy incline to look. The entrance was gone. He could hear the Jólakötturinn no more.

The scratches on his chest were dripping blood faster now. His roll down the pitch must have opened them more. He held the shredded clothes together over the wounds. Direct pressure. That's what he needed. And some rest. Just a little.

The ground swayed as he staggered down to a level shelf and sat. No, that was him. Not the actual ground moving. He'd lost more blood than he thought, maybe. Just a little rest. It was all good. There would be no more deaths. Maybe. At least for a long time. And it was all good. All good. He would be okay. The Jólakötturinn hadn't eaten him.

After all, he had his new socks on.

LUCY

Eric Dimbleby

"How you doin' these days with that there collection of yours, old friend?" Lou questioned his most faithful customer, running his hands along the glass case of weapons that he pridefully displayed. The flickering overhead lighting of his shop pulsed, trying to decide if it would stay strong or burn out. Lou's Guns was as important to the community as was the gas station and the super market. It was hunting season, and business was booming, especially given the unseasonably fat wallets of the out-of-towners looking to drop the hurt upon an unsuspecting deer, moose, pheasant, or bear.

Brock reached into the breast pocket of his bright orange vest, fiddling around with eyes affixed on the hearty display of modern warfare that hung from giant silver hooks behind Lou. Brock considered Lou a more crucial component to his livelihood than he did his family physician, mailman, mechanic, and wife combined. Lou had the best stuff around, and there was no need for price-hunting since Lou was the cheapest game in Maine.

Retrieving from his pocket a can of Skoal, he spun the lid and fingered out a clump of tobacco, shoving it deep into his festering brown cheek. "Well," he said, working the tobacco around in his ruddy fat mandibles, "Got me quite the stockpile going, Lou. You know, the usual necessities. Winchester 1894. Sweet little 44 Magnum Colt Anaconda. Marlin M444- three of them, in fact. I call 'em Snap, Crackle, and Pop, but you already know that, ya' silly old bastard." He chuckled, swishing around the brown tobacco spittle in his mouth, rubbing his thick warm gut with his hands. Something about the moments leading up to a hunt made Brock wiggle in anticipation, as though he was ready to shed his skin and he couldn't tear it away from his bones fast enough- every nerve atwitter with the prospect of taking down a dumber beast than himself. "You know the rest. Beretta. The classic Browning, but I keep that one on reserve under my bed for them there Jews and Mexicans and A-rabs. Thank you, Barack *Hussein* Obama, you son of a gun socialist." His mind drifted and he shook his head from side to side, utterly embarrassed for the current state of his beloved, yet handout-happy, nation. Continuing, he listed, "Winchester M94 and M70. Pretty ol' 527 Varmint. MK-250 crossbow. All that other shit. Trip mines. Grenades. Got everything but an angry monkey in my basement, unless you count my old lady. Sometimes when she vacuums she looks like a chimp just escaped from the zoo. I scratch my pits and make all kinds of jungles noises but she don't have a sense of humor, that's what I always tell her. No sense of humor." He stared straight ahead, retrieved a hankie from his back pocket, and blew a soft phlegmy discharge into it.

Lou threw his head back in laughter, "Well, you best put your foot up her ass, boy. Look there- no better fix to that there issue, right there, over there." Pausing, trying not to ponder over his previous statement for how many times had used the word "there", he (like his friend Brock) blew his own nose into a tattered handkerchief, rubbing it along his gray mustache to sop up the stray mucus. Coughing deeply, he posed the question that had been digging at his mind since Brock walked through the door of Lou's Guns, tinkling the little bell that dangled from the doorway, "You lose some weight there, pal? Looking nice and trim. What you down to?"

"Three hundred *ell-bees*," Brock replied, rubbing at his bloated stomach, spitting his first deposit of chew into his stainless steel traveling mug. "Feelin' damn fine, Lou. Think I just had my rebirth, you know what I mean? Like I don't need no damn gun, I'll punch a doe in her face if she gets too close. You hear me knockin'?"

Nodding in agreement that yes, he heard him knocking, Lou questioned Brock's method for dropping the pounds, something that he sought to do himself, "How you do it? The old crow keeps shoving broccoli down my mouth but it don't make a lick of difference if you ask me. Might as well just eat steak all the same, I say."

"No carbs, Lou. Beef and chicken and fish. No more broccoli in my house, fellah. I don't even let no damn potatoes through that door, and I don't mind potatoes much, especially them crinkle cut fries. Me and the old lady are eatin' like kings, I tell ya'. Grilled steaks with a side of creamed chicken. You can't beat that with a stick. Can I get an amen?" He unloaded into his mug again, winking his left eye simultaneously. Lou mouthed, without sound, the word "amen", as dictated to by Brock.

"It's what God intended, Slim," Lou replied, proud that he had caused Brock's face to light up at his new nickname. *Slim.* Brock liked the sound of that, and it made him feel like more of a man. Lou added, "If God wanted us to eat all them there vegetables and fruits then we woulda' all been born like them vegetarian faggots, right? Makes me sick to think of it. I never saw a goddamned carrot that looked or tasted better than a big ol' greasy hamburger. We can't deny that, partner. We gotta fight the good fight for meat eaters all over the world."

Brock nodded. "Damn straight. Hippie sons of bitches are ruining this pretty country, one whining bitch-fest at a time. The lesbians, the faggots, and the Mexicans-they're all in it for the long run. Not on my watch, old buddy." He snickered to himself and Lou did the same. "So what you got to show me today?" Brock asked, changing the subject to the more important matter at hand, that being his insatiable desire for hoarding fire arms away in his unfinished basement. "I got four hundred bucks burnin' a hole in my pocket and my bills ain't due for two more weeks. Set me up with something bloody and loud, Lou." He banged his fist on the counter, as though demanding something that he felt entitled to.

Lou studied Brock's face. He squinted his eyes in thought, pulling back from his glistening counter of vengeance on display, scuttling away to the back room, advising as he backpedaled, "You wait right there, Brock. *You wait right there, muchacho.*"

While Lou was in the supply rooms of his shop, fishing through his scatterbrained inventory of legitimate and black market wares alike, Brock studied the tough-as-balls array of lock n' stock beauty that adorned the walls, as though God himself had ejaculated his most vicious load of vengeance for all to see. Every gun was an extension of the unsentimental man, a piece of modern warfare that made every glorious soldiering morning through the woods feel like Viet-fuckin'-Nam all over again. Brock had not been in Vietnam, but he often told people otherwise.

Some argued that it was unsportsmanlike conduct to shoot a helpless animal with a gun. *Those people are assholes,* thought Brock. Man invented a gun with his ingenuity and brain, and so the collective species of homosapiens have earned an assumed right to wield its absorbed knowledge in the devastation of any dumber beast that dared step in his path. Sure, a bow and arrow kill was more satisfying, but so much more arduous than any modern man had time for. The sport of wielding a firearm was thrilling enough in and of itself, and with it came fewer hurdles. Sport was sport. Why use a putter when you can use a driver?

"What if a deer kicked in your door one day and walked around your house with a shotgun in his hooves, killing your wife and children right before your eyes?" a bleeding heart twenty-something broad (with pungent lice-ridden hair) had asked of Brock one day at a coffee shop outside of his usual stomping grounds, eying his camouflage and orange garb with utter disdain. Brock had snapped into action and responded to the little dirt-pie, grabbing hold of a handful of itchy sweater, "I don't have any goddamned rug rats, Swiss Miss. And that deer can blast my wife in the mouth if he wants to, no matter to me. All animals deserve what I'm givin' them, and if they don't see me comin', then boo-hoo on their birthday. You like meat? I bet you do. You just eat that tofu crap because Jack Kerouac told you to, right? Fucking faggots. So how about I take you 'round back and show you... oh, high and mighty hippie cretin... what meat tastes like?" Brock had proceeded to nestle his testes and penis in his hands, grinning at the girl wildly, unable to control the shifty machinations of his eyeballs. At this, the dirty little hippie sponge had spat in his face and he could have strangled her for that, but resisted the urge, given that they were airing their grievances in a very public place, while several other hippie scumbags looked on.

Lou sauntered from the back of his store, a long black majestic beauty in his hands. It seemed to reverberate good vibes into Brock's time-worn heart as he made his initial eye contact with it. His reaction was nothing less than love at first sight, if one was to be so moronic as to subscribe to the thought of love in the first place. "*Who is this sweet little lady you got here*?" he asked of Lou, already naming the yet-to-be-purchased object of his affection inside of his mental gun-ventory.

Lucy. He would call her Lucy, named after a middle school teacher named Lucy Patterson, or Mrs. Patterson as she was meant to be called when he wasn't tugging his chowdah-maker in bed at night, whom Brock had been madly in love with during his most turbulent pubescent years. "I don't even recognize the brand," he garbled between choked breaths, running his fetid tongue along the roof of his mouth, the volume of his passion for the weapon overtaking his derelict words. Reaching out towards Lou (who only offered a satisfied grin, the silly bastard), he ran his hand along the long black barrel. The smell of fresh gun oil filled his nostrils and he could feel his salivary glands filling with ripe juices. Lou goaded him on, pushing the gun out further from his chest, allowing Brock to wallow in its glory from any visual and physical angle he so chose. *You can take her to bed if you'd like,* Lou considered saying, but bit back his cockamamie tongue, knowing that the final transaction was not yet complete. "Where did you get this? It's perfect. Nothing fancy. Just.... *perfect*." When he touched the black stock of the thing, he felt a buzz pass through his body, sending rivulets of strange emotions pouring through every molecular manifestation of his body. And for a fleeting moment in time, which brought him great embarrassment, he felt himself go hard in his Hanes.

Snorting in delight, Lou replied, "Picked this little heart breaker up at one of them *Injun* trading posts way up north, in the Isle. The Knick Knack Paddy Whack tribe or somethin' all jumbled up like that. Had some dishy lookin' bows and arrows and homemade bear traps, but this was all I had eyes for. It was the only dang gun they had, and they had no reckonin' of where they snatched her up from. Were right glad to be rid of the thing, seemed to me. Practically gave it away. Fuckin' Injuns, don't know how to wipe their own asses without the white man's help, maybe that's why we sent them packin'. I just hope they don't come askin' for the gun back, you know?" At this, Lou emitted a hearty laugh towards his Indian-giving jab, but Brock could barely hear the words spilling from his friend's vile mouth. For all he could process was the mere sight of Lucy. She was giving off pheromones and Brock was game.

"This looks homemade, Lou. I don' see any markings. No brand, no serial number- nothing. She's a peach. I'm going to call her Lucy I think," Brock stated without blinking his rigid eyeballs, presuming that the gun practically already belonged to him, for all intents and purposes. He could not tear his eyes away from her for fear that they would melt in brokenhearted devastation. It was simply not feasible for Lucy to become "the one that got away".

Laughing aloud, Lou replied, "Well, it sounds like you've already made up your mind, but I never said I would sell it to you, maybe I was just showin' off my new trick. I like the way it feels myself, so you'd have to make a bold offer to tear this puppy away from me. You feel that buzz when you touch it?"

"Yes, I do." He glared at Lou, thinking to himself how many pieces he would shred the man in to, were he to dare not sell the weapon. *I'll kill him for that gun*, Brock whispered inside of his mind's eye, biting his lip to hold back from saying his thoughts for all (that being Lou... *the only other person in the shop- nice and quiet*, as Brock has reasoned to himself in a dark nook at the back of his conscious being) to hear. "I feel her buzzing and I want her. I want her right this moment."

"She's pretty."

Brock scanned his mental bank account for crannies of cash and upcoming bills that he could postpone. He pulled up each cushion in his financial life, rifling through the crumbs and dander for loose change. There was no other option.

"How much? How much do you want for it?" Brock asked, repeating his proposition instantaneously with desperation, sounding like a junkie on the verge of dying from a lack of proper fix.

"Everything you got, buster. I've even got just the right bullets for you, free of charge." Lou winked. "Now empty that there wallet and let's talk business, whaddyasay?"

***

Five thousand two hundred and twenty seven dollars, mostly borrowed from his brain-dead (quite literally, by means of a skiing accident) sister Tammy's bank account, and an hour plus five minutes later, Brock was propped in his tree stand on the eastern edge of Polly Garrett's serene hunting property. Polly's husband had died a few years earlier and rented out buckets of time on her land to local hunters, with hopes that she may supplement the hefty mortgage along with her meager widow's income. Mr. Garrett had likewise been an avid hunting enthusiast, and so the business seemed fitting, and in the spirit of his eternal memory. And Brock was her most loyal and regular customer, from the first day she hung her sign by the road, "HUNTERS WELCOME-FREE BREAKFAST WITH HUNTING FEE!". He had bagged seven deer in the previous three years since Mr.

Garrett's death. The property withheld a perfect conglomerate of subtle openings and trees, hiding spots and clearings, hills and moats and everything in between. A deer could wander through without any legitimate suspicions. And without warning, it would turn a corner to see Brock grinning with a loaded rifle, ready to split Bambi's fuzzy head open like a pomegranate.

And on this day, he brought along a new hunting partner.

Lucy. Sweet Lucy. Lucy in the sky with diamonds. I love Lucy.

He sniffed her solid chamber and studded fore-stock, wondering what he had done to become so blessed by Lucy's presence (besides forking over an unbelievable bundle of cash). She continued to hum and buzz and crackle like AM radio static in his hands, whispering sexy words into the attuned nerve endings of his fingers and hands, seizing his very spirit with a brand of ecstasy he had long missed from so many years of a useless and failed marriage to his repulsive slippers-on-Monday mate. Maybe if Lucy became jealous enough, he reasoned, she could set right his marital situation with one swift tug on her bouncy little trigger. "You smell like roses, Lucy. Aren't you just about as sweet as you can be?" he asked of his weapon, unknowing of the odd words that came from his lips. He could feel her at every pressure point and juncture of his sizzling electric bloated body.

Placing her on the cold icy grates of his prime-pickin' tree stand, Brock withdrew a can of beer from his camouflage mini-cooler, cracking the tab open and slurping a grateful glug of frigid amber beer. "Just refueling, Lucy. I won't forget about you so quick, so don't go off getting' jealous." He nodded his head towards Lucy, who he imagined was scowling at him for his neglect and faltering compassion. "Keep your eyes peeled. We need to bring home a big ol' fat Bambi or the cross-eyed sow will never lemme hear the end of it." Lucy nodded, forgiving him instantly. Maybe he could train her to bring him beers and rub his feet.

Brock leaned forward, laying on his invasive gut with Lucy touching the edge of his elbow, sending shock waves through his mortal being. He peered at the snowy ground with a concrete gaze, sipping his beer quietly so that his prey would not detect him when he pounced upon its soon-to-be corpse.

***

A dozen rattling beer cans later, Brock was cradling Lucy against his chest, motionless like an armless Renaissance statue, only breaking his concentration to urinate his liver-processed light beer from the edge of his ivory castle in the trees. His vision had blurred, but he yearned for a few more suds of Forget It Juice. He grumbled to himself that he should have purchased two twelve packs instead of only one. Brock looked down listlessly at the graveyard of empty beer cans beneath him, circling the tree like stones around a campfire, curious if it had been Lucy who had drank all his beers. "Was that you did that?" he asked of her in broken English, bringing her barrel up to his lips, kissing the cold oily surface in forgiveness. "Can't stay mad at you."

A twig snapped in the distance.

I heard you, thought Brock. *You picked the wrong trail to grandma's house.*

Brock shifted his position, crouching to one knee with Lucy in his hands, worried that the crumpling of his vest and jacket would scare the approaching animal. He accidentally kicked an empty can from the tree stand and it tumbled to the ground to meet its drained brothers,

Brock hoping against all hope that the sound had not given him away. "Smile, you son of a bitch," he recited, his typical mantra when he readied himself to pull his deadly trigger, an ode to one of his favorite films, *Jaws*. "You think God's watchin' from above. But that's just me."

From behind a fallen pine tree emerged a sluggish moose, lumbering forward with calculated steps, its wide hooves crunching the twigs and dead frozen leaves beneath him. A male moose- a bull, antlers and all. It stood, based on Brock's fairest estimate, nearly twelve feet high, from hoof to antlers. It hunched its dopey shoulders forward, dropping its head and sniffing through the snow-covered pine needles, burrowing with its nose for a hidden treasure. Then it pulled its hefty head (perfect for a wall hanging) back up straight, looking left, then right- as though crossing a busy intersection, Brock thought to himself. The moose stepped forward once. Then a second step. Brock had a fair shot at the thing, the only problem being that he had had no permit for a legal bull kill.

Why could it have not been a goddamned deer?

Decisions. Decisions. Decisions.

Every year in Maine, a lottery is held to allow the moose population some sanctity from the drooling fangs of the hunting populace. A prospective applicant is required, in the spring, to submit his personal information to the state of Maine for his or her chance at bloodshed. Then the applicant is required to patiently wait for summer to determine what his eventual fall and winter would allow him. As far as Brock was concerned, it was all a tree-hugging liberal bullshit process seeking to effectively ruin his otherwise pleasant life, save for the old lady who was already managing a fine job in that regard. He had never once in his life won a moose license, and felt as though he may never win. Time was ticking, his blood pressure inflated by one or two points every year, and he wasn't getting any younger- *nobody* was, for that matter. And Lucy simply hummed her throaty incantations, begging him to pull the trigger and end the beast's life where it stood.

A man only technically broke the law when he was caught and Brock would refuse to allow liberal socialist bureaucrats to dictate his existence. If they caught him, it may be well worth the slaps on his wrists, he decided. As long as he could keep his wife's wordy trap shut about the booty he was about to bring home, there would be no further issue with regards to his supposed law-bending. He would dress the monstrous weakling where he lay, taking only what he could haul back to his truck in one or two trips. All the leftovers, he could bury. The widow Garrett's land had hidden gullies and crevices and crags all about, places that allowed for him to do the necessary grunt work without discovery.

He trained Lucy upon the beast, breathing slow as he calculated the distance and wind. Though his target was less than thirty yards away, he hesitated to leave any factors to chance. It may very well have been his last opportunity at a moose, since they were so rare to simply happen across by accident, even with a lottery ticket in hand like a bloody-booted Willy Wonka. "You're mine, big boy."

He applied easy pressure to the trigger and fired.

Mr. Moose dropped like a bag of bowling balls, crying out with three groans and then falling into the abyss of silence, dead forevermore. It began to snow, as if prompted by the gunshot, and Brock was quite sure that he could hear the gentle sounds of snowflakes dripping to Earth, coating his kill like freezer burn.

***

He nudged the massive beast with Lucy's barrel, wanting to be absolutely positive that the thing was indeed deceased. It had an awful odor to it that wafted through his sensitive nose, that which Brock could not discern between the natural smell of a moose (he had only once been so close to an assassinated pile of moose meat) or the smell of its gaping wound. The neck wept rich red blood into the pristine ivory snow, pooling and absorbing into the now quickly growing accumulation of flurries.

The moose had thudded to its right side in its last gasp of existence, his dead eyes still staring straight ahead, wide open. He had received such an overly shocking blow that he could not even shut his big brown eyes before exiting the world for good, and Brock found some form of pleasure in that, that it had faded into blackness while watching him climb down from his tree stand, three quarters of the distance to drunk as a skunk in a Volvo's trunk.

He poked the dead thing a second time, the tip of Lucy firm against the stiffening body, nudging into its expansive motionless rib cage. "This old boy must way fourteen hundred pounds. You done good today, Lucy," he whispered to his newly acquired partner in population control. She did not respond this time, and in fact she had stopped her interminable buzzing altogether. Her essence had faded away as the moose had, absent since the trigger was ignited and their massive furry victim had dropped to the ground. "Lucy?" he asked. Where had Lucy wandered off to? "You must be sleepin'," he concluded. He shook the weapon in his hand, hoping to spark the fervent kinetics of Lucy again, shaking her like a worried parent would shake a blue-faced child that was choking on a strawberry. "Lucy? LUCY?"

Diverting his attention back to the animal, he leaned down close to it, inhaling the aroma of his fresh kill. It was partially repugnant to his senses, but there was a hidden glory inside of it, knowing that he had successfully conquered a wild beast, as was God's will. If those tofu-eating hippie motherfuckers could see Brock now, they might have climbed their favorite tree for a good cry. Praise the Lord. Brock spit a juicy brown wad of Skoal into the snow, intermingling with the reddish patch of Mr. Moose's demise. Brock grinned and leaned back, stretching his aching back. Standing upright again, Brock could not resist the urge to haul back his black polished boot and give his deadened slave a firm kick to the ribs. The crunch of the bones collapsing at his manly beck and call was nearly as satisfying as the foul stench of it. "You sorry sack of shit. Man versus beast, and beast gon' lose every dang time." He leaned back, pointing Lucy towards the sky, and then pulled the trigger.

Nothing.

He had reloaded on his walk over to the moose, and the gun had no safety.

Glaring at his weapon with disgust, he wondered why Lucy had turned into such a frigid heartless bitch. "What did I do to you, whore?"

Lucy's work was complete, and so she had simply checked out, left her keys at the front desk, brought the car around for Brock to load up the suitcases. There was little left to do beyond driving home in silence. Brock tossed Lucy into the snow, spitting at her with his rotting brown spittle, cursing her behavior in his mind. Their relationship had been a beautiful one from the start, but it had both blossomed and come to a burning crash landing over the course of one perfect day.

Mr. Moose moaned and Brock leaped back a step in fright. It turned its exposed eye towards him, studying his attacker with bleary-eyed confusion. The eye had taken on a neon green hue, and it seemed as though something had turned rotten in his eventual dinner and wall-mounting. "There's no way," he gurgled to himself. Reaching down into the side pocket of his pants, he retrieved a holstered Beretta, unsnapping it from the case in one fluid movement, clicking the safety into the *Go Soldier, Go* position. Without any pause as to the process and delivery of his actions, he squeezed the trigger with four consecutive bursts, sending the echo of his secondary weapon bouncing through the wooded glen of the Garrett property. The bullets entered the side of the beast's head, with the fourth bullet piercing the eyeball, sending a splatter of wet pink mucus on to Brock's camouflage pants. "How you like that, you son of a bitch?" he asked of it, offering a final kick to its inflexible neck, chuckling in childish delight.

It lay still for a moment.

Then it jolted back to life for a third go at livelihood.

It started to breathe again, Brock befuddled by the impossible rise and fall of Mr. Moose's chest, heaving in the cold morning air. Brock backed away after snatching Lucy back off the ground (though they were fighting, he didn't dare leave her behind, there was still a reasonable chance that they could reconcile), unable to fathom what was happening to his righteous kill. "You can't be. You can't be alive." He spat on the ground, wanting to relieve the burden of his eyes through his wrinkled itchy mouth. "You can't be alive," he repeated.

As if in response to his statement of disbelief, the moose kicked out his legs, rolling his torso enough to fold his long brown legs beneath him, lying now in the snow like a dog does by the fireplace, his paws beneath his chin and his spine facing God. It groaned in a tremolo of pain, turning its head towards Brock, who was now contemplating whether he should climb back up into his tree stand or head for the Garrett's house, which was less than two hundred yards away. "Stay down, you cocksucker. Stay down. I killed you!" Brock called out, running his hand along a tree behind him, hoping that it would serve to support his wobbling knees.

It craned its impossibly lively neck at him, turning his head in curiosity, once again reminding Brock of a curious dog. The moose was wishing that it could speak to him, to say something pertinent, had it any vocal cords to do so. Perching its two front legs before itself, the moose rose on his haunches, his oozing ocular cavity spitting forth a fresh geyser of membranes and blood vessels as he next dragged his back legs upright behind him. Now fully upright, it stared right through Brock with an unrelenting gaze... at the man who had attempted to take his life only minutes earlier. It groaned low, less like a dog and more like a silly zombie movie that Brock had once been forced into watching by his undignified wife.

Brock looked down at Lucy in his hands, trembling and wet from the snow and spit he had sloshed her with. "What have you done, you bitch?" he asked of the inanimate gun in his mitts, wanting to blame the seemingly infeasible resurrection of his prey on Lucy. "You did this, didn't you? You filthy whore. I thought we had *something special.*" His words ran together with his torrential brain waves of dread, flustered and spinning like tops.

The moose took a lurching step forward, sending Brock back one step in frightful accordance.

When it took off into a steady gallop, directly towards him, Brock turned his back and started off on his own, grunting to himself in trying to convince the less rational half of his brain that *this was no happening- dead is dead and that is that.* He weaved in and out of the lanky trees, turning to see the moose right on his tail, crashing into each tree trunk and limb in stoic repetition, a titanic brain-dead beast without any form of effective coordination or agility. With each crash, it groaned and maneuvered enough to continue on a basic trajectory, that being the soft skull of Brock, his former judge, jury, and executioner. "Stay back!" Brock called into the air, hoping that the revived animal could understand English by means of whatever demon had entered it. Brock quickly gained distance from Mr. Moose's awkward scramble, and that felt reassuring to him. The moose grunted in response, throwing its head back in a howl. "Stay back!" Brock repeated, and it called back, in its own feeble response, with a second howl.

Brock regretted every cheeseburger and fried chicken bucket he had every consumed, gripping at his heaving fatty belly (effectively holding him back from safety) as he trundled though the scattered trees and bushes of the wooded landscape, scanning the hopping horizon before him for the clearing that led to the Garrett house. Once he found the field that led to Garrett's door yard, he was home free, with less than fifty yards remaining by that point. Brock could only hope to keep a growing distance between him and the resurrected mammal that sought to inflict brutal harm upon him. Luckily, Brock informed his racing mind and body, MOOSE DO NOT EAT MEAT. They were the dirty hippie vegetarians of the animal world, and that only served to make Brock ill. They subsisted on pine needles, grass, weeds, twigs, bark, nuts, and roots. This food preference of the supposedly mighty moose displeased Brock, further lowering the moose on his immovable scale of respect. Nothing, in Brock's opinion, was more admirable than a lion eating a dead zebra, and the limp-wristed moose plopped his nansie-pansie ass at the opposite end of that (re)spectrum. The worst damage it would inflict was to trample him, but even that was an ugly possibility, given the sheer difference of mass between he and his pursuer. "Dirty hippie!" Brock shouted over his shoulder, watching the moose barrel into a thin tree, bending the trunk behind its momentum, folding it in half on to the ground as he fought through the next bevy of natural obstacles. It vocalized its growing discontent, scorning Brock with its one good eye.

A dizzy sense of calm had fallen over Brock (for seemingly the first time in his life) as he emerged from the thick woods and in to the clearing that he believed he would never set his eyes upon again. In the distance, he could see the widow Garrett's welcoming home, and he could faintly make out an image of her sitting on the porch, rocking lightly in her chair, a coffee pot and two mugs placed before her on an end table, awaiting his return. She was always so very generous to Brock, even with his bitter words and hatred of dummies big and small, and he could not reach her fast enough, calling out like a siren on a beachhead. "Polly!" he belted out, feeling the stress of his rasping lungs, both of the fleshy sacs on the verge of bursting.

He clambered across the stiff white grass of the open field, encircled by rigid pine trees. The white snow was falling so much harder away from the protective overhead canopy of the trees and branches. He would have guessed that they were at the very beginning of some serious white-out conditions, but returned his mind back to his pursuing zombie maniac, grunting from behind him, the sound of his pounding hooves turning to a thudding- a steady drumbeat on the frozen grass of the field. When it fully cleared the tree line, Brock pivoted enough to see it gaining a new found burst of velocity, trudging with a misdirected erratic vector, most likely from the damage inflicted to the ribcage by Brock's sturdy boot, and he was now pleased with himself for committing that unknowingly proactive act. “Got a little problem with your stride, don't ya'? You winkin' at me or you missin' an eye?” he goaded the undead moose, his voice shaky and wheezy from his laborious sprint towards safety.

His knees started to fail beneath him, feeling as though they would simply snap at any moment, his gut swaying side to side as he reached his hand towards the Garrett house, calling for Polly a second time, but now realizing that his previous image of her sitting on the porch was nothing more than a mirage.

The moose put his head down, the greenish drool drizzling from the edges of his mouth and wet nose. The deviant orange and green harbinger of death was set to die as the moose once (twice!) had, and there was no other conclusion in the cards.

Brock was halfway across the fifty yard clearing of land when he felt the bull moose nudge its antlers into the back of his neck, projectiling him and tumbling his ragdoll-body into the fresh powdery snow. As he lay on his stomach, staring into the bloody snow (had he busted his nose? *Where was that blood coming from?*), he could hear the methodical breathing of the beast behind him, looking him over like a cold dinner before placing it into the microwave. It groaned near his ear, as though it were whispering something to him, much like Lucy had done only a handful of hours earlier. Brock looked to his right, where Lucy lay in the snow, still silent and unwilling to help her master, a sea change in her once gallivanting carefree attitude. “You hippie whore,” Brock managed through choking bloody breaths, now realizing that the bloody one-eyed bastard had pierced one of his lungs with his sharpened antlers. He addressed the moose as well, "You're both a couple of hippie whores."

Mr. Moose wailed in anger, stepping on to Brock's backside with his front hoofs, dancing a silly jig on the soft bony structure beneath him, snapping through ribs and vertebrae like crushing Ritz crackers into buttery bread crumbs. As Brock slipped on his horrified death mask, he could hear the sound of the forest coming back to life, speaking again its eternal words, knowing that it was forever free of his nauseating influence. Though there were many more that followed behind him, a battle had been won, that of a greater war.

The woods and air and creatures breathed in a deep gust of air, then exhaled with relief.

LOSS OF VECTOR

William Wood

Bellamy closed his eyes and counted to ten. The sound of his own breathing inside the bulky, fishbowl helmet was deafening and he was sure he was going to lose the contents of his stomach any second. Or maybe just his mind. Despite of the all the testing and training and even the clean bill of health, mental and physical, from the team of docs on the ground, he was now sure he was unfit for space travel. Not their fault and certainly not his own. Some things you just don't know until you're in the thick of them. And nothing is *thicker* than the infinite vacuum. Knowing all that lay between him and death by explosive decompression was a few inches of metal and insulation would have been enough to send him packing on the ground. But that was almost three hundred miles away—straight down.

We're supposed to be in space, skipper, his copilot and mission specialist, Sam Morales, had pointed out only hours before. Bellamy had made the mistake of expressing his doubts to the gung-ho Air Force major as they crowded around the viewing port of the modified Apollo module. Skylab hung like an injured bug, one wing clipped, in the blackness above the arc of the Earth. The view was beautiful. Too beautiful.

Human eyes were never meant to see this, he'd said.

Hell, skipper. It's 1979, Morales had continued, a grin spreading across his stubbly face. *A century ago we were taming the West and today we're taming space. Now,* this *is what I call Manifest Destiny.*

A bump against his shoulder startled Bellamy and he turned his head inside the helmet. God, how he hated these monkey suits. *How did I ever get into this program, anyway?*

Because you're a damned good pilot, quick on your feet and get the job done, he heard himself answer. At least the brass thought so. After this mission, he was going to retire anyway. Fifty-one years old was no age to begin traipsing to the stars. This was a young man's business.

Bellamy's view was partially blocked by the nontransparent portion of the helmet, but Morales' toothy smile was apparent even through the glare on his visor. The other man pointed at the GO light next to the circular hatch and then at the dogging lever.

Bellamy forced a smile and nodded. They were on a strict radio silence protocol despite the fact all communications were scrambled. An extra precaution deemed necessary by the boys in Washington. Can't have the Russian triangulating even an encrypted signal and figuring out the Americans have a covert manned mission in the sky.

Bellamy swung the dogging handle and felt the pins snap clear. A muted crack and an audible hiss came from all around as the hatch swung in. They were both fully suited up as a precaution. Systems aboard the space station had been remotely activated but no one had been aboard for five years and HQ wasn't prepared to take chances. Bellamy wanted to believe the brass was concerned about their safety, but the truth was, they wanted the package. The science types had discovered over a year before Skylab's orbit was deteriorating far more quickly than could be compensated for from the ground. NASA had pooled their best minds and repurposed unused materials from the abandoned Apollo

Program into a covert sister project, *Artemis*. He and Morales were to stop the loss of vector is possible, and either way, the package was to return home.

Bellamy took a deep breath and pushed himself through the narrow hole into the Airlock Module, tugging along a tethered bag of tools and equipment.

Beams from his helmet-mounted lights stabbed ahead as he drifted down the center of the dark cylinder. Blocks of equipment and other gear jutted from the curved walls, interconnected by runs of conduit and flexible power buses.

Bellamy heard a muffled thump. Using a cabinet protruding from the wall, he spun himself to face Morales who followed a few feet behind. His helmet lights played brightly through the Major's visor causing the other man to squint.

Morales gave an exaggerated nod and shrugged inside his suit. He'd heard it too.

No need speculating, thought Bellamy. In a few minutes they'd be through the final airlock into the OWS, the main body of the station, and they could remove their suits for the duration of their stay.

Grasping the blue airlock handle, Bellamy cycled the lock but didn't swing the lever even though the GO indicator built into the frame showed the pressure on both sides equal.

Another thump came from the other side, from inside the Orbital Workshop. He'd felt the impact through his gloved hands. He twisted to face Morales again who drifted into the wall ungracefully and scrabbled to regain control and orientation. His ever-present smile didn't miss a beat. Everything was one big amusement park ride.

Morales pointed at his left wrist and Bellamy could hear the unspoken words. *We're wasting time, skipper.*

Bellamy took another deep breath and pulled the hatch. White light poured through the opening into the Airlock Module. With a tug against the airlock rim, Bellamy placed his arms at his sides in order to fit through the circular hole. Ideally astronauts would leave spacesuits in the Airlock Module but the brass had spoken again. The suits stay on until the entire station was secure.

Halfway through the hatch, a shadow flashed from his left, something moving fast. He threw his arms up reflexively but too late to stop the wrinkled white tentacle striking his visor with a *crack*. "Shit!"

He waved his arms like a swimmer, attempting to paddle back into the Airlock Module but Morales was pushing him from behind unable to see the commotion, only aware that his flight commander was not making timely progress.

Cartwheeling through the interior of the Workshop, a vast expanse after thirty hours of the cramped confines of *Artemis*, Bellamy managed to snag a rung along the arc of the cylinder wall, stopping his tumble. Turning his body to face the airlock and whatever had attacked him, he saw only Morales floating inside the Workshop a yard to one side of the hatch, turning a valve and re-stowing an insulated hose in a shiny aluminum clip.

Bellamy could hear his pulse roaring in his ears. *What the hell?* A compressed airline? He shook his head slowly and forced his breathing to slow. Probably came lose when they docked. He really was getting to old for this stuff.

Morales pushed himself across the gap between them, his mouth wide in laughter. The sound was more of a cough by the time it reached Bellamy's ears through both of their helmets. Morales made a face of exaggerated terror and mouthed the word *shit*, throwing his hands up in mock surprise before the coughing noise continued.

Bellamy sighed and pulled his tethered tools in, removing a bulky instrument cluster covered in gauges and dials. If someone had told Bellamy the device was the product of a typical over-budget, over-engineered NASA project to build a baby rattle, he'd have believed them.

"Can't wait to hear how you're going to explain breaking radio silence for that one," snickered Morales once their helmets were off.

"Let's just get this done and get out of here."

Suits secured by straps to a bulkhead, they moved through the open hatch to the aft compartment, the crew quarters. The smell of rubber and ozone tickled his nose, unsettling his stomach.

"You don't look so good, skipper."

Bellamy pulled himself into the small compartment, marveling at the sense of disorientation. Nothing can truly prepare one for prolonged weightlessness. The few seconds obtained by freefalling aircraft and submergence in swimming pools, even skydiving, were nothing compared to the sense that something unnatural was shoving your guts up into your throat. He'd studied the prints of the lab and worked in the mock-up enough to have everything memorized down to the placement of individual bolts and rivets, but looking up from his position and seeing the *floor* of the crew compartment as the *ceiling* was unnerving, like the sky was falling.

The space was well-utilized with only enough room for occupants to move around. Future stations would need more openness if man was to ever feel at ease in space—at least Bellamy believed so. Half of the level was partitioned off into smaller compartments, like closets. A tubular shower. A room with a three-pronged table assembly amidst racks and racks of smaller lockers. Another space with three sleeping bags mounted to the walls.

The other half of this level of the station was similarly congested, but with equipment. An electrical distribution panel, a bizarre chair that would put Captain Kirk to shame, an inclined cylinder the size of a 55-gallons drum.

"There," said Bellamy, grabbing a stainless rod protruding from the chair and swinging his feet to touch the floor. He moved to an electrical cabinet, the Experiment Support System, beside the drum and released a latch at its base, allowing the cabinet to swing aside, revealing a smaller cabinet mounted to the bulkhead behind. Unlike the other cabinets and equipment on the station, each bristling with conduit and wiring running to and from them, this object's surface was smooth and white. A silver rim ran all the way across the top and down the sides, two latches on each face, making the cabinet look more like a suitcase than an experiment. Stenciled in small letters between the top latches were four letters. E-PEP.

Extended Preservation Experiment Pod. But the acronym was all that Bellamy knew. The contents were known only by Morales. He *was* the mission specialist, but he probably didn't know either.

Minutes later the package was free and Bellamy hunched against his tethered kit stowing his tools in their slots and sleeves.

Two snaps came from behind like gunfire and he turned to see Morales twisting two more of the eight latches holding the package halves together.

"What are you doing?"

"You don't think I'm going to *not* look inside do you?" His white teeth gleamed.

"Thought you already knew what was in it."

"I do." Two more latches snapped free and the cover pivoted on the last two like hinges. "Still not the same as actually seeing."

Bellamy couldn't immediately see the contents but tensed when Morales gasped. "What?" He touched Morales' shoulder and pushed himself up until he could see over the younger man.

The inside was lined with stainless tubing and small black modules linked by multicolored wires, all surrounding a translucent plastic bag nestled into a rigid copper-colored mesh. In one corner of the box was a yellow can painted with the telltale three-lobed symbol for nuclear radiation.

"Close that thing," snapped Bellamy taking the case's cover floating in the air next to them and thrusting it at Morales. "You trying to kill us or something?"

"Relax, skipper." He reached into the box and released several small catches down the center of the copper mesh. "It's just a battery to power the rest of this contraption. What I want to see is the occupant."

"Occupant?"

Morales pulled the mesh apart exposing the bag within. Two rows of teeth pressed against the inside of the plastic, human by all appearances except for four huge canines. Two milky eyes stared out at them from beneath a heavy brow ridge.

"A frozen chimp?" Bellamy could hardly believe what he was seeing. Why in hell would—

"Not frozen...preserved. His name is Lazy—since he's up here just sleeping the years away, I guess."

A crinkle came from open box, the plastic baggie shifting as it settled without the immobilizing mesh and reinforced cover. They both looked into the face of their evolutionary relative. A small fellow, as near as Bellamy could tell, even for his own species, not that he considered himself an expert on simians. "This is why we're here?"

"This and to—"

A loud clacking erupted from inside case and they both froze, watching as the chimp's jaws opened and closed repeatedly. Two milky eyes twitched and locked onto them.

Morales stepped away from the case pushing Bellamy, still holding onto his shoulders, along with him. The plastic bag expanded like a balloon and ripped down the center. Dust and fibers sprayed from the tear as a spindly arm thrust into the air.

The smell of rotting flowers and formaldehyde washed over Bellamy and he gagged, his own arms extended to stop his spinning motion in the small open section of the room.

A second emaciated arm clawed out of the bag and the chimp squirmed up from the copper mesh. A loose strand in the metal fabric snagged its mangy gray skin, unzipping it and exposing withered brown and black tissues within. It looked at Morales, lips pulling back from its teeth as its mouth gaped. A noise halfway between groan and hiss filled the small compartment.

"Get it back in the box!" shouted Bellamy grabbing the instrument cluster still tied to his waist and wielding it like a club.

Morales took the cover of the package and pushed against the chair with his feet, launching himself at the hissing simian.

Bellamy shoved off the compartment ceiling, struggling to see but the other man's back combined with the large white cover of the E-PEP completely blocked his view of the action. Rapid impacts came from behind the cover as Morales swung the panel like a shield, trying to prevent the ape from completely freeing itself from its hi-tech coffin.

Bellamy collided with Morales and top edge of the cover struck something with a hollow *thunk.* Tiny limbs pirouetted over the cover and Bellamy twisted, narrowly avoiding the clasping fingers as the ape thrashed by. The tiny fingers found purchase on Morales' pants leg and in a flash the ape had latched on with all four limbs and sunk its teeth into the specialist's leg.

Morales screamed. Bright red blood sprayed around the chimp's lips as it ripped a mouthful free and bit into his thigh a second time.

Bellamy flailed, finding a toehold and pushing himself at the fray. His high-tech club struck the ape as he flew by but his momentum was all wrong and he struck the animal with only a fraction of the force he'd intended. The animal lost its grip and spun away, fingers clawing at the air and head tilted back, hissing at them.

Blood flowed from Morales' thigh like a faucet. A cloud of tiny red spheres expanded into the room, globules joining and rippling in mid-air as they collided with one another.

Bellamy could see Morales was in shock. The injured man's face was ashen and his eyes glazed over. His breathing was coming in spasmodic jerks.

Damn! Bellamy looked toward the room the ape had disappeared into. No sign. Probably having trouble orienting just like they were, he thought. He took Morales by the shirt collar and threw him in slow motion toward the hatch leading into the laboratory level and back toward *Artemis.*

First things first. He had to stop the bleeding and to do that they needed to get out of this compartment and seal that thing inside.

Morales bounced against the padded section of ceiling near the hatch as Bellamy swung between handholds close behind. He pushed at Morales, moving him into the hatch as the man's blood misted and pooled in the air around them, beading on his hands and face like water droplets.

"Stop fighting me!" He held a rung with one hand and shoved the specialist with the other but Morales looked at him, his face limp and his eyes unfocused.

"Mars," said Morales.

Bellamy stopped. "What?"

"We need this to get to Mars."

Bellamy clamped his eyes shut and shook his head hard. "Get through the damned hatch, Major." He looked back for the chimp. A shadow was moving inside the room but he couldn't make out the source through the airborne blood.

"Gotta beat the Russkies," mumbled Morales. A milky film had formed over his left eye and specks of white seemed to expand across the other as Bellamy looked on. "I'm going to be mission comm—"

Bellamy snatched the man from his wedged location across the open port and pulled himself through instead, reaching back down and grabbing Morales by an arm and hauling him through. Thank God for zero gravity.

"Special process...irradiated virus...preserve...Lazy..."

"Shut up," snapped Bellamy, tossing the man aside and pulling at the hatch. The hinge, unmoved for years, had seized and did not want to move.

The ape rolled through the hatch and sailed across the expanse between the forward and aft bulkheads of the relatively huge Workshop. At least they should have a few seconds before it could get back to them.

Bellamy pulled a piece of hose from a unit attached near the hatch and looped it around Morales' thigh, cinching it up to his groin. They could do something better in the *Artemis*. Right now, he had to stop the bleeding.

He pulled his shirt over his head, half-wadding and half-folding it as he wrapped it around the wound. Before applying pressure and tying the tourniquet in place, Bellamy pulled the dressing away. The wound had stopped bleeding.

What? He'd been bleeding heavily, yes, but not enough time had passed for him to bleed out. He looked into Morales slackened face, at his limp body. *But how?*

He stared for a moment and then looked across the expanse between himself and the Airlock Module leading to *Artemis*. The simian was nowhere to be seen. He whipped his gaze around the cylinder, eyes raking over the equipment, the compartments, the netting along the walls.

The ape was moving slowly along the far wall, holding onto the netting as it moved, its empty eyes watching him, its teeth snapping together like wood blocks.

He had less than a minute. Taking Morales once again by the collar he launched them across the gulf. A hiss came from behind and he felt a vise clamp onto his wrist. He turned to see Morales, face contorted, milky eyes swollen in their sockets. The mission specialist that never stopped grinning was opening his mouth now but not to make a joke or erupt into laughter.

His intent was far darker, far more primal.

Bellamy spread his legs and twisted hard in the air sending the two of them flying apart but both still on vectors for the Airlock Module wall.

Morales hissed, his voice a deeper, stronger imitation of the apes.

They struck the bulkhead at the same time, hard enough to knock the wind from him. Bellamy scrabbled for a hold before he rebounded from the impact back into the open air. Fingers locking around a ventilation duct, he hurled himself along the sloped wall for the hatch that would lead him into the Airlock Module and then to *Artemis*.

The hatch was closed.

Bellamy forced his toes under the ductwork as he bent at the waist and tugged the blue handle aside, hearing the pins snap clear. He looked up as Morales seized his shoulders with both hands, at once trying to dislodge his victim from his toehold and also pull himself the final few inches toward his prey.

Bellamy twisted and punched his attacker square in the face, hearing the bone in Morales' nose snap. Morales, oblivious to the pain he should have felt, snapped like at animal at Bellamy, still holding onto the older man with one hand. Bellamy gouged at the man's eyes with his thumbs feeling one press deep into the swollen white orb with a sudden pop. Morales tumbled away, hands flailing, tearing at the air between them.

Mission Commander Francis Bellamy took the airlock door in hand and swung it free, releasing his toehold and dropping through headfirst, spinning like a champion swimmer doing a switchback at the pool's edge. Whipping the tethered toolkit along, he grabbed inner airlock door and pushed it home.

But the hatch wouldn't seat into the frame. He braced against a metal strut and pushed harder. He flinched as a tiny arm whipped at him from around the door and a deafening hiss filled the air.

The arm was like a snake and Bellamy drew back as it swatted at him and sprayed his face with compressed air. He laughed and grabbed the hose by its nozzle and opened the door enough to throw the airline into the Workshop.

The ape catapulted through the opening slamming into his chest and clutching at his throat. Bellamy's fists closed around the animal's neck and squeezed as he spun as their combined momentum slammed the beast's skull into the final hatch leading to *Artemis*. A crunch echoed through the small module and the creature's body went limp.

Bellamy opened the airlock door to *Artemis* and closed both hatches behind himself. The automated system would never let him detach from the station unless there was a good seal on both the station and the *Artemis*.

Safety first.

He floated in the warm confines of the tiny Command Module for long minutes before he heard the first thump against the hatch. Checking that the airlock was secure and locked, he began preparations for undocking. Once clear of Skylab, he'd call for instructions. Damned the radio silence.

He pulled the tabbed checklist from its slot on the command board and tried to read the smeared words.

What the...no. God, please, no.

He drifted to a highly polished stainless panel, studded with gauges and lights and buttons. Between the blinking indicators he could see his face only slightly distorted in the mirrored surface.

Gouges ran down his neck on both sides, none bleeding and his eyes had lost their luster, their deep brown fading as he watched.

Bellamy remembered his mission objectives.

Return with the E-PEP package. *Failed.*

Restore Skylab to an orbit-sustaining vector. *Failed.*

And his own personal mission objective. Return to Mother Earth. That, at least, he would do.

ONE MAN AND HIS DOG

Wayne Goodchild

-I-

"Where the hell did that come from?"

"I found him in one of the traps I left in the old Kelson place, eatin' on the other roaches. Ain't he a beauty?" Burt smiled, revealing a couple of missing teeth.

"It's something all right..." Connor continued to goggle at the thing in the glass tank, the old man stood behind it like some kind of proud parent. The cockroach looked to be about three inches in length, a circular plate covering the top of its head with a dark patch in the middle like a face with a halo around it. Translucent wings were folded across its back, jagged veins running through them like pale psoriasis. Its entire body was a queasy off-white, the colour of glow-in-the-dark paint. Everything, that is, except the 'face' on the insect's back, and its own eyes, which shone like black pearls on either side of oversized mandibles. "What species is it?"

Burt grunted. "Nearest I can figure, he's a Death's Head, albeit one who's stuck in some kinda teneral state."

"Like it's just undergone..." Connor closed his eyes as he searched for the correct terms, "ecdysis but its cuticle hasn't hardened yet?"

The old man chuckled. "Glad you been payin' attention." He quickly sobered and pointed at the cockroach. "'Cept this little fella's body has hardened."

"So he's an albino?" Connor caught himself using the masculine term but couldn't be bothered to correct himself.

"I don't think so," the old man mused. "Truth is, I don't rightly know quite what he is. 'Cept a marvel."

"A marvel?" Connor had being working for Burt Sanderson for close to a year, and still couldn't quite figure the old man out. He clearly enjoyed his job as an exterminator, yet held a deep respect for insects that bordered on reverential. Once, when Connor'd asked him about this apparent contradiction, Burt simply offered one of his trademark throaty chuckles and said "because even I realize the world could do with losing a few million of the little bastards."

"I wanna show you somethin'," the old man hobbled over to the miniature refrigerator in the corner of the room; his 'bug fridge', where he stored live specimens in a docile state, ready to study and run minor experiments on. Pulling out and opening up a plastic tub, he said "Watch this." He then withdrew a cockroach, small and placid, and dumped it in to the glass tank with the large pale one. Almost immediately, it jerked sideways and snapped the new arrival up in its jaws. The old man waited patiently for the large cockroach to finish its meal, then slowly slid his hand into the tank.

"Burt!" Connor gasped. The old man held a finger up to quiet him, and gently clasped the pale roach in his hand, before carefully lifting it from the tank. "Now watch this," he said, a smile wrapped around the words. As if handling a piece of fine antique china, he knelt down and placed the roach on the linoleum floor, where it promptly skittered several inches away from him, antennas twitching. Burt waited a few beats, then placed his hand, palm up, on the floor. Making a few 'kissing' noises, he managed to coax the roach back onto his hand, which he then returned to the tank with as much as grace as he'd used to remove it.

"That's about the damnedest thing I've ever seen," his young employee breathed.

"Pretty neat, huh?" Burt grinned with a wiggle of his busy eyebrows.

"You said he came from the Kelson place?"

"Yep. I went back and checked my traps four days ago, found this fella then."

Connor tried to work through things in his head as he spoke. "Surely four days isn't long enough to train a roach-"

"I ain't taught him anything," Burt said, and the tone of his voice made it clear he was as impressed and bemused as Connor was. "He just seems receptive to me, don'tcha Rex?"

"*Rex?*"

"Means 'King'," the old man explained. "As he undoubtedly is."

Connor snorted. "That's what my neighbour calls his dog." He paced around the tank, staring dispassionately at the roach as he tried to pick the right phrasing for his next question. "What are you, er, going to do about...him?"

The subtext was clear to the old man, whose eyes all but blazed with something approaching indignation. "I can't in good conscience kill something as beautiful as this-" he spluttered, holding his hands out towards the tank. "No, Connor my boy, I think I can make good use of Rex. Good use."

The younger man folded his arms across his chest and leant back against his desk. "I can't wait to hear this."

"I've spent most of my working life as an exterminator..." Burt began, his voice edged with nostalgia. "Since 1935. Forty years! Longer than you've been alive, Connor."

"Are you going to start going on about control techniques again?" Connor had heard such stories a million times, and couldn't be bothered to even make a pretence of being interested.

"That attitude will get you in trouble one of these days, my boy," Burt grumbled. "But yes, that's what I'm talking about. I want to find the most humane way to exterminate bugs as possible."

"So you've told me," Connor stifled a yawn.

Burt ignored him and said, "I think Rex here might just solve all our problems. See, I been feeding him a variety of insects an' he loves them all," he proclaimed, a little too proudly. "And it got me thinkin' - you use a mongoose to catch a snake, a hound to catch a fox-"

"Oh fantastic." Connor rolled his eyes. "I get it - use a roach to kill a roach."

"Exactly!" Burt declared. "I heard of the method before, of course - they call it 'Biological Control', when you use a natural predator to eradicate a pest. It's fairly simple to implement if you're dealin' with crops, say, but interior work...that's a little more tricky. But, I been thinkin', and I reckon I might actually be able to use Rex to clear out properties by allowing him to hunt down other pests within a given area."

Connor burst out laughing; he couldn't help it. "I'm sorry Burt, but I can't believe that you - *you* - would even consider doing something like that. I mean, letting an insect *loose*..." he trailed off in dumbfounded amusement.

"I think - no I'm *certain* - it'll work," the old man insisted. "I ain't been training Rex but I *have* run a few tests."

"Oh Lord, what now?"

"I used this room a couple of days ago," Burt admitted, sweeping his arm across the small office they both shared, its walls decorated with framed insect bodies pinned to card, a corpse to represent each stage of a bug's life cycle. "I let a variety of pests out – cockroaches, moths, beetles – and then let Rex loose-" he cut himself off when his associate gaped comically in response to the news. "I wouldn't suggest the idea of using Rex," Burt spoke slowly and evenly, "if I didn't have reason to believe it would work."

"He ate all the other pests?"

"Yes. In record time. A couple, like the moths, he had to wait until they settled down somewhere before grabbing them, but otherwise he completely cleared the room in just under an hour. All cockroaches have cannibalistic tendencies but Rex has a voracious appetite for *all* insects. Well, all the ones I fed him anyways."

"And you watched him?"

"At first. When I saw how *concise* he was being, I stepped outside and left him to it for a little while."

Connor shook his head. "He could have secreted himself in a gap in the floorboards, or anything."

"But he didn't," the old man pointed out.

"Let me get this straight," Connor paced across the office, hands clasped behind his back like he was about to make a deal-making presentation, or solve a crime like Sherlock Holmes. "You seriously want to use Rex to kill other pests. A cockroach. That you've named. Like a pet."

"He's evidently very tame..." Burt shrugged, tired of his young colleague's impertinence. "Plus, we wouldn't have to worry about him escaping an' mating with other cockroaches, because he ain't got no genitalia."

"He – what?"

"I examined him when I brought him back, and apparently he – it – is sexless."

"But...surely that's impossible? How does he reproduce?"

Burt shrugged again. "If you think about it for a moment, Connor, it makes perfect sense. Where did I find him?"

"Kelson's house."

"And what was Kelson?"

"Er...eccentric?"

"Apart from that."

"A scientist?"

"That's right!" Burt stabbed the air with a chewed nail. "No-one knows exactly what sorta scientist he was, though."

"Someone told me he liked to experiment on bums and junkies."

"Pah! I don't quite believe that, but I do believe a few the other stories I heard 'bout him."

"Stories?"

"When he died, David Kelson left no Will. He left no Will because he had no family. Hell, they couldn't even find his body. The State tried to find someone, anyone, to take his junk off their hands, but with no success. So they sold his house, and everything in it, at an auction.

"It was bought by Mary Renmar. She owns most of the buildings in town, and saw the Kelson place as prime redevelopment space. 'I can turn that place into luxury apartments,' she told me, 'but I need someone to clean the place out first'. Thing is, in the time between Kelson allegedly poppin' his clogs, and Mary gettin' hold of the place, a year had passed. And from what I heard, some of his experiments were still going on when the removal men went inside to start shifting furniture and the like."

"What do you mean?"

"Well..." Burt leant in close and adopted a conspiratorial tone, "I've gotta couple pals who work in the town's Sanitation Department, and they were involved in clearing some of the place out. They told me there were all these vines growing on the walls, 'cept when the workers cut them away they bled, Connor. *They bled.* An' they found tanks and cages in the cellar, full of weird-looking...*things.* All dead, mind you. Some had rotted right up but others kinda mummified in the dryness of that place, from what I heard.

"But that weren't the strangest thing. See, I think the creatures were like a hobby for Kelson. No-one really knew for certain what he did 'cept it musta involved chemicals, as that's what they found the most of in his house. Jars an' tubs an' bottles of different substances."

"What's so strange about that?"

"They found branches from the vine trailin' into some of the chemicals, like it'd been feeding from 'em. But that's not all.

"A lot of the workers reported hearing noises in the walls – they thought it might be rats, 'til they uncovered a rats' nest with vines all in it, the rats just as dead as you please. So they thought: Must be bugs. That's where I came into it."

"But you never said anything about hearing weird noises when you came back from sorting the place out..." Connor said, then added, "Mind you, you never told me you'd got a new pet from there either."

"I didn't hear nothing when I was there," Burt admitted, with a touch of disappointment. "Maybe the workers got spooked by the things they saw, or maybe whatever lives inside that house decided to be quiet when I turned up, or maybe Rex ate whatever it was."

"That what you think?"

The old man shrugged eloquently, "I only know what I know."

"Do you think Rex is one of Kelson's-"

"Maybe," Burt interrupted, though he sounded less than convinced. "Except all the tanks and cages they found had something in, even if it was just a skeleton."

Connor grunted, not sure what to say. After a few moments, he asked, "I guess your mind's made up about using Rex, huh?"

"Yep," Burt replied. "An' don't worry, kid. Like I said - I wouldn't try something like this if I didn't think it'd stand a real good chance of working."

Connor sighed. "Okay. If we start small, let Rex loose in confined spaces and under supervision, we should be all right. But I'm warning you, Burt," he pointed at the old man, "if it starts to look like this is even one percent of a bad idea, I'm going to kill Rex. Just like I would any other pest."

"Now there's no need to sound so harsh, kid-"

"That's the only way I'll go along with your screwy idea, Burt." Connor folded his arms defensively. "We need control methods, otherwise we're just asking for trouble."

"Sure, sure," Burt waved a dismissive hand and hobbled around the other side of his own desk. Collapsing into his chair, he began to leaf through a large book on his desk, licking his fingertips in-between each turn of a page. "Our next booking ain't 'til next week. I'll use these next five days to see if I can give Rex a taste for anything other than moths, beetles and other roaches."

"I don't think that's such a bad idea," Connor admitted. "I'm not sure how intelligent a bug can be, but if you can try and get Rex to correlate your presence with food, you might – *might* – actually be able to train him, to a small degree."

Burt looked up from the diary and stared into the glass tank, where Rex casually feasted on the remains of an earlier meal. "I think they're a lot more intelligent than we give 'em credit for..."

-II-

Burt decided to give Rex a baptism of fire, by letting him loose on a wasp nest in a client's garage. "I know he likes the taste of 'em," he told Connor when they arrived at the site, "but I'd like to see just how much of an appetite he has, and how resilient he can be."

"I gotta admit Burt, I didn't think you'd want to risk Rex's life like this on his first job."

"I told you before, he's a King. I just know it," the old man replied. "He'll surprise us, you'll see."

And he did.

Burt released Rex next to the large paper-lantern of a hive once Connor knocked the wasps out with smoke, and knocked the nest down from the roof. The two men, dressed in thick overalls and masks, then retreated a number of steps and waited with a mixture of excitement and fear. The large pale roach skittered eagerly towards its next meal, twitched its antennae as it tasted the air, backed-off a few inches, then darted inside the hive, eliciting a crisp rustling noise akin to the scrape of leaves on cloth. Occasionally they'd come a brief, vicious buzz from inside the hive, but nothing escaped. A little over fifteen minutes later, and Rex cautiously stuck his head out of the bottom of the hive. Burt took this as his cue, removed his mask, and bent down to scoop Rex up, who – just as before – climbed eagerly onto the old man's hand and waited patiently to be placed back inside his glass tank. Connor carefully prodded the hive, tearing ragged holes in its sickly grey skin. Nothing spilled out, not even dead wasps or larvae.

"Holy shit," Connor said, quickly excusing his language in front of his boss.

Burt laughed and said, "Don't worry about it, kid. I kinda feel like cussin' myself."

"It's...it's *incredible*. I don't know how else to describe what just happened."

"Yes sir," Burt proudly patted the tank in his hands. "Looks like Rex here is our dream ticket, all right."

"Let's not get ahead of ourselves, Burt," Connor warned. "We don't know if he'll try to escape once we let him loose somewhere else."

Burt grinned. "Only one way to find out."

-III-

Under the guise of trying-out a new chemical agent, Burt and Connor assured clients that, although there was a chance a job might end up taking longer than usual, there wouldn't be harmful residue left behind. Anyone who was still uncertain or unhappy with the prospect of paying more than they usually did were told the new extermination method would also completely wipe-out any trace of the pests currently causing them misery. Even so, there were still those who showed reluctance or cynicism towards the pair's entrepreneurial plans. Burt decided to run a sweep on their houses and apartments first, at a reduced rate, as a sign of both goodwill and his own confidence.

Thankfully the gambit paid off and business, though it didn't exactly 'boom', did increase. Burt only used Rex in small, confined areas, and in turn Rex repeated his astounding ability to completely eradicate any and all pests within that area. Word-of-mouth spread the revelation that Burt Sanderson and Connor Jenkins had created or discovered a brand new extermination method, one that played out exactly as they said it would.

Rex never attempted to scuttle away and hide whenever he was released, and happily allowed Burt to handle him on a regular basis. Whilst charged with clearing out a basement of roaches, Burt lifted Rex from his tank and faced Connor. "Why don't you have a try?" the old man asked his apprentice, holding a placid Rex out on the palm of his liver-spotted hand.

"No thanks," Connor pulled a face. "Rex looks like he could give me a nasty bite if he doesn't like me touching him."

"You'd never do that, would you boy?" Burt asked the roach. Rex twitched his antennae in reply. "Come on, kid. Hold him. You should be used to him by now."

"Sorry Burt, but I'm not as comfortable around insects as you are. Besides, he's your pet. I think he's more than happy to let you feed and handle him."

Burt made a 'pfft' noise and gently placed the roach down on the cold stone floor. "Go get 'em, Rex!" he urged, quietly. The roach skittered haphazardly around the basement until it decided on a direction. As it darted towards a jumble of old boxes, Connor said, not for the first time, "I hope he doesn't decide to stay down here."

"He'll come back to me," Burt nodded to himself.

"I'll guess we'll see..." Connor muttered, setting up a couple of baited roach traps to catch any potential stragglers.

***

A slow damp hour passed, the solitary light bulb buzzing like a trapped bee, before Rex reappeared with a small roach in his jaws. "Guess he wants to bring a meal with him," Burt chuckled, bending down to pick Rex up.

"I can't help but think we're pushing our luck," Connor said, quite suddenly and with an abruptness uncommon to his general manner. Burt gently placed Rex back in his tank then stood up with a crack of his spine and fixed his rheumy eyes on the younger man. "Change the record, kid. Since using Rex our profits have almost doubled. Rex is good for business."

"Rex *is* our business," Connor replied. "Okay, so let's say he's the tamest roach on the planet and we don't lose him whilst clearing a house. What about if he comes across a natural predator like a centipede or a, a...a parasitic wasp?"

"*If* that ever happened," Burt said, "the other insect would have to be pretty darn big to overpower ol' Rexy." He chuckled and motioned for Connor to carry the roach's tank. "Hold 'im a sec, kid, while I get myself a drink." Reaching for his hipflask, Burt continued, "An' seriously Connor, the way you been carrying on lately I'm startin' to wonder if maybe you ain't cut out for a career in pe-"

Burt was cut off abruptly by the pop of the lightbulb as it died, drenching the two men in solid darkness. Startled, Connor cursed and dropped Rex's tank with a dull crash.

"You, you *halfwit!*" Burt roared, his whiskey-rough voice croaking hoarsely. "Don't move an inch!"

"Shit! I'm sorry Burt – the bulb going out like that made me jump, and-"

"Sssh!" the old man hissed. "Rex! Stay where you are Rex, I'll rescue you."

"You boys okay down there?" Mrs Macready, the homeowner, called from the top of the stairs, the open doorway allowing a jagged slice of weak daylight to filter into the darkness of the basement.

"The bulb went, Mrs Macready," Connor called back, using the diffused light to clear up the broken tank.

"There's a lantern by the foot of the stairs," she called back.

"Got it!" Burt said, fiddling with the lantern as Connor cursed yet again. "What is it now? An' if you've killed Rex..."

"Cut my hand on a piece of glass," Connor muttered. "Rex seems...oh."

"What?" Burt bent over with an ancient crack and a grimace, eyes desperately searching the remains of Rex's tank for any sign of the roach.

"Y'know, it's not as bad as it looks..."

"Quiet, Connor," Burt snapped, eyes widening at the sight of the glass poking out of Rex's back. "My poor Rex..."

"Let me-"

"I'll do it," Burt waved the other man away and moved closer to Rex, who sat apparently nibbling at the piece of glass with Connor's blood on. With infinite care, Burt slid the shard from Rex, who didn't even appear to realise what was happening. Though there remained a noticeable, albeit tiny, mark in the roach's back, the wound didn't leak any bodily fluid at all. The fragment itself was completely clean. Connor frowned at Burt but the old man was too busy fussing over his favourite bug. "Let's get you home and looked at," he soothed. "Get you away from this nasty man."

"Oh for f-" Connor threw his hands up in exasperation. "I didn't do it on purpose, Burt!"

"Clean up in here, an' sort out Mrs Macready's account wouldya?"

"Sure, just-"

But Burt ignored him and slowly clambered up the basement steps, Rex tucked protectively in his hands. He nodded at the old woman, and said "Connor could do with a dustpan, Eda," before leaving the house.

-IV-

Rex, initially never Connor's biggest fan, developed an apparent and severe distrust of him. Connor thought so, anyway. Every time he approached the roach (now housed in a new, fancier tank) he swore the insect moved away from him. Burt, predictably, took the side of the bug. "You gave him a real fright, boy."

"I'm not going to keep apologising," Connor said. "Besides, he's clearly okay. Which you have to admit it is a little weird."

"Clearly, his species can take more punishment than a normal roach."

Connor grunted in response. Talking to Burt about Rex's...uniqueness...only resulted in a kind of stubborn denial from the old man about just how peculiar Rex was. The old man looked about ready to say something when he was interrupted by the office phone. He picked it up and, after a brief conversation, hung up. "It's Mrs Macready," he said. "She's dead."

***

Her husband had discovered her body, collapsed in an uncomfortable heap against the foot of the basement steps, a look of utter shock carved onto her elderly visage. Thankfully, the police had removed her body by the time Burt and Connor turned up, but they still got all the details from the town gossip, who just so happened to also be Eda's neighbour. "Terrible," she said to Connor, hovering around the scene of the crime like a fly around dead meat. "Her face was white as chalk, like she'd seen a ghost!"

"That's quite enough, Julia," Officer Hendricks warned, herding her from the kitchen.

"Thanks for coming down, fellas," he said to Burt and Connor once he returned.

"Why do you want us here?" Connor enquired.

"Far as we can tell, you gents were the last people to see her alive. Doing a job, were you?"

Connor frowned. "You know we were - they're our traps in the basement."

"What sort of bugs were you boys trying to clean up?"

"Cockroaches. And we did."

"What's this all about, Roy?" Burt demanded. "If it ain't important, you wouldn'ta asked us to call by."

"Quite right," the cop agreed. "I'd like you gents to take a look in the basement."

"What about the crime scene?" asked Connor, completely puzzled.

"Just go take a look, Mr Jenkins."

Connor looked at Burt, who shrugged, and motioned for him to lead the way down the steps. Connor obliged and trudged down, noticing the light bulb had been replaced. A noise, small and harsh, greeted his ears and he held a hand out behind him to slow Burt down.

"Kid?"

"Can you hear that?" Connor stepped onto the basement floor, acutely aware the sound was coming from a nearby wall. He peered into the edges of the light bulb's illumination and gasped, feeling a deep, cold calm wash through him.

The wall was alive with hundreds of squirming pale insects.

"Jesus..." Burt breathed beside him. "That ain't right..."

The slowly churning mass of bodies comprised of roaches, spiders and a handful of other insects that shouldn't congregate together. All pale, all black-eyed, all fundamentally *different*.

"Nearest we can figure," Officer Hendricks spoke up behind them, "is Eda came down here to replace the lightbulb, and when the new light came on she saw those bugs. Gave her the shock of her life and she stumbled, possibly banged her head, or had a heart attack. Jerry's doing an examination as we speak to find out which."

Connor said, "How'd you know about the bulb?"

"She was holding a dead one in her hand when her husband found her. Poor fella."

Burt turned to face the cop. "Where's Harry now?"

"At his sister's. Guy's only just holding onto it."

"This is pretty fucking weird," said Connor, turning to Burt. "Pardon my language, but it is."

"No, I agree with ya, kid." Burt shook his head, "Surely this ain't got nothing to do with Rex...?"

"Rex? You gents are using a new pest control technique, that right? Rex to do with that?"

"Rexaprotheen," Connor said quickly, unsure quite why he was lying. "New chemical we've been using."

"You got all the correct licences and whatnot?"

"Of course," Burt replied, indignant. "You trying to blame us somehow, Roy? That's low, boy. Very low. I run a tight ship. Have done for years."

"Nothing of the sort, Burt," Hendricks soothed. "Simply asking questions. That's all."

"What do you want us to do about these bugs? Are they a suspect?" Connor asked with a completely straight face. He was secretly pleased to get a chuckle from Burt.

"Get rid of 'em. I don't think old Harry'll want to live in a house crawling with those things, now will he?"

"Yes sir," Connor saluted. "We've got a job-"

"Whatever," Hendricks waved a dismissive hand. "One of my men'll be here to let you back in."

"Yes sir," Connor repeated.

In the pick-up back to the office, Connor asked Burt "Are you thinking what I'm thinking?"

"I am," Burt admitted, "but I'm gonna pretend I ain't."

"We did the job in Mrs Macready's basement three days ago. I think it's safe to say no other mutant strain of cockroach got in there and...did whatever it did to those insects to make them look and act like that."

"Maybe," Burt held a warning finger up, "but if that's the case, why ain't we seen any other signs of peculiar insects since before today?"

"That's what's worrying me more the most..." Connor replied, quietly. "Because Rex clearly decimated the areas we let him loose in the first few times, we just assumed he'd done the same with all the places since."

"But the back-up traps were clear."

"The ones in Mrs Macready's basement were too," Connor said, maintaining eye contact with Burt until the older man had to pay attention to the road again. "I can recall, off-hand, at least five jobs where Rex appeared to remove all organic trace of the pests we sent him after. Five. And let's not forget the four jobs we've done since being called out to the Macready basement."

"Seven. I did a few extra jobs with Rex without you knowing."

"What? Why did you go behind my back?"

"Because I knew you'd kick up a fuss about it," Burt said, matter-of-factly. "Let's not get carried away, kid. We'll go back, cover the bugs in the basement with some Delta Dust, then head to the job we got booked for this afternoon. We ain't had no other reports from any of our previous clients about the reappearance of insects so I think it's safe to say there ain't been any."

"We'll see," Connor muttered darkly.

-V-

Up in the warm, stale environment of Carl Reinhold's attic, moths had made a home in and around several large boxes of old clothes. "I don't care what you use to kill 'em," he told Connor and Burt. "They've completely ruined all my clothes now anyway."

"So why are you bothered about getting rid of them?" Connor couldn't help but ask.

"Because this is my fucking attic," Reinhold replied, giving the younger man a look that clearly said 'you're an idiot'. Connor shrugged it off and helped Burt lift Rex's covered tank into the attic. "That your new secret weapon that's got ever'body so goddamn excited?" Reinhold smirked.

"Yup," said Burt. "Now if you'll excuse us, Carl, we'll-"

"Yeah yeah," Reinhold interrupted, clambering down the metal ladder muttering "My fucking attic" to himself.

"I really think you should reconsider using Rex for this job. I think the little guy deserves a break."

"Nice try Connor my boy, but I ain't retiring Rex just yet, just because you got some spooky feelings goin' on." He gave a throaty chuckle and gently lifted Rex from his tank. "Moths, Rex. One of your favourites," he whispered, setting the roach down in the empty floor space that dominated the low-ceilinged attic. The pale insect skittered through the layers of dust directly towards the clothes boxes, vanishing in an instant. "Alright, let's leave him to it."

"What? I'm not going anywhere."

"Suit yourself," said Burt. "I'm gonna get that cranky bastard to fix me a whiskey. Rex'll be okay up here on his own for a little while."

"Like hell he will," Connor blustered. "I'm not leaving him up here alone after what we saw earlier."

"Fine," Burt replied, calmly, easing himself back down the attic ladder. "You stay up here in the heat an' dust, overreactin'. I'm getting a drink."

***

"Still think I'm overreacting?" Connor tried to keep the smug tone out of his voice but failed miserably. Together, he and Burt stood watching Rex as he methodically dragged or carried moth bodies from various hiding places into the centre of the floor. This time, Connor didn't even have to voice his opinion because Burt did it for him.

"That is some damn strange behaviour..."

Connor simply nodded in agreement.

"Why you stockpiling the husks, Rex?" Burt asked the roach.

"They're not husks," Connor said, crushing a couple underfoot. No blood or juices leaked out as the furry grey skin of the bugs split to reveal a pale body underneath. "They're more like cocoons."

"What-"

"Rex is *infecting*, I guess, other insects, to turn them into pale versions of themselves. You can't deny the bugs in the basement and these-" he motioned at the crushed moths "don't look like little ol' Rex there."

"There's got to be an explanation..." Burt shook his head, kneeling down.

"There is and I've just given it to you, but the real question is-" Connor paused as Burt started to coax Rex towards him. "Are you sure you want to do that, Burt? Now we know what he's doing, you sure you want him on your unprotected skin? I dread to think what his bite could do to a human."

"Don't be ridiculous, boy," Burt sneered. "Most insects ain't got the muscle power to puncture human skin, and why would Rex decide now's the time to try a nibble of me anyway?"

"I think he might have got a taste for blood. Human blood," Connor replied sickly, watching the old man gently carry Rex over to his tank and lower him into it. The roach happily enjoyed the journey without so much as trying to attack his constant handler.

"When? How?"

"I'm pretty sure he tasted some of mine from a piece of broken glass the other day."

"Pretty sure?"

"Well yeah, I..." Connor faltered. Maybe he was overreacting in that respect - Rex never tried to hurt the old man or escape from him so at least in that sense the roach was harmless. "But the other bugs..."

"We'll crush these, then go check on all the *dead* ones that'll currently be decorating the floor of the Macready basement," Burt said, in a deeply patronising tone. "Come on."

-VI-

The strange, pallid conglomeration of insects were completely unfazed by the liberal dusting of Deltamethrin Burt and Connor had coated them in. "Incredible..." Burt whistled. "This shit's stronger than Hercules."

"Look at 'em; it's impossible every species in this little group would be immune to the Delta Dust, yet there they all are, happy as Larry."

Burt took a swig from his hipflask, wiped his lips with the back of a hand, said, "Guess it's the old fashioned-way..." He hefted a piece of broken furniture from a pile of junk on the basement floor and began to crunch it into the swarm of insects. Connor followed suit, feeling sick at the feel and sound of the activity. After a few hits, the bugs started buzzing/scuttling/twitching in frenzied activity, and Connor noticed a fair few critically damaged insects dragging their bodies along the wall when they should by rights have been slowly curling up in death-throes. "I don't like this, Burt."

"We...just...need t' keep...smashin' 'em," he huffed.

Connor laid a hand on the old man's shoulder and said, more insistent, "We need to leave. Now."

As if this sentence had been the cue they were waiting for, the insects poured from the wall and swarmed towards the two men, herding them out of the basement in a panicked hurry. Burt slammed the basement door shut, keeping the insects behind several inches of sturdy wood. "Okay," he admitted, "we might have a small problem on our hands."

"Unstoppable bugs is more than a 'small problem', Burt."

"There you go, gettin' carried away again!" Burt hobbled across the kitchen. "There're other chemicals we can use. Heck, Rex might even want to eat those little buggers now-"

"Enough!" Connor was surprised at the volume of his own voice and stared unblinking as his boss for a few moments. "I'm sorry, Burt. This is just..." he sighed, "too much. I'll admit I actually thought for a while Rex would be exactly the master-stroke you thought he'd be, and we've had a good couple of months business using him, but this has to stop. He's doing things to other insects, changing them, and I don't like it one bit. He has to go, Burt; Rex has to go."

"It could be any number of reasons," Burt replied levelly. "A contaminated food source, a fungus, anything. Rex's involvement could be nothing more than coincidence."

"Have you already forgotten what your pet was doing in Reinhold's attic?!" Connor shouted in exasperation. "Jesus Christ, Burt. I've heard of denial, but...Jesus Christ."

"It's been a stressful day," the old man continued in the same, calm voice. "Why don't we both go home. I'll tell Hendricks to quarantine the basement off, and I'll come back first thing to spray some Cypermethrin, see if that works. I said it before: no-one from an earlier job's contacted us saying they seen pale bugs, so what we got to worry about? Nothing."

"Maybe the other bugs are waiting."

Burt harrumphed, "Yeah? For what?"

Connor answered quietly, "I hope we don't find out."

-VII-

The room was buried underground, beneath wood and brick structures, down in the darkness and damp where things without colour grow and bloom. Connor's breath fogged in the air in front of him, though he couldn't see it.

Something moved through the subterranean night, close-by. Startled, Connor spun on the spot, trying to remember how he got here. There must be stairs, back to the surface. Hands outstretched, Connor stumbled around for an indeterminate amount of time, all the while acutely aware of tiny unidentifiable noises around him.

Eventually, he bumped off a wet wall, its surface caked in fungus-like lumps. Scrabbling along its surface, Connor came to a set of narrow steps. Carefully, he clambered up their creaking length until his hands encountered something soft and warm; a trapdoor, unlike anything he'd ever felt before.

Afraid, yet certain he was headed in the right direction, Connor heaved the panel up and open, revealing glistening red light. Connor pulled himself into a tunnel, one which sloped gently upwards. The walls here were as soft and welcoming as the illumination that emanated from them, and Connor soon reached the tunnel's end.

Almost reluctant to leave, Connor pushed through the increasingly narrow exit and realised, too late, his hands were covered in thick, white bristles. As he struggled to pull himself free, he also realised his arms were backward-jointed, and curved inwards. Like an insect's. *No,* he thought. *No, this isn't possible.* The tunnel entrance contracted and buckled as Connor struggled to get free, and two instantaneous realisations dawned on him:

He was crawling out of someone's mouth; at the same time something was trying to crawl out of his.

He woke, screaming as hundreds of thick, white legs swarmed over his body. Spiders, pale as Rex and almost as big, filled Connor's bed. The quilt rippled as waves of the creatures tickled and caressed his limbs, his torso, his face. He leapt from his bed in a wild panic, the memories of sleep sliding from his mind like wet mud. Locusts and beetles and a hundred other insects wriggled and jumped from the bed onto Connor. Desperately, he spun on the spot, flailing his arms and swatting at the creatures. *Why are you doing this?* his mind screamed as his body itched with hundreds of bites, turning his blood to fire in his veins.

"Help me!" he shouted, but the horde of mutated insects crawled into his mouth, covered his eyes, blinded and suffocated him. He could taste their pallid skin, and choked violently on the sting in his throat. He had just enough of his wits about him to wonder where they had all come from, only to realise he already knew the answer. *Not like this,* he thought. *Not like this.* In a pain-fuelled agony he collapsed to his knees with a piercing *snap*, just as his mind followed suit.

-VIII-

"Connor," Burt knocked loudly on the young man's front door. "Wake up, kid. Not like you to oversleep." When he still received no answer, he rummaged around under the plant pot where the spare key hid, took it and let himself in. There was a strange, buzzing silence in the house. A sound Burt could feel more than hear, like standing near a railway track as a train approached.

"Connor?"

Burt wandered through the rooms, a feeling of deep unease growing inside him. "Come on kid, this ain't like you. I'll think about giving Rex a break, how about that? Con-" the word died on his lips when he stepped into his young apprentice's bedroom. "*Oh Jesus...*" he whispered, collapsing against the door frame.

Connor lay on the bare floorboards of the bedroom in an untidy heap, his skin swollen and deformed. Web-like vines bloomed from various areas of his anaemic skin. Several different species of insect crawled over and out of him.

"Help..." Burt croaked, sliding away from the bedroom. "Help!"

He hobbled from the house, calling out for assistance. It was only now he realised just how empty the streets were and had been on the drive over, even given how early it was. The unease inside him grew thorns and pierced his guts, filling his throat with the taste of bile. Fighting the urge to vomit, Burt staggered over to Connor's nearest neighbour's house and pummelled the front door and windows with aged fists. "Someone!" he bellowed. "Someone help me!" He pressed his face to a window, cupping his hands around his eyes so as to block out the reflection of the early morning sun. A woman sat in an armchair, fleshy tendrils trailing over the armrests. Her left hand clawed feebly at the air. "Christ, oh Christ," Burt sobbed, hurrying back over to his pick-up.

He drove through street after street, and it didn't take long to realise the entire town had been claimed by insects during one night. Mutated people, not-quite-dead-nor-quite-alive, lay sprawled in awkward positions inside their homes, evidently overcome before they could raise the alarm. To all intents and purposes it appeared as if Burt was the only person who had been spared. "Rex..." he murmured, heading home.

Burt half-expected the roach to have escaped his tank and be out on the streets, leading his brethren in their uprising, but it was with an unrestrained sigh of relief that he found the three inch creature sitting patiently in his glass home. "What are you?" the old man asked, leaning down and staring directly into Rex's opaque eyes. Rex twitched his antennae but said nothing. Burt tried to think things through, feeling his luck was fading fast. "Are you controlling them?"

Still no reply.

"Kelson," Burt snapped his fingers in a sudden burst of inspiration. "There must be *something* I can use in his old place..."

Picking up Rex's tank, Burt carried him out to the truck and placed him in the footrest on the passenger side, before slipping in behind the wheel and kicking the engine into life. Seeing no point in adhering to the speed limit or traffic lights, Burt made straight for Kelson's house, reaching it in record time.

He wasn't at all surprised to find the front door ajar – as far as he was aware, there were still people working on clearing the place out, and with Kelson's creepy reputation hovering over the house like a dark cloud, kids never tried to break-in to or vandalise the place. Burt pushed the ancient oak door open with a ponderous creak, calling out "Hello?"

He was answered by silence and dust.

Then, a scratch. Inside the walls. Burt felt against the wooden panels, trying to locate the source. The sound drew him into the house, into dusty gloom. Half-packed cardboard boxes and overflowing garbage cans filled some of the rooms, waiting to be removed. Down, deeper into the house, the scratching methodical and insistent in its pattern, its clarion call. Burt stepped over the malformed and shifting bodies of workers without batting an eyelid. He knew before he entered the house he'd discover why the house hadn't been cleared on schedule.

Into the cellar, where vines bulged from the crumbling brickwork, some still leaking dark liquid from cuts made by inquisitive removal men. The scratching led towards a far corner of the cellar, beyond the reach of the grimy light bulbs. More vines peeked through the flaking masonry here than any where else in the property. The scratches became staccato and frenzied, aping, Burt realised with a deep coldness, Morse Code. He looked around in the semi-darkness for a blunt object, his gaze settling on a ancient lamp stand. He managed to heft it without too much difficulty, and began to chip away at the cellar wall, the scratches urging him on.

The stonework, long since dried out, crumbled away in easy chunks to reveal a dark recess hidden behind the wall. Fear catching in his throat, Burt stepped back from his grim discovery, the dirty light just enough to illuminate the almost-phosphorescent form secreted away down here.

"*Kelson?*"

A body the queasy white of glow-in-the-dark paint rested inside the alcove. Or rather, it was held up by the hundreds of vines that sprouted from the desiccated flesh and burrowed deep into the brickwork around it. Once, it may have been a man, for it wore the ripped and tattered remnants of a suit, but all trace of masculinity had been erased from its features by the horrendous physical changes that contorted its frame. Its eyes were smooth obsidian rocks fixed in cavernous sockets, its jaw held open by the plant-like growths. From the way the vines looked, and from where they grew from, Burt strongly suspected they were in fact veins, and he staggered backwards and threw up on the cellar floor.

The scratching picked up the pace once again, and Burt chanced a step closer. The body's right arm twisted up above its head, hand grasping the wall in a vicious claw. The nails had long since been ripped away by the constant scratching of the fingertips against the brickwork, thin tendrils twirling from the crusted wounds into the stone.

A bucket filled with cement sat beside the body's feet, or at least what was left of them. A trowel was stuck firmly in the dried mortar, a pile of surplus bricks next to the bucket. A pen and piece of tattered paper lay in the dirt, and Burt bent down to pick them up. He flipped the paper over to read a note written in scrawled calligraphy:

experiment 427 went terribly wrong should have seen this coming no time to make proper arrangements will hole myself up try to keep away from population chance not work but no other choice now must fight it cant die now roots taken hold spread effects of 427 through contact insects insects loose feeding please burn me losing grip dead now still alive find me burn me someone please

"Christ Almighty Kelson, what were you tryin' to do?" Burt breathed.

The body's eyes rotated towards him in answer.

Cursing, Burt began to feverishly hunt for anything flammable. His search took him back upstairs where he grabbed a couple of cardboard boxes, tipping the contents onto the floor, desperately aware of just how alive the walls now were. Hurrying back downstairs, Burt doused the scientist's ragged clothes with booze from his hipflask and crammed the cardboard boxes in the alcove by the mangled feet. "I pray this works," Burt whispered, flicking his lighter and setting the whole thing aflame. He hobbled from the cellar as the fire licked eagerly at Kelson's deformed living corpse.

A horde of insects waited patiently for him outside.

Burt slowed to a limping walk, thousands of tiny black eyes watching him as he climbed into the cab next to Rex. When he closed the driver door the ones who could took flight and swarmed back towards the town; the others scurried away in the same direction. Burt looked down at Rex. "Maybe the fire'll spread an' kill 'em?"

He doubted this though. The only thing he knew was that Rex was a talisman for him, a deterrent to the fate that'd so rapidly and irrevocably consumed the rest of the town. "Maybe I can warn others, stop it spreading?" he asked Rex.

The roach refused to give Burt an answer.

"Maybe..." the old man answered himself, starting the engine.

WHY THE WILD THINGS ARE

Carl Barker

One for sorrow,
Two for joy,
Three for a girl,
Four for a boy,
Five for silver,
Six for gold,
Seven for...

Seven for...?

Lionel stood by the living room window, half-heartedly ransacking the dusty attic of his brain in search of the correct ending to the rhyme. After five minutes of rummaging in vain for words he felt sure were hidden away in there somewhere, he decided to give up and returned his attention to the gruesome scene currently taking place in the front garden. As he continued to sip thoughtfully from his mug of Bovril, Lionel mused to himself that he had no idea whether or not the children's rhyme went as far as thirteen magpies. He was however quite sure that if it did then the correct words were certainly not 'Thirteen for strips of rotting flesh being torn greedily from the dead body lying face-down in my garden pond.'

The rancid cadaver in question belonged to Lionel's previously regular postman and had been loitering in the pond for going on two days now. The algae covered surface of the water lay strewn with discarded letters from the postman's bag. Unable to be delivered, they clustered forgetfully about the partially submerged head like discarded thoughts, the addresses of the intended recipients slowly bleeding into the murky water.

For the first twenty-four hours or so, the corpse had remained relatively unmolested. However, once the late June sun had crawled lazily up into the sky on the second day, the first of the birds had started to appear on the lawn. Small ones to begin with, sparrows and finches mostly, casually strutting across Lionel's neatly manicured grass as if they owned the place.

Standing in the kitchen with a bowl of dry cornflakes in his hands, Lionel had observed with some wry amusement as a particularly bold Bullfinch climbed up onto the deceased postie's head and began industriously pecking into the back of his blood-spattered skull. Within a couple of minutes the majority of the other birds in the vicinity, taking the lead from this first diner, had also clambered atop the body and busied themselves with the task of extracting whatever tasty morsels they could dislodge from Lionel's now defunct mailman.

Barely remembering to chew his cereal, Lionel had watched in morbid fascination as a Blue Tit manoeuvred itself into an inverted position beside one of the mailman's ears and proceeded to peck furiously into the unprotected organ as if it were an upturned half coconut.

Of course, Lionel's first thought had been to telephone somebody to report the abrupt appearance of the body on that first morning, but then the thought had occurred to him that he wasn't entirely sure of whom to call. The two man village police force would have their collective hands full coordinating the recently introduced 'domestic cleansing' policy and would therefore probably be too busy to answer the phone, let alone pop round to investigate. It was also pretty self-evident that the district hospital could do nothing for the poor chap and two days was probably a bit soon to be contacting the undertakers, who might well be as busy as the police at the moment.

So having not come to any satisfactory conclusions as to who to contact, Lionel had elected to give the matter the necessary degree of thought and therefore proceeded to make a fresh pot of tea. It had to be black of course, as the last of the milk had been used up almost a week ago. In fact the milkman hadn't come calling since last Tuesday, on account of what had happened to him.

Lionel had been rudely awakened around seven on that particular day by the sound of screaming coming from the street outside. Running to the bedroom window and pulling apart the curtains, he had been just in time to glimpse the somewhat comical figure of the milkman tearing away down the lane with a decidedly vicious looking jackdaw firmly attached to his head. Though already some distance away, Lionel had deduced that the irate bird must have taken it upon itself to try and penetrate the soft gold-top foil of the man's cranium, presumably in search of the sweet-tasting cream beneath. He understood that the poor fellow had now been made very comfortable in the nearest intensive care ward. Well, as comfortable as it was possible to be with half your face and one of your eyeballs now firmly in the possession of a member of the corvid family.

The tea tasted a little dry without milk, but thankfully there was still plenty of sugar in the cupboard and by half past eleven Lionel found himself curled up in his favourite armchair, stirring the last of three sugar lumps into a reassuring cup of Earl Grey as he continued to eye the telephone in silent contemplation.

Perhaps he could ring the newly rechristened R.S.P.B (Royal Society for the Prevention of Birds, circa May 2012), he had reasoned as he continued to stir evenly anti-clockwise. After all, the fact that the body was now being molested by an assortment of avian pests surely placed the matter firmly within their particular area of expertise? However the more he thought about it, the more Lionel realised that the idea of a bunch of trigger-happy pigeon fanciers setting up camp in his garden with camouflage nets and laser-sighted sniper rifles didn't much appeal to him.

The Royal Mail was another possibility, but then this raised the issue of them sending out yet another postman in order to confirm what had happened to the first and of course now that the local wildlife had acquired a taste for the flesh of Postman Pat and his ilk, that kind of behaviour was most definitely asking for trouble. Not to mention the fact that he felt entirely responsible for the whole incident in the first place.

The removal of the 'Beware Of The Dog' from the garden gate a week ago had seemed the most logical course of action under the circumstances ("...seven for a secret never to be told" whispered a quiet voice in his head), but at the time he had never imagined an outcome of this magnitude and informing the authorities of what exactly had transpired here was certainly not going to help matters any he reasoned.

No, Lionel had decided that if he was going to contact the Post Office regarding the matter then the correct course of action would be to write them a short friendly letter in a couple of days time. That way he could enquire as to whether they were yet aware that one of their postal workers was missing and that if it wasn't too much trouble, would they mind popping round and delivering their late colleague into a couple of black bin-liners for disposal. This would then allow Lionel to kill two carnivorous birds with one stone and find out if it would be possible to request a second copy of his Reader's Digest, on account of the first now having sunk without trace into the thick layer of silt and blood at the bottom of the pond.

By noon that day, the larger of the common variety garden feeders had begun to arrive on the scene; a couple of crows at first, swooping down to land abruptly beside the slowly rotting corpse. The pair had squawked copiously in order to frighten off the gathered horde of smaller birds and then inexplicably chose to fight with each other over the spoils before finally being themselves scared off by the dull rumble of a passing bus.

Lionel was tucking into a rather delicious tuna sandwich with extra mayonnaise when he noticed the increasing number of magpies gathering atop the roof on the opposite side of the street. At first there were just two of them, huddled together beside the TV aerial like gossiping old women, but as word evidently got around this number multiplied rapidly to six, then ten and eventually an even dozen. As a thirteenth and final bird (slightly larger and fatter than the others) swaggered arrogantly past Lionel's garden shed, he did a quick tally and pondered whether or not this number of magpies should be considered unlucky. It was certainly unfortunate for the remains of the late postman, as with a single cry from the largest and nearest of the birds, the whole gang of magpies took flight, sailing down into the garden and descending en masse upon the hapless body like a hoodwink of delinquent grave robbers.

The piebald beasties made quick work of ripping mercilessly into the already tattered remnants of flesh still clinging to the corpse and upon remembering the correct collective noun, Lionel smiled grimly to himself at the thought that this was most definitely a 'bad' tiding of magpies.

Despite his melancholic state, he couldn't help but laugh at the rather gruesome sight of an increasingly frustrated bird furiously trying to remove a shiny Rolex copy from the postman's left arm. The poor bird appeared to be having some small trouble with the clasp and had resorted to solving the problem by attempting to peck the whole hand off at the wrist in order to retrieve its precious bounty. Several of the other magpies, attracted by the flickering reflection of light from the watch, decided to muscle in on this attempted daylight robbery and soon what had begun with a mere cacophony of irate squawking rapidly developed into a thoroughly vicious melee of wings and bloodied beaks.

Throughout this riotous behaviour, the largest (and presumably the leader) of the group remained perched majestically atop the postman's torso, seemingly content to observe the petty machinations of his brethren from on high. As Lionel continued to watch spellbound, the despotic bird glanced up and looked directly at him, its beady red eyes boring into him. The unwanted connection sent a shiver down Lionel's spine and he instinctively took a step back away from the window in fear.

Despite all the publicity and government information films which had appeared in the national media over the last few months regarding 'The Event' and the subsequent aggressive genetic mutations in local fauna, he still found himself distinctly unsettled by the red-eye phenomenon which was common amongst infected wildlife. It was like looking at a badly taken photograph he had decided, but one where the still life in the picture could suddenly leap out at you without warning, intent upon tearing your face off. The self-appointed magpie king continued to glare resolutely in Lionel's direction and finding himself lacking the gall to continue this staring contest, he retreated back to his armchair, leaving the birds to their macabre feasting.

After making himself comfy, Lionel reached for last Thursday's broadsheet (no new deliveries since the paper boy had been left in a coma following an encounter with an ill-tempered badger the week before) on the coffee table. The neatly folded collar lying hidden beneath the paper was an unwelcome reminder that at some point today he was going to have to venture outside and take care of unfinished business. He stared at the collar for just a moment, his eyes lingering on the single word lovingly engraved on the silver clasp, before banishing painful thoughts from his mind and turning his attention to re-reading the lead article in an attempt to delay the inevitable:-

MUTATION SPREADS TO DOMESTIC ANIMALS!

"Scientists still no closer to combating Occold virus"

The name 'Occold' was first coined by the scientific community about a week or so after 'The Event' actually took place and is a reference to the location of the biological research facility where this new and extremely virulent threat to national security was first unleashed.

According to information received by this reporter from a source within the facility; footage from the internal surveillance systems suggests that the current crisis was the result of an unfortunate accident. Whilst supposedly working on utilising recombinant DNA for cancer therapy, a small team of particularly unfortunate boffins somehow managed to create an 'unstable in vivo virus' which had the unexpected effect of 'triggering cascade genetic alterations in living cells at an alarming rate'.

This mutation in itself might not have presented a particularly large problem, given that all experimentation on the project was being carried out in a sealed lab environment as a precautionary measure. However, the fact that patient zero happened to be the heavily tranquilised 450 lb male mountain gorilla lying on the lab operating table at the time proved to be a much more serious matter. One which was complicated further when the rapid genetic alterations taking place also apparently neutralised the substantial dose of tranquilisers present in the silverback's bloodstream and the rather bewildered animal arose suddenly from slumber to find itself trapped in an eight by twelve glass cage filled with sharp pointy instruments and three extremely terrified scientists. The understandably upset animal proceeded to butcher his gaolers in particularly gruesome fashion; crushing skulls and rending several limbs from bodies before making his exit through the nearest glass wall and running amok through the facility.

Through a series of further unfortunate mishaps, it transpires that the enraged gorilla then managed to escape from the facility itself into the surrounding countryside, leaving behind a trail of bloody carnage and destruction in its wake. Realising that this could no longer be classified as a simple internal security matter, the research company was left with no choice but to contact the local authorities and notify them of the somewhat alarming prospect of a large genetically altered primate running loose in the English countryside.

Of course the national media was alerted to this too-good-to-miss story within the first hour and by noon that day, the majority of the county of Suffolk found itself being closely scrutinised by a combination of law enforcement officials, zoological experts, animal rights campaigners and journalists. Along with these assembled professionals came an assortment of enthusiastic members of the public armed to the teeth with a variety of entirely useless paraphernalia, ranging from cans of pepper spray to over-sized fishing nets.

Given the contrasting ethea of the various factions, co-ordination of the search unsurprisingly proved to be a nightmare. The scientific experts present decided that getting as close as possible to shoot the possibly rabid animal up with tranquilisers was the best course of action, but found themselves at odds with the animal welfare types as to whether chasing the poor creature around the countryside for several hours would cause it unnecessary distress. The gun-toting authoritarians were of a mind to simply put the crazed animal down as quickly and efficiently as possible so as not to endanger the general public, but had a great deal of trouble preventing said general public from heading off half-cocked to track the gorilla down before them.

In the end, none of the assembled groups were able to lay claim to having tracked down the over-sized ape. That rather dubious honour went to a short, balding and decidedly plump, bespectacled gentlemen from Tunbridge Wells (who it later transpired was only passing through the county on a day-trip), after he somehow managed to hit the gorilla head-on with his 1983 Volvo Estate.

Despite having saved the surrounding populace from a severely dangerous biological menace and generally being hailed by most local people as a hero, the quiet little man seemed strangely more concerned as to which of the assembled parties was going to compensate him for the substantial damage to his vehicle's radiator and front headlights. Sadly, this fortuitous traffic accident did not take place before the afore-mentioned rogue science experiment had rampaged through half the county, infecting almost every genus of wildlife it came into direct physical contact with.

Thankfully it seems that at this point, the virus has chosen not to mutate further into an airborne variant. However the numerous small animal carcasses, upon which the evidently hungry ape fed during those first few hours of freedom, were unfortunately not discovered soon enough to prevent a host of other opportunistic creatures from also feeding on the same infected flesh.

The mangled body of the ape was of course disposed of immediately by a government biohazard team and the surrounding area rigorously sterilised, but after about a week, the reports of further sporadic incidents began to appear and it quickly became clear that something had gone terribly wrong.

Like a bear stirring from deep hibernation, the parliamentary bureaucracy slowly and painstakingly began to take steps to decide as to what was the best course of action. The debate raged back and forth in the House for days as the virus continued to spread unabated across South East England. By the time a plan was finally formulated, the authorities could no longer hope to contain the contagion and instead, regional animal control teams were hastily assembled from the ranks of local law enforcement and animal control organisations. Dispatched into the ever-widening infection area with orders to incinerate anything that moved and wasn't human, these zoological death squads set about their own particular brand of pest control with extreme prejudice.

Alas, despite essentially razing the majority of Suffolk to the ground in a matter of days, the authorities soon came to the terrifying conclusion that the underlying problem was going to be the birds. Having fled the immediate area as soon as large-scale extermination began, the birds had the potential to travel great distances in a short space of time, thereby rendering any predictions about the overall map of infection completely useless. In addition, many varieties of common garden bird are located towards the lower end of the food chain and might soon find themselves fodder for a number of larger predators, thereby exacerbating the problem.

Beset by an increasingly rancorous barrage of public criticism, the severely cash-strapped government has finally elected to hand over responsibility for controlling any new infection hot spots to individual county councils, giving them complete freedom to deal with the matter how they see fit. Parliament of course maintains overall control via a small number of national 'clean-up squads' placed on high alert, ready to be dispatched to any areas encountering severe difficulties, but essentially our government has courageously decided to wash their hands of this whole sorry business.

In practice, this strategy has met with considerable success within the inner cities and other highly populated urban areas where the ratio of people to animals is particularly biased in favour of humans. However, the plan quickly breaks down when employed in the more rural areas of the country, where the scales are decidedly more biased in the opposite direction.

Having reached the end of the article, Lionel neatly folded up the paper and replaced it carefully on the edge of the coffee table. He had heard all of this several times before of course, choosing as always to take everything he read in the papers with a large pinch of salt. With no new deliveries having come through the door for several days and television reception down here in the valley being as poor as it is was, he had no other current providers of information with regards to the national crisis and so had read and re-read the same newspapers over several times.

Usually, his primary source of knowledge was via word of mouth; more specifically via Mrs Garrett next door. At the grand old age of eighty-five, Lionel's elderly neighbour had only two main interests in her life; namely caring for her inordinately spoiled miniature poodle, FiFi, and the relentless acquisition of village gossip from anyone who would spare her the time of day. Visitors to the house were encouraged to stay for afternoon tea and often a cucumber sandwich or two, whilst being subjected to intense interrogation ordeals that would have given even the most sadistic SS officers the willies. Throughout the conversation, Mrs Garrett would sit eagerly hunched forward on the couch, surreptitiously feeding the occasional morsel of Ferrero Rocher to Fifi, whilst she herself hungrily devoured the tasty titbits of information on offer from her guests.

Yes, on any normal day, it would have been safe to say that whatever goings-on related to the dreadful Occold virus had transpired in the village of late, Mrs Garrett would have been able to give Lionel a detailed and precise breakdown of it all, possibly over coffee and custard creams.

Unfortunately, the usually placid Fifi had become infected three days previous and helped herself to a large chunky titbit of Mrs Garrett's right hand before escaping into the garden and disappearing through a gap in the hedgerow.

At the sound of the first scream, Lionel had come running out into his backyard, just in time to clumsily leapfrog over the fence and catch his blood-soaked neighbour as she feinted clean away onto the patio. The emergency services had been called almost immediately and by the time the ambulance arrived to take her away,

Mrs Garrett had regained consciousness and begun chatting with the local constabulary, who had decided to put in an appearance.

The first line of business had of course been to ascertain how the poodle had managed to avoid being culled as a precautionary measure during the compulsory domestic cleansing policy instigated nationwide well over a month ago. Mrs Garrett had managed to remain remarkably elusive on this subject, partly due to her being a little disorientated from the attack and claiming to be suffering from mild shock. It was also partly due to her being a wily old battleaxe, who was as practiced in the retention of information as she was in its acquirement.

During this rather official conversation, Lionel had chosen to keep very quiet on the periphery of the scene, hoping to God that Mrs Garrett would not choose to mention his own particular infidelities. Thankfully she had seemed far more concerned as to the fate of her escaped pet than with placing him beneath the same public scrutiny as she now found herself uncomfortably squirming.

A thorough search had been made of the immediate area, but no trace of Fifi could be found. Mrs. Garrett had seemed quite beside herself at this, desperately unhappy at the thought of her 'poor little baby' being forced to spend the night out in the dark all alone. But when informed that she would soon be en route to the district hospital for a series of blood tests, the old dear had actually perked up a little (presumably buoyed by the thought of adding more new faces to her dense network of informants).

Once the paramedics had finally managed to shut Mrs Garrett up long enough to bundle her into the back of the ambulance and depart the scene, the remainder of the clean-up operation had proceeded with merciful swiftness. Lionel had given a short statement to the attending constable whilst the crime scene (if one could call it that) had been carefully screened for any relevant items, which were then carefully bagged and tagged for removal to the station.

Being himself an intensely neat sort of fellow, Lionel had been heartily impressed with the general speed and efficiency of the forensic officers, who having checked and rechecked the scene several times, had also had the presence of mind to secure the house before they left. One rather pleasant young man, kitted out in clean white overalls and face-mask, had even been so good as to hose the rather unsightly blood stains from the patio flags, so that if you ignored the yellow and black tape hung about the place like webbing, it was almost as if the whole incident had never happened.

Finding himself eventually alone once more, Lionel had returned indoors and immediately headed to his kitchen pantry, knowing that Saxon would almost certainly need to answer the call of nature, having been kooked up inside for so long a period of time. He had opened up the pantry door to find the twelve year old Alsatian sitting patiently in the corner waiting for him.

Due to his ageing years, Saxon's coarse fur was a mixture of mottled browns graced with sporadic patches of faded grey. This patchwork of bland colours contrasted noticeably with the bright blue bandana which Lionel had recently substituted around his neck upon discovering that Saxon's collar was beginning to cause a mild skin irritation beneath his thinning fur. Upon seeing his master, Lionel's only true friend in the world had let out a single solitary bark of annoyance and then sidled past him in the direction of the front door.

Of course, Lionel always had to be his usual cautious self before letting Saxon out into the garden; performing a cursory inspection from every vantage point in the house to make sure that no-one was in the immediate vicinity to observe what he had now come to think of as nothing more than a harmless minor legal transgression. Whilst he did so, Saxon would follow at his heels, nuzzling his warm nose affectionately against the palm of Lionel's hand as he peeked out through the net curtains.

As he stood in the porch that evening, leaning casually against the doorframe and watching Saxon evacuate his ageing bowels onto the grass, Lionel mused to himself that it really wasn't as if they were a pair of dangerous master criminals or anything. One read in the papers all the time these days of foolish city types who, having chosen to keep their 150 lb Rottweiler hidden from the authorities and letting the animal out unsupervised under cover of darkness, were then somehow remarkably surprised when their once cuddly canine companion returned home later that same night with two gleaming red eyes and a new-found penchant for human flesh.

It was different with Saxon of course. For starters Lionel always made sure that at every instance, he kept a very close watch on his faithful companion and at the merest hint of any approaching wildlife, he would immediately call Saxon inside so as to avoid even the remotest possibility of contamination.

Never once during the last few months had Lionel even so much as once contemplated turning Saxon in to the local authorities. In his opinion, the bond between a man and his dog was sacrosanct and in the case of this dog, he was entirely sure that if the roles were somehow reversed one day, then Saxon would choose to stick by him as well. Sure, the both of them were becoming more than a little irritable in their waning years, but at the end of each day, Saxon was always to be found contentedly curled up across Lionel's feet as he dozed in his armchair before the hearth.

As he watched, Saxon padded slowly round the edge of the lawn, pausing momentarily to sniff at movement in the rhododendron bushes before deciding to push his snout in amongst the large pink flowers for a closer inspection. Lionel sighed at this, rolling his eyes in the manner of an exasperated parent, for if he'd told the dog once, he'd told him a hundred times to leave the damn bees alone unless he wanted to get himself stung. Of course the silly animal never listened and more than once Lionel recalled having to gently apply ointment to a swollen nose as Saxon lay whining pitifully in his lap like a baby.

'Serves you right!' he muttered under his breath as he observed Saxon yelp and withdraw his now pollen-covered muzzle sharply from the bushes, shaking his head repeatedly as he did so. The Alsatian turned and came skulking back across the lawn with a rather sheepish expression on his face and having no sympathy for him, Lionel merely stood to one side and watched his old friend slink back into the house, presumably in search of some quiet corner to hide himself away in whilst he licked his wounds.

Lionel sat motionless in his armchair now, his eyes once again lingering on Saxon's collar on the coffee table as he recalled that same scene from three days ago as though it had just occurred. 'It wasn't my fault' cried an indignant voice in his head. 'How was I to know that Saxon discovered something other than a bee in the bushes that day?' But beneath the tarnished sheen of his supremely righteous ego, Lionel found himself unable to ignore the thick grimy layer of shameful guilt deposited by the young postman's death.

Up until the moment the lad had come calling the morning after all the commotion, he had honestly thought nothing of the fact that Saxon had been keeping a low profile all night. He had assumed, incorrectly, that his four-legged friend was merely skulking about upstairs in order to hide his embarrassment at once again coming off worst from an encounter with an insect only a fraction of his size.

The familiar sound of a cheerful whistle meandering through the chorus of 'Moon River' had signalled the arrival of the post at around eight-thirty and being already up and dressed, Lionel had headed to the front door, intent on saying a brief hello as he collected the mail. The postman had waved in recognition, a handful of letters already in his hands as Lionel unfastened the door chain and grappled clumsily with the dead bolts. But as the door swung open, Lionel had seen the youth's cheery expression rapidly turn to one of confusion and then abject terror as he stared past Lionel into the house.

The next thing Lionel knew, he was being thrown roughly against the now fully open door as a bedraggled mass of blood and fur barrelled past him towards the open-mouthed postman. Lionel's first thought had been that some wild animal had somehow managed to force its way into the house during the night, such was the difference in appearance between the hellish creature that blurred past him and the beloved friend he knew so well. Every inch of Saxon's body dripped in copious amounts of a sticky fluid, which appeared to be a syrupy mixture of blood, saliva and pus. In places, the dog's fur was matted into thick clumps of hair, clustered together in groups across his back like angry carbuncles. Amongst these congealed dark knots, patches of fur were missing, apparently ripped out by Saxon himself, the skin beneath ragged and bloody where the distressed animal had bitten deep into his own flesh.

The postman was already beginning to back away, but had hardly moved in the direction of the gate when the thing that used to be Saxon was upon him. He managed a brief yell of panic before the Alsatian leapt up at him, hitting the terrified man square in the chest and knocking him to the ground with its considerable weight.

Lionel knew now that he should have done something at that point. He should have darted forward and tried to pull Saxon away, or perhaps even tried to drag the postman inside and away from the dog before it was too late. But he hadn't done either of those things. In fact to his shame, he hadn't moved at all. Instead he had remained motionless in the doorway, paralysed with a mixture of shock and fear as the now feral blood-crazed creature that used to be Saxon had wrapped its wide jaws around the flailing postman's exposed neck flesh and torn out the screaming man's oesophagus in one great bloody chunk.

Lionel had felt his mouth drop open and the ineffectual words "down boy" weakly escape his lips, but the sound could have reached no further than the doorway as he watched a fountain of blood erupt from the postman's body, coating the Saxon-Thing in a fine crimson mist. The sight of four rapidly twitching limbs and the low gurgling sound coming from the body made Lionel realise in horror that the poor man was still alive as the creature bent its maw and began to lap voraciously at the exposed hole in his neck. Lionel felt faint and lurched sideways, grabbing hold of the door jamb just in time to stop himself from tumbling out of the porch. His stomach convulsed repeatedly as he fought back the urge to retch and he felt sure he would have passed out had it not been for what had happened next.

At the sound of Lionel slumping against the door, the Saxon-Thing had lifted its blood-soaked head and turned to gaze in his direction. In that moment, Lionel had felt his whole world implode as he found himself staring with disbelief into the two red unblinking eyes which looked out at him hungrily from the centre of the face he had raised from a pup and loved so unconditionally over the last twelve years.

With no evidence of recognition, the Saxon-Thing had uttered a low growl and taken one meaningful step back towards the house. The creature had bared its teeth as behind, the still moving postman flopped over onto his side and began to crawl desperately in the direction of the pond, leaving a trail of fresh blood and entrails in his wake.

At that point, Lionel's underlying survival instinct had finally taken over. Having slammed the door shut, he was instinctively crouching into a protective foetal position on the floor when he felt the Saxon-Thing's full weight slam into the outer wood of the door. The blow almost flung the door back open, but instead it caught Lionel full in the side of his ribs, knocking the wind from him and causing him to collapse flat onto the ground. As he fought for breath, a nose appeared through the crack in the door, followed by twin rows of teeth foaming with blood and fresh sputum. Operating solely on instinct, Lionel desperately threw his weight back against the door just as one malevolent red eye appeared through the gap. As the edge of the door slammed back hard against the Saxon-Thing's face, the wood cut a deep groove into the exposed flesh of the dog's face and it let out a loud yelp. Lionel's heart wrenched at the sound of his best friend in such pain, but still he found himself desperately kicking at the dog's face and then fumbling with the lower dead bolt as the lacerated snout withdrew and the door slotted back into its frame.

Lionel reached up and pulled himself into a kneeling position by the handle just as a second loud thud shook the door and this was followed by the sound of scratching and gnawing as the infuriated creature tried to force its way back in. Once the chain was slid securely back in place, Lionel slumped defeated onto the floor, his trembling body finally letting go of any remaining composure as he both soiled himself and puked his guts out onto the rubber welcome mat.

Unable to force the door, the Saxon-Thing remained outside, pacing angrily back and forth and as Lionel lay there weeping into a pool of his own urine, an unearthly howl which no longer sounded anything like a dog filled the air. He covered his ears, attempting to block out the agonising sound, but as the Saxon-Thing turned and raced away into the nearby woods in search of an easier kill, Lionel could do nothing but lie in a desperate heap and sob.

It was nearly nine-thirty now and finding his body stiff and unwieldy, Lionel realised that he had been sitting motionless in his armchair for the entire afternoon. He looked down to find that Saxon's collar had somehow found its way back into his hands. He reached out as if to place it back on the coffee table, but then stopped. Taking the collar in both hands, he wrapped it slowly and painstakingly around the palm of his right hand with grim determination, pulling it tight before threading the clasp through the last hole to secure it in place. For a reason he could not fathom, the symbolic act gave him some kind of new-found courage. He stood up, letting his hands drop to his sides and as he did so, the tiny silver disc bearing Saxon's name tinkled slightly against the metal clasp. The sound was somehow reassuring to him and noting that there was very little daylight left out there, Lionel swallowed loudly and headed into the kitchen.

Despite everything being in its proper place as always, it took him several minutes to locate what he was looking for, his over-wrought mind struggling to perform even simple tasks. With a trembling hand he carefully withdrew the nine inch kitchen blade from the utensils drawer and held it up to the fading light. The warped reflection of a scared old man, who had cried far too much that day, stared back at him from the unblemished metal of the blade.

Returning to the front door, he turned the dead bolts and removed the chain as quietly as he possibly could. A little voice inside kept telling him that it might be ok, that maybe the virus would have worn off by now and that good old Saxon would be fine ("...eight is a wish"), but in his heart he didn't really believe it.

Lionel had not set foot outside the house since the encounter with the Saxon-Thing two days ago and the door had evidently become slightly wedged into its frame since then, for he had to take hold of the handle in both hands and yank firmly several times before it finally juddered open. Immediately the sickly sweet smell of death wafted through on the in-draft and he reflexively gagged at the appalling stench.

The pond was easily fifteen yards away at the other end of the garden but even at this distance, the smell emanating from the postman's remains was almost overpowering. Lionel's eyes watered slightly as he pulled the door fully open. Taking the knife firmly by the hilt in his left hand and gripping tightly onto Saxon's collar with his right, he stepped gingerly out into the porch.

The outer door was not shut, instead hanging precariously from its hinges and it seemed evident that the Saxon-Thing had vented its frustration at not being able to get into the house. The garden was eerily quiet, the majority of the birds thankfully having already gone to roost for the night. A barn owl screeched somewhere off in the distance and Lionel shuddered at the thought of a winged carnivorous predator that could turn its sharp jaws through 360 degrees.

Feeling as if he was being watched, Lionel glanced up and immediately jumped at the unnerving sight of thirteen pairs of glowing red eyes glaring at him from the roof across the street. He could just make out the outline of the troupe of magpies in the dusk, not one of them moving as they sat clustered together on the slates, keenly observing his movements. At first Lionel couldn't understand why they didn't just swoop down to attack, but then it dawned on him; they knew what was about to transpire down below and were simply waiting until he became easier pickings.

"Yeah, well fuck you too" he whispered in the direction of the roof as he stepped carefully onto the lawn and began to tiptoe towards the pond.

Glancing around him, he peered carefully at every long shadow, squinting to try and make out the crouched shape of a dog lying in wait for him. The garden overflowed with darkness and he struggled to make out any definite shapes in the remaining light. His hands were slick with sweat now and he could feel it running down the hilt of the kitchen knife as he clenched it tighter into the ball of his fist. Stalking forward, he shook his right hand slightly so that the silver name tag jingled against the collar, the slightly off-key note ringing out clearly in this silent graveyard like a summons.

Sensing a rough outline in the shadows beside the pond, Lionel raised the blade up in front of him and leant cautiously forward to get a closer look.

"Come out, come out wherever you are" he crooned smoothly as he bent lower, brandishing the knife before him.

A low growl came in answer from the rear and Lionel froze, feeling a single bead of cold sweat uncomfortably trickle down his back. The Saxon-Thing was directly behind him he realised, the sound seeming to come from slightly above him and he now knew that he would have only a few seconds to get this right.

Tensing every muscle in his body, Lionel dug his fingernails resolutely into the leather collar and abruptly spun round. Above him, on the flat roof of the shed, the Saxon-Thing's hulking form stood silhouetted in the partial moonlight, its blood-red eyes burning with primal hunger as it glared down at Lionel. The laceration caused by the door had cut a deep groove across the dog's face, leaving an angry battle scar crudely sliced through its hellish visage. Around the beast's neck, the tattered remnants of a dirty blue bandana were just visible amongst the dense mass of crusted hair.

As the creature launched itself in his direction, Lionel felt the knife rise up in his hand. The Saxon-Thing was a snarling black ball of teeth and fur as it hurtled through the air towards him, its eyes locked on his and then there was a sudden wet puncturing noise as the creature's soft underbelly slid onto the outstretched blade. Still though, the Saxon-Thing's momentum carried it onwards and Lionel let out a loud "oof" as the dog's weight slammed into his upper body.

His knees gave way under him and he found himself falling backward onto the lawn, the wounded beast collapsing on top of him with the kitchen knife forced into its chest right up to the hilt. Not quite dead yet, the creature immediately began to claw and bite at him as it writhed in agony and Lionel desperately grabbed the dog by the throat, forcing the snapping jaws away from his face. Tears streamed down his cheeks as he grappled with the murderous nightmare that had once been his only friend in this world and as the life finally drained out of the creature, just for a second as the evil red glare in the animal's eyes faded, he glimpsed Saxon's pleading face behind big brown eyes as they dimmed to nothingness.

Lionel felt the body go limp and still weeping, he wrapped his arms around his dead companion and hugged the dog tightly to him, burying his head into Saxon's matted dark fur.

After he could cry no more tears, he laid his head back onto the blood-soaked grass, exhausted and stared up into the night sky. Between wisps of dark cloud he glimpsed the solitary brightness of Sirius and let out a low whimper of anguish. As he did, there came a rustle from his left.

Turning his head, Lionel found that he had landed next to the rhododendrons and he now watched the oversized leaves at the base of the bush began to softly jiggle as something slowly pushed its way towards him. He tried to get up but the dead weight of the dog had effectively pinned him to the ground with his upper arms trapped at his sides and he could only stare in horror as the leaves parted and a familiar face appeared beside him.

Beneath blood-streaked white fur that had been tied up in an assortment of garish ribbons and brightly coloured bows, a tiny set of sharp teeth parted into a wide snarl as the Fifi-Thing growled threateningly at him ("...nine is a kiss"). The disagreeable bouquet of carrion mixed with chocolate-coated hazelnuts washed over him as fear took him in its rigid grasp and he opened his mouth to scream.

The poodle lunged hungrily forward at his prone unprotected face and as the dreadful sound of torn flesh and Lionel's high-pitched shrieks filled the night air, thirteen magpies took flight from the rooftop across the street and as one, soared up into the darkness in search of fresh meat.

TWO DAYS BEFORE THE END OF THE WORLD

Ryan C. Thomas

Nick steered his pickup truck into the dirt driveway of the Robinson farm and parked it behind his friend Gavin's beat up Ford 150. He had no idea what Gavin had been crowing about on the phone, or why he needed to be here so early, just that he needed to git his ass on over here like right now. A cloud of dust, kicked up from the tires, engulfed him as he opened the rusted truck door and stepped out into the scorching August heat. With the sun directly overhead, and the air conditioning in the truck busted all to hell, his insides were jonesing for something cool and refreshing.

The farmhouse's driveway-side door was wide open but the inside screen door, warped from years of being kicked and slammed, was wedged shut. Nick cupped his hands around his eyes and peeked in through the mesh at the kitchen beyond. Same old same old. Place looked like a tornado had hit it. Dirty dishes stacked precariously high near the sink, empty beer bottles lying all over the floor, faded and wrinkled copies of *Guns & Ammo* tossed willy nilly on the countertops and the kitchen table. If the stench of trash could win awards the smell coming from inside would have a case full of trophies. Every surface, including the chairs, was coated in some kind of ochre stain that you didn't dare touch unless you had the CDC's number on speed dial. Some of it was food, some of it dirt, but the rest... God only knew. The place had looked like this since Gavin's brother Jessie took off two weeks ago with some whore he met at the Box Seat Tavern.

Nick announced himself. "Yo, shitheel. I'm here already."

He waited a second, but no one answered. A good yank got the screen door open. He stepped inside and started for the sink to pour a glass of water, saw the flies buzzing about it (ain't no screen gonna keep flies from getting at a meal, that's for sure) and opted for a beer from the fridge instead. It was cold. At least Gavin had remembered to pay the electric bill. Either that or the electric company offered a generous grace period to delinquent bill payers. As he was shutting the fridge door, he spotted his friend sitting on the stoop out back. "Hey, you deaf? I said I'm here." He used the top of the kitchen table to pop the beer cap off. "I'm taking a beer."

Without a word, Gavin waved an arm in a "come here" gesture. That was strange, Nick thought. Gavin was usually a pretty boisterous fellow. Could be he was just hung over or something. God knew that happened often enough. 'Course he hadn't sounded hung over on the phone when he was telling Nick to git his ass here pronto.

Nick passed through the breezeway, accidentally kicking over a pile of porno mags and a shoebox of old Junior Brown cassette tapes, and opened the screen door to the back yard. The heat slammed him once again as he sat next to Gavin on the stoop. "Well, here I am. What the hell's so damn important I gotta get out of bed at ten o'clock on a Saturday morning? I don't work on a farm, in case you forgot. I don't need to be up right now."

Gavin shushed him with a finger and pointed across the small yard to where the rows of corn began.

"Yeah, I heard this one before. The corn has ears? Hardy fucking har."

"No, douchebag. Hush up for a sec and wait."

Nick waited, sipped his beer, waved a gnat away from his face with his baseball cap. The corn was doing a pretty good impression of being corn. He gave it five out of five stars--top rate mimicry. "Well now I see what you mean," he said. "Corn this exciting shouldn't go unwatched. Pregnant women should avoid this ride."

"Hold up," Gavin said, a smile now starting to curl up at the corners of his mouth. "I think it's coming."

"What? Winter? 'Cause if we sit here long enough—"

"There." Gavin thrust his finger out toward the corn, a little to the left.

Nick could see the stalks swaying a bit as something walked through them, moving slow and kind of low to the ground. He took another sip of the beer just as a mangy sheep came walking out, its wool coat matted and muddy and housing various bits of corn stalk. It walked like someone had put new legs on it. Splotches of red goop were streaked across its body. Looked like blood.

Slowly, Nick put the beer on the stoop and stood up for a better look. "Shit, ain't that—"

"Harley," Gavin said.

Harley was Gavin's brother's pet sheep. Nick rarely paid it any mind when he was over; the thing was smelly and loud. Poor thing must've gotten attacked by something. Sometimes coyotes from the nearby mountains ventured down at night. And there'd been rumors of mountain lions out past the river, but no real proof.

"What the hell happened to her?"

"Honestly?"

"No, make something up. Direct answers are for pussies."

Gavin waved him off and ignored the wiseass reply. "I killed her."

"What?"

"I said I killed her."

"Well, don't take this the wrong way or nuthin', but looks like you screwed up."

"That's just it. I didn't screw up. I took my slugger and—"

"Hold up. First things first. Why you want to kill her? You that hungry? Thought you guys didn't slaughter animals?"

Gavin stood up now as well, and both of them watched the sheep amble around the small yard in front of the cornfield. "Nah. She was sick. I mean like real sick. I tried to put her down, you know. Last night I come out here and she's puking up a storm. She was like a ruptured hose, spraying fluid every which way. Blood, shit, puke. You name it, it was comin' out of her. It wasn't natural. And the way she screamed at me... she tried to bite me. I think maybe she got a case of rabies or something, and I ain't taking chances with no rabid sheep, pet or not."

"Could just be some kind of animal flu. You shoulda just called that farm vet out by Millford, maybe taken her in? Your brother's gonna kill you when he finds out you messed her up."

"First off, it ain't some flu. It's something else. Second, Jessie ain't gonna do shit because Jessie run off with that cumdumpster Brandy. The way he'd been talking about getting away from here, I know he's washed his hands of Indiana for good."

"You think he went to Vegas?" Nick asked.

"What am I, his secretary? He could be on the moon right now for all I know."

"Doubt it. You need a degree to get to the moon."

"Well, then, he sure as shit ain't on the moon."

Nick took a step off the stoop and stood on the grass, inched his way toward Harley but kept a respectable distance. The sheep was staggering like a wino, its head lolling sideways like it was too heavy to lift. "He always was talking about Vegas, is all."

"Don't need to tell me. He fancied himself a craps genius but I think he was confused by what he did in the bathroom and what the casino game is."

"Maybe he's getting hitched. A real wedding with Elvis impersonators and everything."

"I hope not," Gavin replied. "That girl is too hot to take off the market. I tried getting on her a few times myself. I can't fuck her if she's my sister."

"Well, technically speaking..."

Gavin wasn't listening anymore. His eyes were glued to the ravaged animal before them. "You see the wound on Harley's head?"

Nick walked a bit closer, bent around the sheep and looked at the gaping hole behind the animal's ear. Runny scrambled brain oozed out of the split skull. No wonder the animal was staggering around, it had to be in some sort of awful pain. "Dang. That's pretty fucking gross, man. We should really put her out of her misery."

"You're missing what I'm saying. I already did. I did it twice already. She won't die."

Harley swung her head in Nick's direction and gave a feeble bleat. It was more like a burp than anything else but it freaked him out so he trotted back toward Gavin and gave a little shudder.

Gavin spit hot summer phlegm into the dirt by their feet. “Don’t be scared, she can’t move fast enough to bite anymore.”

“I ain’t scared.”

"Looked it to me."

Okay, Nick admitted to himself, she had scared him. But come on, the thing's brain was about to fall out of its skull, who wouldn't be scared? He still felt bad for the poor animal. That hole in her head, there was no way a vet could fix her now. And if Gavin wasn't going to put it down correctly he was gonna have to do it himself. "Don't you have Jessie's gun or something?"

"Nope, he took it. All I got is my slugger. It's right over here, still covered in Harley's blood." Gavin walked over under the kitchen window and picked up the baseball bat that was leaning against the house.

Nick took it from him and examined it, ran his fingers across the dried blood. Man, he couldn't imagine getting slugged in the head with a bat hard enough to crack his skull open. The pain must be killer. And it wasn't like he gave much of a damn about a smelly sheep but it still seemed like a cruel way to go. Poor Harley. Sometimes euthanasia was just the best option. "All right, I'll take care of this. Stand back."

"I'm telling ya, it won't matter," Gavin said.

Harley was standing near the cornfield now, her legs rickety like a poorly made coffee table. Something in her eyes said she knew what Nick's intentions were, but something else said she wasn't too concerned. There was a distant spark of life in those eyes that didn't know enough to call it quits. He got around the side of her where her brain was exposed, raised the bat over his head, and said, "Hold on, Harley, it's all over now." The bat came down with a *crack!* and knocked the sheep to the ground, four legs splaying out at varying angles. Harley's neck broke under the impact of the swing and her head rebounded off the ground and flipped back over her shoulders, her tongue drooping out across her wool coat. She's definitely dead now, thought Nick. Nothing could have survived that blow, not even a rhino. He came back across the small yard and handed the bat to Gavin, picked up his beer and took a sip. "Done. I'll bill you in installments."

"I'm waiting for proof."

"Proof nothing. She's dead. Just don't tell Jessie it was me. I don't want his crazy ass chasing me down 'cause you played vet with his girlfriend. I'm getting another beer. This one's warm already." But before Nick could get back into the house, Gavin put an arm on his shoulder and spun him around.

"Lookie there, Mr. Grim Reaper."

Turning back, Nick just about dropped the beer on the ground. Harley was back up on all fours, more wobbly than before, her head swaying down between her two front legs. She did her best to turn toward Nick and Gavin and let out another bubbly bleat. Nick felt his gut do a somersault. There was no way that animal should be alive. He'd hit her harder than he'd ever hit anything. A real strong blow with complete follow through just like coach had taught them at practice. Now, for the first time, he felt a bit uneasy about everything. "Gav?"

"Yeah?"

"Gimmie the bat again."

Gavin handed Nick the bat and followed him as he took up position behind Harley once more. "I told you something was up," he said.

There wasn't much for Nick to say to that. Something was definitely up, and whatever it was, it couldn't be good. "Let's put her on her side," Nick suggested, "come at her from an angle."

Nodding his head in agreement, Gavin pushed the bloody sheep to the ground, got it on its side. He put a foot on it to hold it still while Nick prodded its head with the bat, getting it into a good position for a direct blow.

Then he raised the bat up and brought it down on the side of the animal's head.

CRACK!

Blood spit up onto Nick's clothes, splashed him in the forehead. Bending down, he took off his hat and cleaned his face with it. Looking into Harley's eyes, he could still see that spark of life shining out. Finally, he put the bat down and said, "She ain't dying."

***

Six o'clock rolled around quicker than they'd expected. They'd been sitting on the stoop ever since that last swing of the bat, trying to figure out what the problem was with Harley. So far, they hadn't come up with shit. And they were out of beer to boot. At least the heat had died down. "You think Jessie's really getting married?" Gavin finally asked, breaking a ten minute bout of silence.

"Nah," Nick replied. "I doubt it. If he was wanting to get married he'd have done it long ago. He's probably just out having fun. You know how them whores can be."

"Yeah, I know."

"Who are you kidding? No you don't."

"Man, eat my nuts." There was a long pause. Finally, Gavin said, "I can't run the farm without him. Ma and Dad's will said Jessie is in charge of the estate." Gavin banged his fist against the side of the house to show how dilapidated and un-estate-like the home really was. "If he don't come back I don't even know if I can sell the place."

"Yeah, but look at it this way. How many other people our age get their own house."

Gavin picked up a rock and tossed it out toward the sunset. It landed near Harley's body, which was still twitching and bleating every now and then. "You wanna move in if he don't come back?"

For the first time, Nick could see genuine concern in Gavin's eyes. It wasn't like Jessie had never taken off for a couple of days before, but this was two weeks, and that was something to think about. Could be he really was gone for good. He'd spoken about it enough times—going to Vegas, leaving Indiana in his dust. Maybe he'd finally convinced himself. "I can't," he replied, feeling a bit bad as he said it, "this place is too far from the city and I'd be late to work every day."

"You call that work, being a waiter?"

"It pays the bills."

"What bills? Your parents don't make you pay rent?"

"It gives me money for weed and video games. Point is, I don't exactly have the best resume, so waiting tables is what I can get right now." That probably wasn't what Gavin wanted to hear, so Nick dug deep into that part of his male psyche that forbade him to have emotions about guys and turned it off for a second. "Listen, you need help, you call me. My folks and I...we got an extra room."

"I can't leave here. This is my home."

"I'm just saying."

"I can't."

"Suit yourself."

They sat in silence for a few more minutes while Harley's legs kicked in the grass. The sheep tried to roll over a few times but didn't make it up. "So how did she get sick?" Nick asked.

"Harley?"

"No, the old woman in the shoe. Yes Harley."

Picking up another rock, Gavin shook his head, pitched the rock in to the corn. "No idea. She just showed up at the door that way last night. Animals get sick, you know. Had some blood on her, though. And some bite marks. We got mountain lions 'round here. That's why I was thinking it's maybe rabies. Funny thing is the couple of bite marks on her belly...couple of 'em are round, like a human bite mark. I can't think of an animal that has a round mouth print."

"Probably something small like a raccoon. They have rabies. I saw one on the news once. Thing was hissing."

"I never much cared for her, you know. But she didn't exactly bug me neither. Jessie loves her pretty hard. Said she's a better pet than a stupid dog. I was surprised that he left her."

"Loves her? You mean like in a baaaaad way?" Nick mimicked a sheep.

Gavin chuckled, but it was half-hearted. Nick could see he was still worried about his brother and about the future of the homestead. "Aw hell, who knows with my brother. I wouldn't put it past him to get so drunk he wouldn't come out here and make Harley his woman."

Nick's eyes perked up. "Serious?"

"No."

"Aw, I bet he did at least once, the sheepfucker. Your brother is a beast humper."

"Well he did do your mama."

"Hey. Mama jokes are no fair. I can't make them back to you."

"I know, that's what makes it such a sweet deal for me."

Nick indicated the sheep with a nod of his head. "So she got out of her pen somehow?"

"Yeah, I checked it earlier. Looks like she just chewed through the wire. Her teeth are all ground up in her mouth, so that pretty much confirms it. Considering her state last night, she must have gone mad or something."

"I gotta admit," Nick said, leaning back and stretching out his legs, "this is pretty weird. You think we should call someone? Maybe the cops?"

"And tell 'em what? We been hitting a sheep with a baseball bat all day and it won't die? They'll think we're nuts. My brother already has a reputation 'round here, I don't need one too."

The sunset was dipping below the horizon now, the last bands of golden light bouncing off Harley's blood-stained fleece. Nick thought of an old movie he'd recently seen on TBS. Bunch of Greek guys looking for something similar. The effects were crap, but he'd liked it anyway. Harley was even moving all herky jerky like the claymation figures in the movie.

"Well, you want to try some more? Maybe get an axe and chop her head off or something?"

It sounded cruel as he said it, but he felt so bad for the creature he wanted to find a way to finally let it move on to the great, peaceful sheep pen in the sky.

Gavin considered this, but ultimately shook his head. "You know what I think? She obviously don't want to die, and she don't look worried about the pain. I think she's earned the right to live. I say we just let her go."

"You're kidding?"

"Nope. Let's pick her up and see if she can still walk."

Together, they crossed the grass and looked down at the pathetic animal. Her eyes moved to follow them despite the fact her head was bent at the completely wrong angle and her brains were starting to ooze out of the fist-sized hole in her skull. Some chunks of gray and pink meat dotted the ground nearby. They bent down and got their hands under her belly and hoisted her to her feet.

"No way she's gonna stand," Nick said.

But when they let go, sure enough, Harley stood. Wobbling, swaying, kind of staggering even, with her head swinging down between her legs like a grandfather clock's pendulum, but standing by definition. "I don't believe it," Nick said.

"Your parents cooking dinner tonight?" Gavin asked, rubbing his hands together to get the stink of death off them. It was clear he was hungry, and judging by the state of the house, Nick could tell there wasn't any food inside.

"Yeah, grab your jacket. Let's get out of here."

Before they got to Nick's truck, they looked back at Harley one last time. Slowly, on shaking legs, the sheep pushed its way into the rows of corn, let out a feeble farewell bleat from its dangling head, and disappeared from view. The corn stalks swayed for a bit, then slowly went still. Harley had left the building.

"Damn. Strange sheep," Nick said.

"Yeah. Strange sheep."

They climbed in Nick's truck, backed down the driveway and turned onto the road, narrowly missing a disheveled, staggering drunk who looked liked he'd spent the last three nights sleeping outside. The man moaned in protest, moved a bit like Harley did, Nick thought. The man's sallow eyes were glazed and his mouth was stained with crimson. Nick flipped him off. "Watch out, you idiot."

A minute later, the truck was speeding down the road toward the center of town, jokes about beer and girls lifting out of the open windows and disappearing into the summer night sky.

GIFT HORSE MOUTH

J Gilliam Martin

Lightning lit the sky every thirty seconds or so. The rain was gentle, but the thunder was deafening. Between claps, Terry could hear a faint slapping sound outside the window. Wood on wood, creaking and cracking. He rose from his chair, spilling his sour mash as he stood.

"Oh motherfucker," he shouted at the broken glass. "Janet! Clean up this mess while I see what the fuck is making all this noise outside."

He was sure she wouldn't budge. Ever since their six-year-old son, Levi, was slaughtered by a truck while riding his bicycle on the main road, Janet hardly made the effort to breathe. Terry kicked shards of glass under the coffee table, and made his way to the window.

Upon looking outside, he noticed the yard gate ajar, whipping open and shut in the wind.

"What in the fuck? It better not be running around the field goddammit. "

The farm was anything but a farm these days. A few pigs, too many chickens and a goat. Just one goat, with its pen door swinging wildly in the storm. Terry crossed the living room and tore his jacket from the coat-hook, cursing with each arm he put in it. Mumbling obscenities illegibly under his breath like a cartoon character, he made his way outside and into the yard.

Sure enough, the goat was not in his allowed area. Neither could he be seen anywhere in the visible vicinity of the farm. Terry yelled the goat's name into the dark a couple of times, until the lightning flashed so bright, he was given a daylight view of the scene. On the corner-post nearest the loose gate, he spotted Billy's collar, complete with an annoying bell. It had not been snagged or torn on the fence, it was hung there neatly like a successful ring toss. The goat hadn't escaped, someone had taken it.

"Janet call the fucking sheriff, someone's run off with the goat."

She stared through him, bottom lip quivering.

Terry reached under a cabinet pulling tape from its bottom, releasing a key. He unlocked the cabinet and withdrew his shotgun, checking the chamber and cocking it for action. He looked at his wife, still drooling in a depressed half-coma, shook his head and went back outside.

"Useless cunt."

Part 1: Don't Look

Willy Marsh sat in his room scribbling through some homework, staring out the window at the barn below. It was math, various algebra problems, to which he made guesses at the value of "x" and declined to show his work. A guaranteed grade D paper, since Ms. Wilkins would never fail him due to his misfortune over the last year.

Willy's father, Leroy Marsh, was locked away in the county prison after coming home from the bar in the early afternoon last May. He was not only drunk, but had passed out at the wheel before his truck went off the road into a tree, pinning a little boy and his bike to it. In these parts they lock you up for a good long time simply for a driving while intoxicated offense. Never mind getting out of prison at all, should you add manslaughter to it.

Since Dad's incarceration, Mom was never home. A promiscuous whore, Silvia Marsh filed for a divorce almost immediately, and spent her time a couple hours far, in the city, fucking *with* or *for* drugs. She came home every Sunday to drop off groceries and some money, and a brief interrogation into Willy's life during a grilled-cheese and tomato soup dinner, which Willy prepared. Before sundown she was gone back to the city, but not before a short ride on Willy's horse.

Black Beauty was the horse. Not an original name, sure, but Willy had received the horse as his seventh birthday present, to satisfy a child's obsession from after seeing the movie. B.B. certainly fit the part: a muscled and long-legged jet black horse the family had bought during better times. No one knew what kind of horse he was, but his size and strength suggested they had paid far less than he was worth. Without a single hair on him in any other color than black, and with a patient temper that made him a gentle companion but an energetic mount, he matched his namesake perfectly.

After finally deciding that the final "x" was four after you took "a" from "b" and whatever, Willy grabbed his music player and ran out to the barn. You might think a thirteen-year-old living by and raising himself would skip homework altogether, but the agreement he had with

Ms. Wilkins was that she would not fail him as long as he made an attempt. Willy had no desire to fail at anything. He had grown up seeing both his parents fail at almost everything, time and time again. They were a gap between Willy and his very successful and hard-working Grandfather, the farmer. The farm itself was too far gone for Willy to save, but he was determined to keep house, barn and horse in working order.

The horse was more than thrilled with the visit. Some carrots were exchanged as Willy equipped Black Beauty with the necessary gear for riding. He fiddled with the music player until heavy metal filled his ear-buds, hoisted himself into the saddle, and rode the evening away with his best friend.

There were trails throughout the woods behind his house for riding. Parts of the trail were extremely rough, but Willy and B.B. had rode this exact course every day for six years, so the horse did not hesitate to jump a downed log, or take shortcuts through rougher terrain past the muddy areas. On the drier parts of the trail the horse dug in and achieved great speed, hooves pummeling the path with great haste and force. A horse, black as night, raced through a road carved by nature (and frequent riding). Dust and dirt kicked up behind them and trees slapped at Willy's torso, their pace kept by fast and raw heavy metal, house and homework left behind.

Hours passed before Willy was ready to turn his steed around and head for home. Sleep came easily that night, as it did most nights he got a good ride in.

The next morning while waiting for the bus, Chad brought him a new album to listen to. Something about "coffin nails". Chad was a metal-head through and through, and possibly the only other in the tri-township.

This made friends of Willy and Chad by default. The world of heavy metal music was vast. Willy had preferred the faster, violent metal like thrash and death, like his favorite band, Splatter Infection, a gruesome death metal band, each song themed to the murder of some undeserving wretch. The faster the drums and guitar, the more adrenaline Willy felt while riding Black Beauty through the trees.

Chad indulged in black metal, a branch of metal coming mostly from Scandinavian countries, full of hate and Satan worship. The artists often donned "corpse paint", bland combinations of black and white face paint, often used to illustrate permanent expression of sadness or anger, as well as to portray the wearer as deceased.

Chad Barry hadn't had life any easier than Willy. When he was seven, Chad's sister took her own life, claiming in the note that she was regularly molested by their father. Chad's older brother Curtis took it upon himself to punish his father, caving in their father's head with an aluminum baseball bat. Curtis now rots in the same prison that houses Willy's father. Chad and his mother got by with a mix of marijuana, merlot, and music. Both denounce people, society, and God. While Chad's mother simply ignores all of these things, Chad has taken the alternative route seriously, and vows loyalty to Satan. He truly believes that through his commitment to evil ideals, the Devil will eventually embrace him and bestow strength upon him to deal with life as he pleases.

"I found this CD in my brothers old shit. I looked into it a bit on the internet and this was their only recording before the entire band ended their careers in a suicide pact. How cool is that? It was in the box I had been looking for, with all these ritual texts."

"Ritual texts?" Willy asked, staring at the album cover.

"Yeah, fucking Satanic rituals. Like 15 of them, from making a girl love you, to causing an enemy to choke to death on air."

"You really believe all that possible? I mean, if it were really that easy to take someone out, don't you think your brother would have left a trail of corpses behind him? Or anyone else, for that matter?"

"There have been plenty of people to walk this earth and leave a trail of corpses behind them. Anyway, you need people to assist with most of these rituals, Will. My brother had no friends, and neither would I if it weren't for you. But together, I think we could actually pull off a couple of these incantations, and fuck some shit up!"

Willy shrugged as the bus pulled up. He put the compact disc in his player and went to the back of the bus. This was no different than any other school day. Chad and Willy had slight conversation before the bus arrived, then both proceeded to the rear seats and strapped on their respective headphones. They wouldn't talk again until math class, last period of the day.

This new stuff was definitely some pure-evil music. The lyrics were totally incoherent, but the low tones they accompanied were so dark, Willy felt a hatred seething inside him, boiling just below the surface, on the low flame of this music. He listened to it twice on the ride, before handing it back to Chad as they stepped off the bus, and it remained fresh in his mind all through the morning.

Until lunchtime, when Sarah crossed his path.

Sarah was, in Willy's eyes, not only the best looking girl in school, but the only one worth looking at. For years he spent much of his waking state thinking about her, however unreachable she may be. Today, for whatever reason, she chose to sit with him.

"I didn't know you rode, Willy."

He said nothing, still shocked that after six years in school together, this was the first time they shared words.

"I had Chad as a volleyball partner yesterday in phys-ed, he told me all about your Black Beauty."

Still no reply. He couldn't imagine Chad talking to anyone.

"I'd like to meet her."

"It's a him," he finally replies, "and you know where I live, stop by anytime."

That seemed reasonable to Willy. Rather than indulge in conversation and risk saying something completely stupid, he simply corrected her mistake and extended an invitation.

"I just may come by," she smiled. "Maybe even tonight after band practice."

She played the flute. She had the blackest hair, running down to her ass-cheeks. She was a scrawny girl, with a funny nose. She was a nice girl, a band geek. She never got less than a "B" in her life. She had a normal life, and a normal family. Every word and every motion she displayed overflowed with kindness. She was perfect in Willy's eyes, and she was talking to him.

"Just let me get your phone number, Will," she said through a blush. "You know, in case I can't make it."

"I don't have a phone, Sarah. But no worries, B.B. is always there, even if I am not."

He was proud with not leaking his excitement. Not showing her how much he was anticipating her visit. He wouldn't be leaving the house tonight, in hopes that she did make her visit.

"No phone? I can do it tomorrow if that's better, no band practice."

"Whatever."

At the end of the school day, Chad and Willy never took the bus home. The walk was over two hours, but this was when they spent their chunk of time together, talking almost solely about metal. Today was no different.

"That album you had me listen to this morning, its almost too dark."

"It really fucked me up when I listened to it last night," Chad explained with an enthusiasm Willy did not know him capable of. "I'm sure a lot of its effect is from knowing that these fuckers killed each other practically during the recording, but something about it gave me hope."

"You mean 'un-hope'."

"I suppose that's exactly what I mean. Un-hope for meaning to life. If I ever get good enough at guitar to record an album, you can be sure I'll kill my band-mates. Shit, I'll do it mid-recording so you can hear them screaming in the last track."

"Just make sure you give me a copy before you do yourself in, you know I won't be able to afford it."

"Oh I won't be offing myself. I owe Satan my life, and I'm pretty sure he wants me alive for it. By then I will completely be his instrument on earth. Suicide is no longer an option from me, since I refuse to take what is not mine."

Willy brought the subject to a change, knowing that once you get Chad going on talk of Satan, his soul, life and the after-life, he would go on for the remainder of the walk.

"Sarah Clark talked to me today at lunch. "

"No shit?" Chad laughed. "You've been staring at that girl for how many years, and she finally noticed?"

"Actually, I think *you* finally noticed. She said you had Phys-Ed together."

"Guilty. She insisted on talking. If I had to talk to someone, it sure wasn't going to be about me. I told her about your obsession."

"It's not an obsession, asshole. It's just the only fucking thing good in my life. Anyway, she says she wants to stop by and meet my horse."

"Well look at you, gonna get some pussy are you?"

Willy scowled at Chad, and sighed away the immaturity. "Well, maybe the horse is."

"Gross."

The conversation was interrupted by some yelling behind them, as three kids on bikes were pedaling fast towards them.

"Fuck, it's Tim."

Tim Roper and his two goons, Mike and Greg twisted their bikes to a stop, spraying Chad and Willy with dirt. Tim was the first to spill shit from his mouth.

"Well, well, well... You fags haven't found a good bush to fuck in yet?"

Tim, Mike and Greg were, simply put, bullies. They patrolled the roads after school, looking for people to fuck with. For a long time, Chad and Willy would take off-road trails to get home. Today, with the conversation more real than ever (not just about music), they hadn't really been paying much attention to where they were walking.

Tim grabbed Willy by the collar.

"Give me that fucking player, keep your shitty headphones. If you got any money, you know the drill."

Mike and Greg stood by, laughing, watching Chad for any movement. A minute went by and not one of them moved, but Chad was the next to speak.

"We're still looking for the bush with your Mother in it. Get the fuck out of here."

Tim drew back his right arm and pounded his fist into Willy's eye. "Every word you say, faggot, gets Lil' Will here a smack. Now hand over the shit."

Willy, eyes clouded with tears, face throbbing, cast his glance at Chad, who shook his head and emptied his pockets. Willy handed over the music player, and assured the trio that he had no money. They were well aware of his situation, and did not disbelieve him. Chad gave them his last few bucks, and they gathered their bikes up and pedaled off in search of more victims.

"I think in the past we made it much further down the road before we had to change course. I guess they really wanted to see us." Willy said through a shaky, pain-laden voice. "Let's not fuck that up tomorrow."

"First of all Will, I have an extra player you can have. And second, I will never stray from this road again for as long as I live, and if they pull this shit again tomorrow, I will fucking cut them."

Willy wanted to remind his friend that he would probably never cut anyone, but wanted more to leave the whole thing behind him. The rest of their walk was uneventful, and only talk of music.

There was no homework that evening. In the time he would have allotted to his schoolwork, Willy was in a panic about a potential visit from Sarah, and his black eye. After an hour or so of cover-up attempts using his mother's abandoned make-up, he decided that she would not be coming, and sat down in the kitchen to a bowl of beef-flavored Chinese noodles. She rang the doorbell after his third bite.

"What happened to your eye?"

"My eye? Oh, Chad and I exchanged some blows on the way home from school. It's a boy thing, you should see the other guy. I suppose you are here to see Black Beauty, let me grab my coat."

Black Beauty turned around in his stall at the scent of approaching carrot. Not a word passed between Willy and Sarah en route to the barn, and she was just as speechless when she stood before the massive horse, black as night. There was a slight gasp from Sarah, and Willy shivered with pride that his own horse could be so beautiful as to captivate such a girl.

"Will, she's beautiful..." Sarah whispered.

"It's still a he..."

"I'm sorry, I am just predisposed to thinking of horses as 'she'. Plus, with a name like Black Beauty..."

"I was six, I saw the movie and wanted my own Black Beauty. He's a boy in the movie. I don't see how 'Beauty' makes it a girl's name by default. Do you want to ride him?"

"Could I? It has been years since I have ridden, can She... *He...* hold us both?"

"Could he, yes. But he doesn't want to. But you are welcome to a ride. There are trails all through the woods, B.B. knows them all."

Sarah agreed and after Black Beauty was saddled, she climbed onto his back. Willy explained everything he could think of to make the ride a safe and pleasant one. He encouraged her to ride as long as she wanted, explaining that Black Beauty would come home when he was ready. Sarah, though giddy with excitement, looked down at Willy with a bit of disappointment, and said something that changed his whole life in a moment:

"You should also suppose that I came here to see *you,* Will. "

His horse and his favorite girl left him standing there, feeling the first bit of joy in his life that was not obtained from the back of the horse. He blushed and smiled, threw some metal on the speaker system in the barn, and cleaned up the stall.

Sarah was in a heightened state of enjoyment, like a dream you didn't want to end. From the back of Black Beauty, she felt almost as though they were flying. It was a calm ride, for the horse was well aware of its rider and her comfort, though there were a few stretches he could not resist picking up the pace and jumping a stump here and there. There was a bond between the two, Sarah could feel it, and she tried her best to reciprocate the feeling to the horse.

The rain started about a half hour into the woods, but it didn't slow Black Beauty, and so Sarah did not care. They were soaked, but both still enjoying themselves to the fullest. It wasn't until another half hour or so that the trails became so muddy that Sarah noticed the horse's difficulty traversing the paths.

At the point that they had been close enough to the edge of the forest to see a building, Sarah offered for the horse to wander off the trail, into a grass field. It was still difficult to manage, though nothing to the mud. Black Beauty picked up his pace a bit and pounded down tall blades of grass, until Sarah saw the road.

"There we go Beauty," she told the horse, "get yourself on the road, and solid ground."

The rain was coming down so thick and heavy at this point, though the sun was not yet set, the sky was nearly as dark as the dead of night. Visibility was limited to only a few feet in front of them as they reached the road, but Sarah could feel the relief in the horse as its hooves hit a more solid surface.

"Do you know which way is back? I bet you do."

The horse never questioned direction, and set course for shelter. The biggest problem with the visibility, however, was that it also seriously affected the oncoming truck.

Terry was lost in thought, taking in the similarities of this rainy night to the one when the tragic loss happened. His eyes were on the road, but his brain was preoccupied with flashbacks of the event so clear, it felt almost as if he had been driving the truck on the night past. More similar it became when he caught not a glimpse of the horse, but a buckle on the boot of the rider, and his reflex thrust his foot to the brake pad. However quick his response, his grill smashed into the legs of the mount, and its body came nearly through his windshield. The truck hit some thick grass a bit off the road, on that same curve not so long ago, where the grass matted previously had not yet managed to catch up in growth to its neighboring grass.

Shock grabbed Terry, and his head thumped the steering wheel. An indefinable amount of time went by before he remembered the shining buckle.

Black Beauty had tossed Sarah just before the impact, and when she hit the ground a few feet away, the wind was knocked from her chest and her lightheadedness kept her from reacting for a small time. She pulled her face out of the mud and coughed some sopping dirt from her mouth. When she put her arm down to prop herself up, it slid quickly along a muddy rock and brought her face slamming to the ground again. Between tears and the rain, she could see nothing. She lifted her head and screamed into the night sky. Rain washed the mud from around her eyes, though water leaked into her nasal passage and forced her coughing. She opened her eyes to find the lights of the truck shining on the body of Black Beauty, twisted and broken, face smashed, and most definitely, literally, lifeless.

When Terry finally did remember that it wasn't just an animal he had hit, he pushed open his door and stumbled into the mud. He saw his lights on the horse, and shook his head. The horse was dead, and without its flesh to hold it together it would have been smashed into a hundred pieces. He quickly shook his sight around until he saw the girl in the road.

He helped her to her feet, and shook his head at another death on that curve.

Part 2: In the Mouth

In the pitch dark of the night, a goat lay writhing on a table-like rock, its legs bound together with duct tape. Two boys stand on either side of the rock, one armed with a book in one hand, a knife in the other.

Willy was always skeptical of Chad's obsession with Satanism and occult rituals, but having been robbed of his only bond to a life worth living, he was willing to try anything to bring Black Beauty back. He missed two days of school before Chad realized how upset over the loss Willy actually was, despite Chad doing his best impression of cheer to liven the situation. Sarah made a visit on day two, a cast on one arm and stitches across her face, and did her best as well to convince Willy that all was not hopeless.

Here now, they stood, as Chad prepared to read from his texts, the same found in his brother's closet just a week before. He knew it would work. He had devoted his life to evil within bounds of the law, and he knew that whatever dark forces were responsible would come to his aid this day. If not, he had done everything he could to help Willy, and would continue support. Willy was Chad's Black Beauty, the only living being keeping him from withdrawing completely into loneliness, with hatred for all living things. Given the same situation, Chad would be out here in attempt to raise his friend, perhaps with a higher level of offering. Maybe a cheerleader tied up on the rock, instead of this screaming goat. For a moment, lost in this thought, Chad heard the wailing of the cheerleader, and something inside him sparked motivation to continue.

Black beauty lay in the sleep of absolute death on a tarp next to the rock. Willy cried next to him, anticipating the far shot that Chad's ritual might succeed. Chad had lectured Willy a couple of times already on the topic of crying.

"We're here, reaching out for help from all that is evil. You need to turn those tears into hate, Will. The demons will respond better to a ritual fueled by hatred or sin. They are not a very sympathetic bunch, and I fear the sadness will drive them off."

Willy kept this in mind, of course, but the pain of seeing his greatest friend in its current state was too great. Every time he imagined putting a carrot to the mouth that was now lifelessly agape with a swollen tongue pushing at the teeth as if trying to escape, or the eyes that were filmed over with a cloudy, dry mucus that seemed to attract every buzzing fly in the county, he was unable to fight the sadness. He did make his best attempt for Chad, since he wanted to take this whole event as seriously as possible, in the unlikely event that it should succeed.

Chad performed his chanting, eyes rolled to the back of his head, a self inflicted cut across his forehead oozing blood across his face. The self-inflicted cut could have apparently been on the hand or anywhere, only a small amount of human blood was supposedly needed for this ceremony, but Chad was so deeply into his believed reality of the situation, he thought a more dangerous, severe cut would help convince the Un-Gods of his serious commitment.

His words were not of any language Willy recognized. The clouds above them seemed to close in as the ritual went on. Rain started again. There was more rain this year than Willy could ever remember, and gave him hope that the winter was cold and bleak. Since he spent most of his time indoors and alone, he appreciated the scenery outside when it looked inhabitable. When there was snow and ice covering leafless trees and the roads and wires, and the sky was always gray, Willy felt a bit less alone when he thought of other people not leaving their houses either.

Black Beauty was in rough shape. It was a short time since the accident, but he was a stiff heap of broken limbs. He could be mistaken for a stuffed horse, if not for the expression of anguish across his equine face, and a couple of patches of missing hair where meat and bone were exposed. There was a particularly large chunk of it missing on his chest, exposing a few ribs. Willy wondered if these wounds would heal in this resurrection, but did not care to dwell on it.

As Chad's voice got louder, he raised the knife above his head with both hands. He looked like a fucking warlock out of a horror fantasy. Of course, instead of any ritual robes, he was wearing his usual all-black outfit , save the chrome studs and spikes. He was yelling now, screaming incoherence, not at the top of his lungs, but more from the bottom. On what became the last word, he carried out the last syllable, shouting it into the sky as he brought down the knife into the goat. Willy swore a sole bolt of lightning came out of the sky and struck the blade before its descent, but dismissed it as hope and did not mention it.

Terry and Janet sat at the dinner table. Janet ate slower than ever, her eyes up towards the corner of the ceiling, as if watching a bug. Terry enjoyed a steak and most of a baked potato, and washed it down heavily with whiskey. He spent most of the day driving around town looking for the goat. The goat had been like a yard-gnome before it went missing, just a decoration that ate more of the lawn than Terry would have liked. Now that it was gone, however, he too stared off for most of the meal, wishing he could have it back. He mentioned it once during the meal, and for a second he realized how it must sound as Janet sit there wishing for something they both wanted back more than anything. For a moment, he pondered the possibility that he was the cause of her silence. The rest of his thoughts on the situation were kept strictly to his head.

I'll bet it was that fucking Marsh kid. Trying to get back at me for running down his horse and girlfriend. As if the score were evened out, much less toppled into the Marsh's favor. At least your girlfriend didn't die, you little prick.

By the end of the evening and the bottle of whiskey, Terry had convinced himself that William

Marsh was butt-fucking his goat in that barn of his all day, and tomorrow he would do something about it.

Sarah had gone to Willy's again that night. He wasn't there. She felt responsible for the death of his horse, and she was sure he hated her for it. It was so obvious that Willy would only ever care for his horse, yet that drew her to him. Something about the commitment was attractive to her, and before she had taken it away from him, she thought maybe he had some to share for her. He was a good looking kid, though not as hygienic as people might like. He had a general bad attitude about things, but it seemed realistic after the shit he had been through. She knew about his dad, everyone did. Even though he was entirely at fault for killing that little boy, he was under the influence and ill equipped to make any sort of judgment to change either of their fates. She, and a lot of people in town, were sympathetic to this on some level. They were all guilty of drunk driving, a lot of them more often than not. Leroy Marsh had been unlucky, and had a disadvantage living out on that curve. The event straightened out some people for a couple months. The bar was almost vacant every night for the duration, and people just got drunk at home. Time goes on. They forget, and life has a way of reverting back to normal, for most people.

She walked around the yard and went into the barn. It was exceptionally clean. Much cleaner than when she had been by yesterday. She imagined that poor Willy was obsessively cleaning his empty barn, unable to stop thinking about the horse. She stepped into Black Beauty's stall. A nice bed of fresh hay lay in the corner. The smell of horse hovered in the air, and Sarah lay in the hay thinking about Black Beauty, and Willy, and started to cry.

Chad had lost consciousness almost immediately after burying the knife into the goat's gut. He lay on the ground, the rain washing the blood and make-up off his face. Willy had run over for an attempt at catching him or breaking the fall, but had not gotten there in time. He shook Chad a bit, and gave him some pats to the side of the face. Once satisfied by finding a pulse under his neck, he shook his head at Chad, and went to the horse.

The first thing he saw was the black of the horse's eye moving around in its socket. He lost his breath, fell to his knees next to the horse, and lost himself in tears. The horse moved its head very slowly, and Willy could tell that it was entirely unaware of its surroundings. Upon investigation of the wounds, he found that the fleshy holes had not closed, but the damage to the face had been lessened, the tongue withdrawn back into the mouth. The hair that remained, reflected a moon that was not seen on this evening in its blackness. The legs were straightened. Willy was shaking with joy. He would mend the open wounds somehow, it was of no concern while his horse lay before him once again amongst the living.

He comforted Black Beauty with soft petting around the head and gentle words. He calmly tried to talk him into standing, warning the horse to move slow and easy in case his legs wouldn't hold. The eye stared at him, as if taking in every word, and the horse let out a snort. Heat had come back to the body very quickly, Willy could feel it radiating. He stood up slowly himself, still saying his soothing words of encouragement.

Before Black Beauty stood up, which was done quickly and with ease, the eye blinked shut for a few seconds, and upon re-opening, it was no longer black, but a glowing, traffic light red. The horse reared in the storm, filled the area with a shrieking whinny to end all, and motioned its head at Willy, as if to say, "Get on."

He took some time to hoist Chad up on the horses back, and gathered their things. Just before mounting himself onto his returned from the grave, demon-horse, Willy noticed the goat still moving. He was pretty sure Chad had mentioned the ritual calling for a sacrifice, not just a stabbing. Yet it had worked just the same. Chad's final blow had been insufficient and poorly targeted, and left the goat suffering on the stone. Willy picked up the knife, still hot from the lightning - Willy was now sure he had not imagined it. He brought it across the goat's throat, opening veins and arteries across it, and watched it bleed out until it was no longer breathing. He thanked and apologized to the goat, in what he believed to be its final moment.

He climbed upon his Black Beauty, who seemed annoyed with anticipation, and they headed home. The horse ran like it was his first time, with a speed and dedication that Willy had never felt.

Tim, Mike, and Greg, had been excessively bored the last couple of days. Since the last score on goods when they had crossed Chad and Willy, they anticipated finding them again. However, yesterday and today they had not been in school. Tim knew that Willy all but lived alone, and wondered if maybe these two clowns had finally grown up and were skipping school to get drunk or stoned. Mike and Greg agreed that the three of them should be included in such an event, and decided to pay a visit to the Marsh farm. Of course their intent would not be to share in any of the activities, but claim them for their own.

Sarah was asleep in the hay when Willy walked into the barn. Chad remained unconscious on the back of the horse. Willy wondered why Sarah would pick such a spot to sleep, and suddenly felt very sad for her. The poor girl had been in a serious accident and could've been severely hurt, as well as had the horse underneath her smashed to death. Willy felt guilty for just letting her go off without him. It was his fault that these things had happened to her, and he was angry with himself for it. He wanted nothing but to see Sarah happy, and to be able to do things for her. Now she was laying alone in his barn, mourning his horse, so depressed that a sleep had claimed her. He woke her gently.

"Sarah...", he touched her shoulder. "Sarah, wake up, there's something you should see."

She opened her eyes to see Willy and immediately started crying again.

"No, no, no, don't cry", he comforted her as she threw her arms around him and buried her head into his chest. "C'mon, Sarah, there's something you need to see."

She started an apology as he stood up and headed for the barn door. He wasn't listening, but she was going on anyway. There wasn't a second between when he opened the door and she caught sight of Black Beauty. She would have fainted instantly, had her instinct not told her that Willy had found an identical horse, and somehow afforded it. But quickly evidence came up to prove otherwise. Aside from her knowing Willy would be unable to just replace his horse, she saw the wounds in its side and some flesh missing from around the knees. The red eyes and the unconscious passenger told her that something had happened. Something was different, and somehow, they had brought Black Beauty back from the dead. She looked at Willy, who was staring at his steed, sporting a very satisfied smile. To see him happy, brought a smile to her face as well.

"Help me get Chad inside, and I will explain."

When Chad came to, he was laying on a couch inside the Marsh home. He rubbed his face with his open hands before he noticed Willy and Sarah sitting across the room from him, staring.

"What the fuck happened?" He asked. "Did it work?"

Willy held back no excitement as he gave Chad the update. He explained how Chad had passed out at the same instant he completed the ritual. He also told him how the goat was not quite terminated, and that he had finished it off. Chad interrupted at this point.

"That is why I passed out. My stab missed its mark, and I think the demons tried to claim me as the sacrifice. With no proper sacrifice, they would be really pissed off. It's a good fucking thing we weren't resurrecting a person."

"It *did* work though, Chad," Willy countered. "Black Beauty is in the barn as we speak, standing on all four and looking better than ever, never mind all the gashes and lost flesh, anyway."

"Will, listen. The ritual works on a demon possessing the corpse of the deceased. These particular demons we summon are rather harmless, especially in the body of an animal. They long to be summoned like this to exist in our world. If the ritual is fucked up though, like ours was, they don't get to use their full arsenal of power. Had we been trying to revive a human in this case, the possessing demon would have means to punish us for such a screw up." Will considered all of this, and argued, "Chad, the horse is resurrected. I can see the demon in its fiery red eyes. I finished off the goat and I think these 'demons' were satisfied with that, because B.B. let us on his back and took us home. And he performed better than I have ever seen him, running faster and harder than he ever did, even at his youngest and best shape."

Sarah listened to the boys argue, her mouth hanging open in a combination of shock and disbelief. Had they really summoned demons to bring back Willy's horse? Had they actually killed some innocent goat in a sacrificial trade-off? She wasn't sure how to react to any of this information. A part of her wanted to leave and put the two of them behind her. She didn't really want to be any part of demonic summoning, especially if it was real. On the other hand, Willy was the happiest she had ever seen him. The last thing good in his life, as he said, was taken away from him, and now he had it back. She continued listening, staring into Willy's smile and excitement.

Chad slid into a sitting position, felt the start of a scab across his forehead, then shook his head as he explained further to Willy. "You say the eyes were glowing red? The demon is there then, which means they had not fully realized the failure of our sacrifice. Or maybe they have let us slide, and you killing the goat was sufficient enough. We need to check on her. If, in fact, the demon came to Black Beauty without knowing the summoning was incomplete, it may have left all the same. If that is the case, your horse will be dead again in that barn. "

Willy sighed at Chad's refusal to acknowledge that everything had worked out, however shady, their ritual had been performed. Sarah agreed to make something for the three of them to eat, while Chad and Willy headed outside to the barn. Chad was sure that Willy was soon to be devastated again, while Willy was sure Chad would be amazed. They left the house still arguing, as Sarah started water to boil for some pasta.

Janet stared out the window. Terry had decided to take one last drunken stroll around town in search of his goat, before finally putting all the blame on William Marsh and confronting him. Janet had her first thought about anything other than Levi in a long time. She thought about Terry, and what all of this had done to him. She wished he would talk to the Marsh's and learn some kind of forgiveness, because from what she could tell, both Will Marsh and Terry would probably benefit greatly from each other's company. One was a father without a son, the other a son without a father. Something happened to her during this thought, and the potential of her imagined companionship motivated her. Terry had been on a path of heavy drinking and uncontrollable anger at the most trivial of things, and she was sure her mourning in silence for so long had contributed to both. Right then she decided that best for her, Terry, and even the spirit of their son, Levi, was an end to life the way all of them were living it. A new start, and maybe a new family.

As she stood up from her chair to grab the phone and make a call to her husband, something caught her eye out the window. The first time in too many months she would have spoken words to Terry, she was distracted, and never got the chance.

The goat was in the yard. She laughed and shook her head. It had taken a leisurely walk it seemed, and returned home all the same. Meanwhile her husband was driving all over town, too drunk to stand up properly. She grabbed her coat, intending to get the goat inside and out of the rain, where she would then make her call with more good news aside from her plan. The return of the goat would help her break the stubborn ice, weakening Terry's surly defense, and allowing her to present him with her thoughts and ideas.

When she walked into the yard the goat was just standing there, staring up at her. It seemed to be staring through her so much that she cast a glance behind to see that there was nothing else the goat may have been looking at. She called to it, but it did not come. It simply stood and stared. She advanced towards the goat, still calling words (her first in a long time) to coax it to her. It remained still. Finally, when Janet was only a foot or so from the goat, she stepped down to one knee and extended her hand with a bit of lettuce she had grabbed from the fridge. The goat still did not move, but she was close enough now to see why. There was a bit of blood coming from its stomach, staining the grass below, and a slice had been made across its neck. Small amounts of blood came from this wound as well, though not nearly as much as there should have been. She gasped at the sight and lost balance on her one knee, falling over into the grass below the goat. At last it moved, with a swift and savage lunge of its mouth to Janet's throat, and quickly tore her to pieces.

Tim, Mike and Greg had gotten to the Marsh farm shortly after Willy and Sarah had carried Chad inside. They made way to the door, but stopped when they heard a whinny from the barn.

"Didn't his fucking horse die? I didn't think this asshole could afford another horse," said Greg.

Tim had processed the exact same thought. "There's no fucking way, this kid is as poor as they come. He doesn't even have a fucking family. "

Tim was furious. He never could grasp the reality that anyone else should have something he wanted. Granted, he had never wanted a horse, but he had always wanted the money to be able to replace his problems instantly. As always, when as angry as he felt at the moment, Tim formulated a plan.

"Come on, let's check this out."

The three of them went into the barn to find the horse in his stall, leaning against a wall. Tim's plan was to steal the horse and make Will Marsh cough up a ransom for it with all this money he was clearly sitting on. When they got closer to Black Beauty, they saw his wounds.

"What the fuck," Mike said.

"Is this," Greg stuttered, "the same horse?"

Tim shrugged. "It sure fucking looks like a horse that has been mowed down by a truck, doesn't it?"

Black Beauty did not move during their approach, nor during conversation. Tim looked around for something to lead the horse out of the barn with, determined to persist with his mission. He had imagined Will to have more money than originally thought, because now, rather than a new horse, it seemed he had paid some amazing doctor or vet to revive his horse. Anyone who could afford to fund the works of a science not yet mastered, and give up such money to keep such an animal, would cough up more money to see it again after Tim and his goons had taken it.

"Mike find a leash or whatever so we can walk this fucking thing out of here. Greg you take those carrots on that bench and feed it a few, earn its trust. I will keep watch at the door in case those fags show up."

He grabbed a pitchfork next to the door and stood with the barn door cracked open just a tiny bit, and stared into the windows of the house, watching for any movement. Mike searched the barn for whatever it was Tim wanted. None of the three knew anything about horses, but Greg, who was gently petting its nose and offering it a carrot, knew that it wasn't supposed to be this cold.

"It's freezing Tim, there is no warmth to its body at all." Upon further investigation, he was also able to discern that the horse was not breathing. Yet there it stood, its pitch black eyeballs fixed directly on Greg, leaning against the wall, clearly distributing weight off its legs which were wrapped in cloth and duct tape. It had moved its head slightly at the first carrot offering, but did not take the vegetable. Greg turned to Tim to suggest he come take a look himself. His carrot-arm rested on the stall gate, he used his other arm to motion for Tim to come. During that motion, the horse's head came down and bit into his rested arm.

Tim and Mike both dropped whatever they were holding as they turned quickly to Greg's scream. The first thing they saw was blood, then this kid's arm caught in the mouth of a horse. Greg thrashed and yelled, tears practically shooting from his face.

"Let go! Let Go! Motherfucker!"

Mike grabbed Greg and pulled, slapping the horse's face. It would not let go. Tim picked up the pitchfork again and dashed the distance of the barn, putting all of his force into a thrust of the pitchfork. It buried into the horse's neck, but the horse seemed unfazed. As he removed his weapon for another strike, Greg and Mike both managed enough strength to pull Greg free from the clutches of the horse's jaws. They fell backward and hit the ground with a hard thump. Tim looked down at them, and gasped, his face twisted in disgust. When Mike and Greg stood, they examined his forearm, which had a huge stretch of flesh missing from it. The bone was exposed, blood soaked his arm, and muscle was torn all around the hole. The flesh had literally been ripped from his arm, and when they looked up, the horse was again leaning against the wall, chewing the last bits of meat it had stolen. They fled from the barn, and headed to Mike's house, which was closest, to patch up Greg. They couldn't take him to the hospital, they did not want to admit to the trespassing or their purpose for such.

Tim, his anger at a full boil, did not want the authorities involved anyhow. Will Marsh would fucking pay for what his horse had done, Tim would see to that.

When Chad and Willy entered the barn, their first sight was of the red stains throughout the hay on the ground. Willy looked up at Black Beauty and his heart stopped. The eyes were no longer glowing. The wounds had gotten bigger, and flesh seemed to be falling off of the horse. The horse leant against the wall of his stall, and looked just as dead as when they had carried it into the woods earlier that day. Chad was right, the demon had left Black Beauty, who now seemed no more than an animated corpse. Chad hung his head in disappointment.

"Will, we failed. The demon is gone. Your horse is but a corpse again."

Will did not understand. If the demon had left its body, then why did the horse not fall dead again? It was clearly suffering, barely able to hold itself up, and seemingly unaware of anything around it. "What now then, Chad?"

"I say we try again. Right here. There's a bit in my book somewhere about failed rituals and how to correct them. Unfortunately that book is at home, so I will need to go grab it. You should come, I don't think it's good for you to stay and see Black Beauty like this. Plus, my mom might not let me back out if you don't come. With you I can convince her that we are doing homework or some shit. Let's move."

Willy did not argue, and ran inside to tell Sarah where they were off to, and they left.

Terry pulled his truck into the Marsh driveway, and left it idle. He grabbed his shotgun, mumbling curses upon the Marsh farm and family as he walked up to the door. He was unsure of his intentions. His severe inebriation had rendered him unable to reason with himself, or even think ahead. Up to this point it had only led him to banging on the door of the house with his shotgun in his other hand. He was well aware that his mind may be aiming in the direction of emptying a bird shot into this kid, and somewhere in the back of his mind that was not fueled completely by trauma and hate for this family, he was happy that no one answered the door. There was a light on in the kitchen, and upon investigating through the window, he saw a table set with a bowl of spaghetti in the middle, but there didn't seem to be anyone inside, and the dinner remained untouched.

Satisfied that he had gone through with coming to the house, he started back to the truck when he noticed the barn door slightly ajar, and a light on inside.

Of course, Terry thought, *he's sitting there in the barn, crying over the loss of his fucking horse. A fucking pet.*

Terry's biggest issue with William Marsh was that he hadn't experienced a loss half that of he and Janet, yet to the kid, the death of his horse was the end of his world. Terry knew that as time went on, there would be other horses, other pets for Willy, whereas for he and Janet, there would be no other kids. Terry stood outside the barn, all of the thoughts from dinner earlier racing through his head once again, and he raised his shotgun and kicked open the barn door.

When he saw the horse, his disbelief almost entirely clouded his purpose. Here was this animal he had seen dead, and was personally responsible, yet it stood alive somehow, though it looked more dead now than when he had hit it. Its face was covered in blood, its ribcage almost totally exposed. Some organs were falling out of the gap in its chest and stomach, and one of its legs was completely bent in half, its hoof nowhere near the ground.

What the fuck have they done? He thought. The horse turned its head towards Terry, its hunger motivating it much more than the last time it tasted flesh. Black Beauty was no longer a horse, but some kind of monster. Terry couldn't imagine how this all had come to be, or why William Marsh would do this to his horse. Surely this could not be better than death?

Selfish fucking bastard, Terry said under his breath.

Terry pulled his cell phone to call the police, but he realized how crazy he would sound explaining the situation, and hesitated. Standing there with his phone open and the numbers punched in, a call-button away from turning over this horror to people far more prepared, he considered what he would say. The more he tried to organize his thoughts and words, the more insane the whole thing had sounded to him. In all truth, he really had no idea what was happening here, but as he remembered his goat, and the fucked up kid Willy was always hanging around with, he started figure it out. The cops would never believe this story, and would probably write it off as the horse never was dead, despite how absolutely sure of that Terry had been at the time.

From the opposite corner of the barn, a moaning grabbed Terry's attention. He looked over to find the other victim of his accident. Sarah sat balled up in the corner, covered in blood herself. Terry quickly put together that the horse had attacked her. She was making noise, but her head hung between her legs rested on her knees, and he could not see exactly where her wounds might be.

Without any further consideration of the scene, Terry brought his shotgun up and emptied its chamber into the horse's skull. In a second movement, the length of a breath, he reloaded and pumped two more shells into Black Beauty. What remained of the body hit the floor, and evidence covered the wall behind it. The body twitched, just enough for Terry to reload yet again, though this time as he did, Sarah lifted her head.

Her eyes were pitch black, void of any emotion. Her mouth was agape, and she seemed to be hissing at him. He saw that her neck and shoulder were all torn up, he guessed by the horse's teeth. The neck wound was no doubt fatal, and most of her shoulder missing, yet she stood there, eyeing him like some wild animal, threatening him with her open mouth and raspy growls. Terry had seen shit like this in a movie once, and his instinct took over. In the exact second that she leaped for him, arms out, mouth stretched more than humanly possible, he emptied his last two rounds into her, splattering almost her entire torso throughout the barn.

THE ROO

Anthony Wedd

He wasn't sure why he'd picked her up. He was glad though; it was working out.

When he'd first seen her at the roadhouse outside Keerawarra, he'd thought she looked scruffy, like most backpackers do. The proprietor had said something about her wanting a ride and asked where he was headed. It would have been easy to lie and say anything, and he almost had. Misgivings had flooded into his mind. She might have friends waiting in the dining room. Or - equally intimidating - she might not. What would they possibly talk about? He pictured hours of awkward silence, made worse by infrequent attempts at stilted conversation. What if she wanted to use the toilet, or get food? She might want to smoke in the car. She'd probably smell.

But the town the man had mentioned *was* where he was headed. The girl had looked over at him and her face was curious, not sullen and expectant. Without thinking about it further he'd nodded and said "sure." Her face had lit up and she'd bounded off her stool like a kelpie.

He'd gone outside to warm up the car while she paid for her food. An anxious expression flickered across her face as she exited. Maybe she thought he'd driven off without her. Her breath misted in the night air. He'd leaned out of the front door and waved and she gambolled over, opening the back door to stow her pack. Finally she'd thumped into the passenger seat and flashed him a thankful smile.

They'd gotten underway, abandoning the beacon of the roadhouse for the engulfing pitch of the outback. To his relief, it wasn't awkward. The girl, Shane as it turned out, chatted with him amiably. She was from London, where she worked as a technical writer. That pleased him. She must be older than she looked. She'd flipped through his CDs with seemingly genuine interest, and even played one. She *did* smell a bit, but it wasn't too bad.

His high beams lit a strip of grey roadway and gravelly shoulder that scrolled endlessly past the nose of the car. Anonymous ranks of roadside markers filed past on either side, their cyclopean red eyes gleaming blankly. The car formed a sanctuary against the vastness that pressed against the road like a chill shroud. In mid sentence, Shane pulled off her hooded sweatshirt with a single motion, revealing a faded T-shirt that read BAD KITTY. There was a picture below the caption, but he couldn't make it out without staring at her chest. She continued talking about her travels as if oblivious to his glances. She swore quite a bit, but her accent made it oddly appealing. Her hand wriggled through her hair like worms in dark earth.

Incandescent moths streaked and weaved out of the gloom, giving their juicy lives against the windscreen with the soft tap of a fingernail. A white glow lit the horizon for minutes before its source appeared – a distant array of lights like a deep sea behemoth that lazily swelled towards them until suddenly its dazzling eyes filled the world. The humped dark shape dwarfed the car as it roared buffeting past, threatening to send them twirling skyward in its lingering musky wake.

"Wow," said Shane. "They're awesome." She would be sick of them before the night was out, he reflected.

She sniffed. "Is that animals it's carrying?"

"Yeah," he replied. "Sheep or cattle, probably. You know, cows." The nervous qualification felt a bit stupid. Of course she would know what cattle were. But she nodded without comment.

They soon approached a turnoff the GPS had heralded for some time. It was unsigned and looked quite desolate for a major road, but he took it with outward nonchalance. Something was dead there – a small thing, half bulbous and furry, half pressed road flower. Its shadow slid wraithlike across the ground suggesting movement, but it was just the turning lights of the car.

They picked up speed again along the narrow road. Stunted bushes punctuated its verge like distorted grey bodies. Beyond them the dark unknown spread out to a featureless horizon blacker than the sky. Shane slumped down in her seat and put her feet up on the dashboard. That perturbed him a bit – her shoes might leave marks - but he didn't want to jeopardise the rapport they'd developed. He didn't think his glance had been noticeable, but she withdrew her legs almost immediately.

The CD finished, leaving a vacuum of silence. Behind the monotonous sucking hiss of the car's motion, he wondered if Shane had fallen asleep, but then she sprang upright. "Can I put one of mine on?" she asked, he assumed rhetorically, for she was already unbuckling and twisting around. "Sure," he said redundantly. She half crawled into the back seat and zipped and rustled around with her pack. He reached over her and turned the interior light on. There was a muffled "thank you," more rustling, then she thrashed and lunged forward with her prize.

He put the light out, allowing darkness to flood the car once more. Shane's CD started with a crash and screaming. She had the volume louder than he usually liked, but that was a bit exciting. He found himself accelerating in response. Shane leaned down to worry at something near the floor and then her feet, bare now, appeared on the dash again. That was tolerable, he decided. She was never still, head nodding to the music, now mouthing the words, now drinking from a plastic bottle. She had a small tattoo on her ankle which held his gaze for a moment, but he couldn't tell what it was.

He turned back to the road and a kangaroo lurched from between two bushes, as though flushed out by the music. He saw its head in profile, eye blazing, way too close. There was no way they wouldn't hit it, yet his instincts spun the wheel and crushed the brake as his conscious mind emptied of everything but vertigo and panic. He felt a sickening juicy crunch and veered further. The wheels shuddered as they left the road. A tree loomed, its pale trunk lurking behind grey billows of foliage. Then somehow they were past it, still on the road, accelerating again.

Chest hammering, he looked across at Shane. She looked back at him and abruptly broke into song, her mouth wide, wailing along with the CD as though trying to drown something out. He wasn't sure what to do, and let his gaze drift wordlessly askance with a half smile. Her ankle tattoo caught his eye, and he saw clearly that it was a cat, stylised and in repose. BAD KITTY.

His head ached excruciatingly from the shock of the ordeal. At least the car seemed no worse for wear, rushing smoothly and silently through the night. He was slightly disturbed by a burning smell. *Must be the brakes,* he thought. A leafy eucalyptus smell also invaded the car, unnaturally strongly. Perhaps something in Shane's pack had spilled. Her voice trailed off and he noticed that the

CD had stopped too. In the silence he heard something much quieter – a choke, or maybe a sob. Was she crying?

He glanced over at her, and she let out another hitching moan. He was about to say something, but her tattoo distracted him again. How had he thought it was a cat? It looked nothing like one.

"What's that on your leg?" he asked. He shifted in his seat uncomfortably and suddenly realised he was cold. The heater was blowing icy air right into his face. Shane's only response was a muffled whimpering. He hazarded another glance. The thing on her ankle was a kangaroo in profile, like the road signs.

He fiddled with the heating controls but it didn't help. The air was freezing. Perhaps that was what was making his head ache so badly. Surely Shane had noticed it too. Still and melancholy, she seemed fragile, as though a twig could break her. He wondered if she had anywhere to stay after this. That might be what was upsetting her. Should he offer to share his room?

Shane leaned towards him. "Um... when we get there? Can I... stay with you?" she asked, as though reading from his thoughts. "I don't really have..." Her lower lip was trembling. She was crying again, small breathy squeaks of distress. What should he say to her? It was so cold. They had to get this heater working. Dust obscured the road ahead. His head pounded. Her face was very pale in the soft glow of the dashboard lights.

"God, it's freezing," he said. The leafy sap smell was very strong.

"Yes, it's... don't worry, I'll... can I tell you..." she began, leaning even closer to him.

...and coughed a hot spray of blood into his face.

His hands had left the steering wheel. Lunging to return them sent him flopping against the driver's side door. They weren't moving; the car rested at some kind of crazy angle. The windscreen had dissolved into a crazy mass of cracks swimming against the opaque milkiness of the car's airbag. Nothing beyond it but swirling brightly lit dust.

Frigid air poured in. Blood slopped thickly like black treacle from Shane's lips. She was a spectre, all pale face and wide terrified eyes, coughing and sobbing up blood. Somehow, there was a tree in the car. It grew in through Shane's half of the windscreen. Her face, inches from his own, was pressed awkwardly against the jagged stump of a branch.

Crashed. They'd crashed. How? It didn't matter. They had to get out. Something might explode. How badly was Shane hurt? For that matter, how badly was *he* hurt? The glass beneath his face was a web of striations with a bloody spider at the centre. His temple pulsed with agony, overriding any other signals his body might be sending. He moved his arms experimentally, then lifted one to touch his head. Sticky. Painful. He didn't want to press because of the pain, and because whatever it was like up there, it felt *soft*. He gripped the seat belt instead, feeling its comforting constriction. It couldn't be too bad, he was conscious and moving. Shane was the one he should be worried about.

"Can you move?" he asked. She didn't reply. Her unfocussed eyes stared past him, blinking as rapidly as her breath. Sinister broken cusps flashed white in her swollen mouth as she coughed again, speckling his cheek and lips with more warm gobbets. One side of her face was rent by a black gouge from which a flap of skin dangled like a peel. Her sobs sounded choked, as though her real cries were too big to get out. Perhaps she had more injuries that were preventing her from screaming or even breathing properly. He forced himself to look down at her lower body, a nightmare of crushed mince and diced bone fragments parading across his mind. What he saw looked OK, though much of it was obscured by bits of the tree. Maybe she could get out too, with his help.

The engine ticked like a cooling corpse. His door opened straight into the ground, but the gap was just wide enough. He wrenched himself out into the freezing gloom like an astronaut, staggering as his footfalls sent ripples of dizziness and pain across his perception. Steadying himself against the roof, he surveyed their plight.

Half of the car was angled upward as though it had tried to climb the tree. Most of the front was crushed into a steaming concave metal grimace. A big complicated branch impaled the windscreen on Shane's side. Their one remaining headlight stared vacantly into the clearing nebula of dust. Surely this couldn't really be happening. He wanted to snap out of this nightmare and go back to the world where they were speeding along, whole and intact. He wouldn't crash this time.

He should help Shane, get her out of the car. Or should he not move her? He tried to remember what you were supposed to do. All he could summon was the title of an unread leaflet – BEFORE HELP ARRIVES. Had there been another vehicle involved in the crash? He couldn't remember. But if there had been, there might be other injured people nearby. Or people who could help.

He set off down the road to look. Outside the artificial car world everything was exaggeratedly real and ponderous. Distances were no longer ephemeral but lingered and fought him with drifts of snarling gravel and clutching tussocks of wild grass. The cold bit into him like a shark. Surfaces and objects became less distinct as he moved away from the hazy glow of the car, as though the darkness framing the road was seeping onto it. The sky glowed and burned with a million white needles, blasting down a deafening wave of vastness.

Something was lying on the road ahead of him.

A piece of flotsam washed up low and vague in the diffuse starlight glow. He opened his mouth to call out to the shape but his voice choked against the silent vacuum. He would just walk up quietly and see for himself. A piece of tyre? Too big. An animal?

He smelled it just as the suggestion of fur and muscle coalesced out of the haze. A dead animal. The heavy stench spoke of something half decayed, of noxious emissions through torn orifices in matted hide. Of exposed bony secrets mottled with dried decay and flies. It got worse as he approached, but he wanted the closure of seeing exactly what it was.

With an unexpected stab of dread, he saw it was a kangaroo. Jumbled images from before the accident flashed across his mind. Had they hit this, or crashed trying to avoid it? No, it had obviously been dead for quite a while. It wasn't just the smell. Now that he was close he could see other things. Some of the skin around the face and mouth had been eaten away. Lower incisors jutted in an expression made blank and savage by the eyeless crater above them. The entire pelt was wrinkled and split. He imagined if he tried to move the carcass, it would tear like rotting carpet. Whoever had hit this kangaroo had done so some time ago.

He should get back to Shane. He might walk forever looking for some phantom vehicle or animal they had hit or not hit, and she needed his help *now*. Yet something was odd. He looked at the kangaroo again. At the mangy chest, partially ruptured and sunken as though from an impact. At the black textured mess, glistening faintly, strewn from the body as though it were a dropped jar. The thing was certainly not in great shape, but nor was it flattened with days or weeks of inattentive tyre tracks. If it wasn't for the stench and decomposition, you would almost think -

He jumped backwards, flesh bristling, watchful. The entire corpse was teeming with surreptitious movement. Tiny sections of fur bulged and relaxed as though something underneath was shifting about. Where fur and skin were missing, the darkness exposed seemed to shift and undulate. Maggots, he thought, or some other parasite. He stepped forward again in spite of himself and saw what it was.

Worms. The entire thing was infested with long, dark worms. He couldn't make out much detail but they definitely weren't maggots, at least not the ones he knew of. They were much larger, long gelatinous threads ringed with segments like beachworms, oozing thickly under gaps in the hide like glistening rivers. In the silence he imagined he could hear the putrescent squirming warren that must exist inside the kangaroo. He vomited, the heavy throbbing in his head reaching a grey crescendo with the effort. Looking down, he saw that even the stain on the road writhed with worms. The thought of them crawling blindly around his feet sent him stumbling away, kicking and stomping in revulsion.

Despite the pain he half jogged back to Shane and the car, disgust and urgency compelling him in equal measure. Nothing had changed. He opened the passenger door and there she was, half hidden by the branch, forlorn and still. Had she died while he wasted time? No, her head lolled semi-conscious towards him when he spoke softly and threaded an arm through to touch her shoulder. Time to get her out. He snapped and peeled twigs and small branches to clear a tunnel. Leaves rustled like dead insects. He could see more of her body and for a horrible moment he thought a branch had impaled her, but she was just wedged behind it. He ducked under the main limb toward her. Urgent broken agony rolled into his temple like blood, but he pressed forward and gathered her in an awkward one-armed embrace. Her breath rasped unevenly in his ear, a hopeful sound. She'd looked slight but she was so heavy, and he had to be very careful. Each time she shifted, hellish images plagued him - internal trickles exploding into bloody fountains, splintered ribs sawing against organs like violin strings.

Her legs probed tentatively at the ground as he brought her out, but took no weight. He lay her down on the gravel near the tree as gently as his screaming muscles could manage. Her eyes were open again, but she was still not fully conscious. He remembered her sweatshirt and retrieved it to make a pillow for her. Kneeling over her, he took stock of her injuries. He knew about the swollen face, the smashed mouth, the crude slice out of her cheek. Elsewhere there was a deep cut on her upper arm, and that wrist was also swollen, her hand cocked oddly. Her shirt was torn across her upper abdomen and he cringed as he lifted it and looked there. To his relief it just looked skinned, though deeply bruised. Did that mean internal bleeding? Nothing he could do about that now. He smelled faint decay. Surely her cuts could not be septic already. She was trembling. Was she having a seizure, or was it a symptom of infection? No, of course, she was just cold, freezing probably, wearing only her BAD KITTY T-Shirt. He tensed to get up and find something to put over her, when her head moved and she said something.

"Mmmmmnnoo. Back. Back."

"It's OK. You're OK," he crooned, touching her. "We crashed but it's OK. Let me get-"

She was shaking her head weakly, lifting her good arm. "Own. Pack. In... there." She curled her hand to her ear. "In my. Pack."

"Don't try to talk," he whispered gently. It obviously pained her. He was reaching for her hand to put it back – it was better that she didn't touch her injuries – when he understood. Phone. In my pack. Of course. Phone. Call for help. That was what they needed to do. He felt very stupid. He would give her his jacket – it was better that he was cold than she was – then he would get her phone and they would be saved. He stood and turned around, and there was the kangaroo.

He knew it was the same one. Even at that distance behind the car he could see its awkward stance, misshapen trunk, and the variegated textures of decay. It was emaciated beyond even the hard gauntness of wild animals – just bones and ripped hide, mounted and stuffed with handfuls of worms and rotting ordure. Ribs shone feebly like stripes. One of its ears was mangled and mostly gone. It stood motionless, its flayed toothy head facing them as though watching.

How was it still alive? It was rotting, too decayed even to stand properly. Barbs of pity and revulsion pulsed through him. He didn't want to look at it. Surely the vehicle and his presence should drive it away eventually. He forced himself to count to ten staring at the ground to give it time to make its escape unobserved. But when he steeled himself to look back, it was still there, rigid in the same attitude. It had followed him; it wanted something. Perhaps it had been attracted mothlike by the lights of the car. Or was it dangerous, driven crazy with pain by its condition? Would it attack in this mangled state?

The open passenger door beckoned. If he was quick, he could be safe there in seconds.

But then what? There was no-one else out here. Shane needed medical attention. He had to get to the back and find the phone, be brave for her. The kangaroo was just a sick animal. Very sick. It might have followed him because it wanted help. Once he had gotten help for Shane he could call someone for the kangaroo as well – the RSPCA perhaps.

He inched slowly, pressed to the car, keeping his eyes fixed on the kangaroo. Its smell washed over him like poison gas – the miasma of rancid tissue expelling its final secrets as it glazed and leathered. Staring at it he imagined he could discern the tiny movements of worms as they curled through its rotting craters and fissures. Finally it began to retreat before his approach. He expected a slow awkward kangaroo limp, but it moved in clumsy inefficient bursts like a spider, its hind legs almost spasmodic with the horrible asymmetric gait of something half paralysed.

Once it was out of sight he turned away as much as he dared and lifted the hatch. Shane's pack was out of reach and he had to half climb in after it. He had no idea where to look for the phone – the top of the pack was branded with seemingly dozens of zippers. The first two he tried were stuffed with underwear and socks. He paused between each, lifting his head like a gazelle drinking to search for the kangaroo. Nothing but stark roadway and gravel and hints of furtive bushes. The smell was still there, but fainter, perhaps just lingering in the air or his own nostrils. The third pocket looked more promising – money in loose notes, a camera, a small booklet, and a phone.

He jabbed at it and Shane's smiling face lit up. She was on the beach, one of a trio of laughing girls huddled for the camera. Above their heads was the time – 1:47 – and next to that some words.

NO SIGNAL

He continued staring at the screen. Shane's hair was different – reddish brown rather than dark, and a bit longer. That kangaroo wasn't alive, he thought randomly.

The worms. The worms were the only thing alive in there.

Was it really 1:47? 1:48 now. How long had they been driving? How long since they had crashed? He watched the screen intently. These other girls must be Shane's friends from England - he recalled her speaking about them. Which meant this must have been taken... where? He thought back, trying to picture her telling him. There were no obvious landmarks in the picture, just green ocean and blazing white sand. A sail. Probably in Australia. Had she mentioned her favourite beach?

The screen had dimmed while he... what had he been doing? He thumbed the button again. 2:02. Still NO SIGNAL. Perhaps if he took the phone outside, he might get a signal. Something in the car's structure could be interfering somehow. He looked around as if he could spot whatever it was, and realised he could climb from here to the rest of the car, just like he could have climbed back here from the forward seats. He hadn't had to confront the kangaroo after all. But that was OK, it was done now, and he was glad he had driven it off.

Even without the phone, someone would come along eventually. He just needed to look after Shane until then. He searched the pack for a while longer and found a nice big coat to put over her. Perhaps she had a first aid kit, or at least some antiseptic. He would search after he had covered her up. He climbed out and went around to the driver's side to turn on the hazard lights. His head ached harder as he bent, but the rhythmic, strong beating of the lights reassured him. He went around the car again, back to Shane, and the stink ambushed him, pestilential, thick as death, gagging. The kangaroo was there with her.

Hunched over Shane's prone body as though sniffing her, it hadn't reacted to his presence. What was it doing there? He hadn't seen it this well lit and the surprise and the putrid walking roadkill sight of it paralysed him. Everything was orange-grey-orange-grey. The kangaroo's head and upper body hitched and jerked. Chunks of dark offal dropped like faeces out of the face and open mouth with its jutting lower teeth. Squirming. Onto Shane.

God, how long had it been doing that? He could see worms on Shane's face and upper body. Surely this was not real. Where was he really? Nonetheless the sight sent him lurching forward, yelling inarticulately. The kangaroo swung around, crouched as though it was going to attack, and for a moment he went right out of himself. He realised that this must indeed be a different world. Not the real one, but one he could leave whenever he liked. These things were not happening to the real him.

The kangaroo hissed at him. The sound seemed to come from all through it in hundreds of bursting fetid exhalations, travelling through the chewed rotting labyrinth like a wave. The mutilated head was still as a dummy's. If it attacked he knew he would not move or fight. But before his helplessness, it fled. One start. Two. Gravel spraying. Tail dragging like a broken, rotting snake. It was gone.

He went to Shane. She was conscious, struggling, pushing herself to a sitting position. Her head and neck were slick with putrescent grey syrup. Worms were everywhere – he could see them all over the vomitous ground around her, on her clothes, on her skin. Especially her face. They seemed to stick as she rose to her knees, clustering around the gash on her cheek. Crawling onto it, and, horribly, into it.

He had to get them off her. Should he go to her and rip them off, or should he get something from the car? If only he'd found the first aid kit. Some tweezers, or antiseptic.

Incredibly, Shane got to her feet. She swayed, balancing, looking at him wide eyed through the curtain of filth. Her expression was puzzled, questioning. She tried to speak. "Wha... What... What?" One hand went to the side of her face and recoiled as if from a hot stove. The worms were very thick there now, clinging and throbbing. He watched another one find the cut and ooze into it, a little less of it visible after each pulse. That was okay. This wasn't real for either of them.

She was shaking her head, still watching him pleadingly as though for answers. "I... what's... I don't... aaah!" Her expression clenched in pain and her hand flew to her cheek, feeling herself there this time. She screamed and staggered.

He couldn't watch. He would go and get the first aid kit and help her. "It's OK," he said. "I'll get something." He sprinted around to the back of the car and ripped open the biggest zipper he could see in Shane's pack. Clothing. All clothing. What was at the bottom? Nothing. A box. He wrenched it out and upended it. Photographs and postcards scattered like dead leaves.

Shane squealed, piercing and agonised. He looked around and saw her stagger onto the road. One hand clutched at her suppurating face, as though trying to pull worms out of herself. Each attempt brought an agonised retch and her hand lifted, trembling. Occasionally her progress was checked as she grabbed at some other part of herself through her clothing and cried out. The smell of the kangaroo thickened as she approached. Abruptly she turned away and ran off into the bush, hyperventilating, her body racked by shuddering convulsions.

He opened his mouth to call out but hesitated, and once she was out of sight it felt too late. But he had to bring her back – she would die without help. Her injuries from the accident alone could be life threatening, and those worms... an image of the kangaroo flashed into his mind, how it had looked in the sullen orange illumination of the hazard lights. Shane could end up like that. He launched himself from the back of the car and went after her.

She hadn't seemed fast when she took off, but she had already disappeared into the black scrub. He stopped running and listened. A faint snapping and rustling was audible from somewhere in there. Leaving the road behind, he struck off through spiny urchins of arid grass and the scraping limbs of bushes. Visibility dropped quickly away from the car, and he was soon occupied with the ground at his feet, plotting a route that wouldn't trip him. Gnarled stumps lurked amongst the scrub like sea mines. Rabbit burrows gaped like the smooth throats of giant snakes.

A faint, blood curdling scream came from the bush ahead of him. Shane's voice. So far away. So lost. He had to get to her, now. Heedless of his own safety, he sprinted. Tussocks whipped his ankles, and saw toothed sapling twigs slapped him. An iron talon clutched his head, flexing with each pounding stride. Light flashed and sparked at the edge of his vision. His foot kicked something hard and unyielding, stopping it with a burst of new pain, and he flew forward into the unknown. A large log with crumbly mold-bark rushed up towards his face.

He got a hand down just in time, breaking his fall. Still his temple seemed to burst with a crushing wave of disorienting pain, the worst yet. Just how bad was it? Visions of slapstick horror, bits of brain falling onto the dirt from his lowered head. The ground writhed with a boiling dimness that wanted to become everything, but he knew that he mustn't faint. Not out here, no matter what. The kangaroo would find him.

He remained crouched on his haunches until the worst of the faintness receded into mere agony. Skewers of wild grass became bright points of irritation along his hand and forearm. He got to his feet slowly and looked around. For the kangaroo, for Shane, he wasn't sure which. Distant light flickered, yellowish. Their car, he assumed, but why did it seem to move? It must be another vehicle, far away on the horizon.

A surge of elation made him want to run back to the road, but he forced himself to move carefully. He could flag down the vehicle and save Shane as long as he didn't fall again. He picked his way along as quickly as he could, trying to pinpoint the source of the light. It was never quite where he was looking, fluctuating as though screened by vegetation. Then he smelled the kangaroo, its rotting blood and bone odour unmistakable over the earthy dropping smell of the ground. Still he suppressed the urge to run. It wouldn't attack if he stayed on his feet. He was almost at the road now. Could this be over?

He stepped onto the shoulder and looked, ready to wave down any approaching vehicle. But the light remained insubstantial, now waxing and waning furtively, now sparking and flashing like a cloud of moths. All in silence. He was seeing things. The only real light came from the sky and from their car, which he could see a short distance down the road.

He still couldn't see the kangaroo, but the strength of its putrid fog placed it very near. Where was Shane? She was lost to him, swallowed by the infinite night outback. What was she like now? He didn't want to think about that. He should get back to the car – he could make himself safe there.

The stench of the kangaroo seemed to follow him. When he reached the car, he looked around and saw it, about twenty metres behind. It had been stalking him, keeping its distance. Waiting for him to die, or faint. He wouldn't give it the satisfaction. He climbed into the back of the car and closed the hatch. Only the branch-pierced windscreen could betray him now, and he didn't think the kangaroo could get in through that. He curled up against Shane's pack and watched through the rear window. The kangaroo approached in a series of lopsided lurching bursts, then simply stopped moving. Its head stared uncomprehendingly at the car. Whatever that creature was, he didn't think it could see. He didn't think anything out there was even a kangaroo. He wondered again if Shane was still Shane. He hoped so. She might have stumbled onto an isolated farmhouse with a telephone and gotten help. Perhaps she had come back to the road somewhere else and been picked up. Hopefully they would come for him soon. Once he'd been rescued, he'd find Shane and make sure she had recovered. Perhaps he would visit her in hospital and bring her some of her things. What would he bring her? Her phone, of course. Some of her CDs. They could listen to them together while he visited. He heard the *thump* of the bass, pictured her singing and nodding to the jagged guitars and raw lyrics. *Thump* went the bass again.

He came back to awareness and the roo's head was over him. A blind skull thinly veiled in mangy corruption, loose worms swaying like ropes. It lunged at him, striking with a sloppy thump. He convulsed. *Get it away.* Thrashing, hands going to his face, brushing and tearing. *Get them off.* He banged his head but didn't feel it. Pulled at his cheek, clawed through his hair. His exposed skin stung and writhed. Legs kicking, driving him back away from the kangaroo. Seats blocking his retreat. Kicking at the window. Fingers protecting his eyes.

Window. The window was there.

Nothing was on him.

A spray of viscous blurry fluid streaked with obscene twisting forms oozed down the glass. The car's blinkers lit a stark ochre nightmare - multiple overlapping stains, lingering worms coiling and sliding. Their heads bristled with complex hooked mouthparts wider than their bodies which flexed and closed continually. Could they chew their way in?

The kangaroo could sense him in here. He had to make it go away, scare it somehow. He banged on the window and yelled. “Get out! Go!” But his voice was weak. The roo stood unmoved like an obelisk against the uncaring sky. When you thought about it, the idea of *him* scaring *it* was ludicrous. So ludicrous that he actually laughed. But he wasn’t helpless yet. He wormed his way between the front seats as he had seen Shane do. Leaves dragged across his cracked china head like the fingers of a broken hand. Once in the front seat, he held down the horn. The strident electronic bray was shockingly loud after aeons of near silence. He withstood the pain in his head by imagining he was inflicting the same on the kangaroo. Eventually he released the horn, turning painfully to look. The 'roo had still not moved. At least it had stopped attacking the glass. He faced the front again and saw another figure outside.

Shane was back. That was good. He hoped she was OK. Perhaps she’d even brought help. He was getting very tired and hungry, and his head needed attention. It was comfortable here, and safe, but he'd better go out and see her. He would be safe from the kangaroo with two of them there. He opened the door and pulled himself out again, not minding the fresh onslaught of pain and lights. This would be over soon.

Shane’s head was lowered but he recognised her dark pageboy hair. “Hello, you beautiful.”

She came closer, but her approach was the lopsided, stuttering hobble of a lame animal. She started to raise her head and he didn't want to see, because he could smell her now too. She was like the kangaroo. What was left of her face confirmed it. Had the worms done that, or - he had an unwanted vision of Shane tearing at her face to get them out, trying not to scream but doing so anyway, digging deeper, more and more flesh coming away each time, peeling herself, teeth and bulging eye exposed skull-like... All in vain, though. He could see them on and in her. Her whole body must be infested.

Like the kangaroo, she stopped once she was within a few metres of him and just switched off. Did they know he was going to die? Perhaps they could see or sense how bad his head was. The cold and pain mingled and clutched at his stomach, but determination shot through him. He'd show them otherwise.

He slid slowly back into the car like an injured grub. Shane was dead. There was nothing left of her in what was out there. He had to survive for her and be rescued, so he could tell her family what had happened. Otherwise she would never be found and they would never know. How would he find them? He had her pack, her phone. Surely their numbers were stored on there. He had postcards too. Probably her passport. It would all be taken by the authorities when he was rescued, but he could write down some contact details first. In fact he should do that now - who knew how soon they might come. Was there a pen in the glovebox?

He caught himself this time. Drifting off with the door open. Stupid! He whirled, but neither Shane nor the kangaroo were there. The road ahead of him was glowing again, diffuse and white now. Was he getting worse? He closed the door and watched the play of phantom light grow brighter and brighter, then resolve itself into four glaring orbs. There was a low buzzing or droning in his ears. He shook his head gingerly to try and clear it. The droning stopped, but the lights remained, appearing to hang over the road. Something tapped hard on the window.

He jolted away, expecting the kangaroo. But it was a person. Shane. The door was opening. He lunged for the handle and pulled, but she was too strong for him. A flood of night poured in to consume him. That was wrong, it wasn't allowed in here. Someone was speaking to him, loudly, insistently. Not Shane. It was a man, staring in at him like a grizzled owl.

"Jesus mate, look at your head. Ya have a prang?"

Was this real? He nodded.

"Anyone else with ya?"

He started to nod again, then shook his head. The man looked momentarily puzzled, then shrugged.

"Well, Jesus, ya'd better come with me eh?"

He allowed himself to be helped out of the car - "Steady. Steady. Ya right mate?" – and led across the road towards a ute with an array of rooftop spotlights. He broke away from the man to circle behind the ute, towards where he'd last seen the kangaroo. He got to the back and a gamey musk of blood and shit froze him.

The tray of the ute was full of dead foxes, draped haphazardly across each other as though frozen in mid spring. Inanimate furry muzzles pointed in false innocence. Tongues trailed like scraps of organs from between mindlessly bared teeth.

He wasn't going to get in there. He decided to return to his car. At least there he'd be safe, and could wait for a more appropriate rescue. He turned away and began walking.

"Where ya going mate? What's the problem?"

He pointed towards the tray.

"What's that? You need something?"

Clearly he needed to explain himself further. "Foxes," he said, pointing again.

The man too looked back. "Yeah," he agreed. "What about em?"

"I can't... I won't go with them."

"Whaddaya mean?"

"It's dangerous."

"It's all right mate. They're dead."

Of course that didn't make any difference. If anything, it just made things worse. He shook his head mutely.

"Look, they're bloody dead. I bloody shot 'em."

He had reached the car. The handle of the door was cold in his hand. It was still open. Could the kangaroo have gotten inside while he'd been distracted? That stopped him. He peered intently through the splintered window.

"Jesus. OK, Jesus. Bloody hell."

He heard the sound of metal slamming behind him, and turned to see the man unloading the tray of its burdens. They flexed limply in the air and hit the ground with solid meaty slaps. The last one bounced writhing off a tree, and only then did he gingerly approach the ute. He investigated the tray to make sure there was nothing left, then climbed into the cabin. A rifle was scabbarded between enormous front seats. A christmas tree hung from the rear view mirror.

They got underway. He closed his eyes, safe at last. He was glad they had gotten rid of all the foxes, but anxious about leaving them strewn on the side of the road. His consciousness drifted away to visions of the road covered in mangled furry bodies, broken forelegs trembling, shattered heads thrashing, spines flexing and undulating as though trying to rise.

DEAD DOG TIRED

Anthony Giangregorio

Rufus rolled over in bed, smacking his lips as he tried to figure out what had woken him. His eyes were still closed, and as he slowly cracked them, bright white light sliced into his retinas, causing him to snap them closed.

His head began to pound and he knew he'd drunk too much again.

A squealing came to his ears, and he opened his eyes once more, turning away from the one window in the room with the ragged shade and no curtain. This time his eyes adjusted as he slowly sat up, the room spinning as his hangover took over his consciousness.

Rubbing his head, he looked around the room, smacking his lips once more. It felt like he'd chewed on sandpaper and then spit it out and tossed in a handful of dirt for good measure. The room looked the same as it always did; dirty laundry piled everywhere, a few crushed beer cans lying in one corner, the spouts gaping at him like one-eyed cats.

There was the distinct smell of unwashed bodies in the air, but Rufus didn't notice. He thought he smelled fine, and besides, it was still three more days till the standard weekly bath.

Standing up, he scratched his butt and stumbled to the bathroom, which looked like someone had carried in a bucket full of shit and had then begun tossing it in every direction. A Rorschach painting of feces, Rufus would have thought; if he had the brain power to think in such terms.

But Rufus had managed all of the second grade, and in his family he was considered a college graduate.

After finishing in the bathroom, and deciding not to flush—the water was only a little yellow, he'd wait till it was a full brown—he felt his head pulse with pain as another bout of squealing floated into the house.

Looking around, he knew what it was immediately, and he waddled to the kitchen to look out into the backyard.

"Damn dog, always complainin'," he said to himself as he grabbed his jacket and opened the back door. Stepping outside, the chill air caused his testicles to crawl up inside him and he shook off the cold, watching his breath coalescing in front of him like a miniscule wraith.

Across the yard was his dog, chained to the old oak tree with gnarled branches and a rotting core. The tree should have been taken down years ago, but at the cost, it wasn't worth it. Better to let it die, and when a good storm came, Mother Nature would see to upending it right out of the ground. Of course, if it fell the wrong way Rufus might find out he had a new sunroof, but he wasn't bright enough to think that far ahead.

The dog, a rather large pitbull, woofed its displeasure at being chained up for the entire night.

"Shut up, ya damn mutt," Rufus snapped. "The only reason you're here is 'cause I made sure my bitch of an ex-wife didn't getcha in the divorce."

The dog woofed again and whimpered. Though a large animal, the ribs of the dog poked through from lack of food and its paws were raw from where it had scratched the frozen earth to escape its chain. The collar to which the chain was affixed had dug into the fur until it could barely be seen. Sores festered around the collar where the leather was biting into the animal's flesh and flies buzzed about; feeding on the spots of blood that would appear each time the dog flexed or pulled on the chain.

Attached to the collar, hanging under its neck, was a dog charm. The charm looked like an upside down ampersand, and had small writing scrawled along the metal. Rufus didn't know what it was as it was from his ex-wife, the woman having bought it from some old voodoo shop in town.

The dog lowered its head and growled low, sensing Rufus wasn't here to help it. The two had never gotten along, and when Rufus' wife had filed for a divorce on the grounds he was a lazy, good for nothin', wife beating, vagabond—her words—he had made sure to get a lawyer with enough teeth to stick it to her good.

So what if he'd slapped her around now and then. It was only when she deserved it, such as when dinner wasn't ready or the house wasn't clean. A woman needed to know her place and Rufus' knew they needed it, craved it. Though they might not admit it, women like to be dominated by their man, to be told what to do and when to do it.

Well, he had fixed her wagon in the end, the bitch going and spreading lies and rumors about him.

The only thing she had ever loved while with him was the dog and he had made sure to get it in the settlement. He got the house, too, and to this day he didn't know what his divorce lawyer had managed to do to get away with that one. Last time he checked, his ex was living in a studio apartment in the city—not the good part, either, and she had a job waiting tables at some dive of a diner on the east side.

Rufus didn't work, thanks to a disability check from the government. In his file, it said he was mental, though in reality he was just an asshole.

Couldn't work with others, didn't listen to orders, and couldn't complete tasks given him. That's what it said on his discharge papers from the army.

None of that had to do with him getting his brains fried in the war, though it could have. No, Rufus was just an asshole who thought he knew better than everyone else.

Still, he took the check and cashed it once a month and smiled while he did it.

The dog growled again and Rufus chuckled at it. The dog had been his for all of a week and he had fed it twice when feeling charitable. But now, with his head pounding, he could give two-shits for the damn mutt.

"Shut the hell up, you mangy dog, or so help me I'll come out here with my shotgun and end you once and for all."

The dog lowered its head so low to the ground its chin scraped the soil, its small tail pointed down. The eyes were creased in what seemed to be anger, and as Rufus chuckled malevolently, the dog lunged for him, only the chain stopping it from tearing out Rufus' throat.

As for Rufus, he jumped back and screamed like a girl, falling in the mud beneath him. He quickly looked around to make sure no one had seen him act the coward. Of course there was no one, the next yard more than five hundred feet in each direction.

Slapping the mud under him with his hands, the cold water soaking into his pants, he raised a muddy fist at the dog and snarled, "You'll pay for that, you no good mutt, just try and get another meal out of me."

Pulling himself to his feet, he took a step forward, just to the limit of the dog's chain, and sent a kick into its right shoulder blade. The dog rolled across the dirt and jumped up a second later, only to lunge and become halted by the tight snap of the chain once more.

Rufus spun around and headed back into the house with an evil grin creasing his lips. He glanced over his shoulder once to see the dog watching him, its hackles still raised. But Rufus wasn't scared. The chain holding the dog had inch thick metal links, and as the dog grew weaker from hunger, he knew the fight would go out of the animal.

It was just a matter of time.

The next four days were one of absolute suffering for the dog as it slowly starved to death.

Rufus would sit on the back porch and watch the dog whimpering as its ribs became more pronounced. As the dog slowly died, he imagined it was his bitch of an ex-wife he was making suffer.

A pile of beer cans lying on the porch showed how much time he'd spent watching the dog succumb to death.

One time, when he was feeling particularly evil, he had taken a cooked chicken leg leftover from his dinner and placed it exactly six inches from the dog's face. Though the animal tried to stretch the chain to get at the food, it was an impossible task. Rufus chugged another beer and laughed hysterically as the dog tried to reach the chicken leg. Its eyes rolled up into its head as it whimpered with desperation, but it could never quite reach the food.

Finally, when Rufus became bored, he kicked the chicken leg into the dirt, where it rolled and came up against the fence. The dog's eyes followed it roll, then lowered its head and whimpered like a sad boy who had dropped his ice cream cone. Rufus laughed and went back into the house, and as he lay in his bed, he drifted off to sleep hearing the melody of suffering that was his ex-wife's dog.

On the fifth day he woke up to hear only silence.

Scratching his butt as he made his way to the kitchen, he grabbed a beer out of the fridge and went out to the backyard. The beer tasted sweet, and though it was only ten in the morning, he finished it off and planned on getting another. But first he wanted to check on the mutt and see if it was dead yet.

As he crossed the denuded yard, he saw the animal was lying on its side, its mouth open, the tongue hanging out. The eyes were wide and glazed and dozens of ants were crawling on the carcass.

Rufus took a swig of beer and nodded to himself, seeing the dog had died sometime in the middle of the night.

Finishing his beer, he wiped his mouth with his sleeve and went to get a shovel.

Deciding the less work the better, he dug the hole only two feet from the dead dog. It took him almost an hour, as he had to rest continuously. Manual labor was not his forte, and by the time he was finished, he was sweating profusely and panting the same way the dog had done when it tried to get the chicken leg.

The hole was three feet deep, and he figured it was good enough for a dumb mutt.

Bending down, he unclipped the chain and carelessly kicked the body into the hole. The dog landed muzzle down and to add insult to injury, Rufus unzipped his fly and pissed on the corpse, spraying his stream up and down the matted fur.

When he finished, he zipped up and filled in the hole, slapping the dirt a few times when he was done. He had some leftover dirt now so he spread it around the yard, using it to cover the few piles of feces the dog had left before finally unable to expel anything, as there was nothing going inside its stomach to fuel the machine.

He tossed the shovel to the side and let it clatter in the ground, forgotten as soon as it landed.

Letting out a burp, he stumbled back into the house to grab another beer. He idly wondered what he was going to do now to keep himself occupied now that the tortured dog was dead.

But for now he wanted to go lie down. The digging of the whole had tuckered him out and he was dead dog tired.

There was a thunderstorm that night.

The wind buffeted the trees around Rufus' house as lightning crackled in the sky. The rain came down in sheets, washing the earth clean.

In the backyard of Rufus' home, the muddy soil began to shift and undulate, as if a giant worm was just under the surface.

Like a light switch had been flicked, the rain stopped and the thunder ceased, the storm over, now only the smell of ozone and the drenched soil left behind.

As the leaves on the large oak tree sagged with moisture, the soil below it continued to move.

Ever so slowly, a mud-covered paw broke through the mud to flail back and forth, as if searching for a hand to pull it free. But there was no one in the shadow-enshrouded yard, the moon hidden behind the clouds, and the porch light off.

As the paw flailed back and forth, another paw soon shot forth, looking like a spear stabbing the earth in reverse. In between the two paws, the mud still shifted, and ever so slowly, a dog's head appeared, the muzzle oozing mud as the tongue flicked slightly, resembling a snake tasting the air.

Ever cautious, the dead dog wiggled back and forth as its paws began to scrape the mud, carving long furrows in the wet soil as it began to haul itself out of its shallow grave.

The eyes seemed to glow with a hatred unknown to this earth, and the talisman on its collar moved slightly, as if it was an appendage, a third tale, that twitched when the dog was pleased or angry.

The muzzle cracked and mud spilled forth, the dog puking up more than a gallon of foul water and soil, all that had seeped into its maw as it lay in the sodden grave.

With a groan, the dog stood on its four legs and shook itself, mud flying off in all directions as the matted fur managed to keep some of the soil within its knotted clumps. The dog looked up at the night sky and howled, a long mournful wail, one of loss and frustration.

As the cloud cover began to break apart, the moon sliced through and illuminated the yard, casting the back porch in its pallid glow. The dog's head swiveled toward the back porch, and when it saw the rear door, its hackles raised and its growl vibrated from within it like a cyclone ready to explode.

There was a beer can on the ground and the dog leaned down and sniffed it, not detecting a scent thanks to the rainstorm, but despite this, the animal knew who the can belonged to.

Legs cracked as rigor mortis began to fade, and with halting steps, it began to stumble drunkenly towards the back porch.

As it moved closer to the house, thunder rolled from the north, the storm now out of range, but soon about to pummel another part of the county.

With eyes glowing with hatred and hunger—a hunger for vengeance—the dog padded toward the back door and the oblivious sleeping Rufus waiting within.

The back door was made of cheap wood, with a brown baize on the inside. With its left paw the dog began to scratch at the wood, its sharp claws digging in and scratching long gouges into the facade. This continued for more than hour, each swipe of its claw slowly taking away more of the wood. On the inside of the door, the brown material began to slowly undulate as pressure from the opposite side increased.

Then the baize ripped and the paw could be seen as it wiggled back and forth, tearing and pulling at the edges.

By the time the hole was large enough for the dog's head to fit, the paw that had done the scratching was a bloody nub with bone protruding at the tip, gobbets of flesh and fur hanging from it to slap the porch as the dog continued to worry at the door.

With a hole now present, the dog forced its head inside, then slowly began pulling its torso through the opening. But the edges of the hole was jagged, thick wooden splinters jutting at odd angles, and as the dog slowly crawled into the kitchen, the wooden daggers sliced into its fur, its flesh, tearing large gashes that seeped congealed blood like cold maple syrup on a winter's day.

One such dagger, jutting at an odd angle, managed to pierce the dog's left eye. The spear sliced into the orb, penetrating more than an inch; a pinkish ooze seeping out of the socket to drip onto the floor.

Finally, the dog's hind legs were through the hole and it plopped down on the floor. The animal lay there, acting as if it was catching its breath, which was the farthest thing from the truth; for it no longer breathed.

As it lay there, covered in mud, large gashes in the animal's hide, one eye now missing, it paused, for a moment not moving, as if it had returned back to death's door.

For the space of half a minute, the dog was immobile. Then a snore carried through the house from the opposite end, causing the dog's head to snap up. Slowly, it pulled itself to a standing position.

It now stood at an odd angle due to the missing paw, now nothing but a bloody stump, and as it began to walk through the house, there was an odd, *slap, slap, click, slap, slap, click*, for each time the exposed bone connected with the kitchen floor.

The snoring called to the animal and it slowly made its way through the house, not rushing, silent as death itself.

At the doorway to where the snoring was emanating, it paused, then used its muzzle to cautiously push the partially opened door wider. The room was wretched in darkness, only a wan spear of moonlight creasing the shadows, cutting through the tattered window shade of the lone window.

The dog entered the bedroom and moved to the bed, where Rufus lay in a drunken stupor.

The dog woofed once, softly, as if it was warning its victim, giving Rufus a chance to wake up and defend himself, but even if the dog had barked with its loudest volume, Rufus was out for the night.

The dog glared at the man who had tortured it, killed it, its one eye seeming to glow in the dull gloom. Then it placed the worn nub of its leg onto the bed and pulled itself up, its rear paws kicking and scratching the bed frame for a second as it hopped onto the mattress.

It slowly walked over to Rufus, standing so its legs were on either side of him, its head even with Rufus' face, and it stood immobile, looking down on the man who had killed it, had let it starve to death for the simple joy of being cruel.

The hours passed silently, the dog never moving, only the viscous ooze from its gouged eye dripping onto the pillow next to Rufus' head. As the night began to recede and the first hint of dawn touched the sky, the mangled body of the dog remained still.

It was waiting for something to happen, but what that might be was locked in its dead brain.

Dawn slowly vanished to be replaced by full morning, the rainwater slowly drying as the grass blades glistened with moisture.

It was going to be a beautiful day, and as Rufus slowly opened his eyes around 11:30 in the morning, his alcohol-tinted orbs gazed up at the muzzle of the dog—the one he'd buried only yesterday.

At first he thought it was a dream, something from his drunken binge that had seeped into his mind, perhaps a small kernel of guilt at what he'd done.

But no sooner did the idea flood his mind that he pushed it aside. He wasn't remorseful. Hell, he'd do it again if he could have figured out how to bring the damn dog back from the dead.

But he never had to consider that again, for something or someone had done that for him.

As his eyes pushed away the grogginess of sleep, he stared up at the muzzle of the dog he'd killed, its teeth flaring in what seemed like anger. Bits of mud dropped off the dog's face to sprinkle Rufus' cheeks and brow, and he realized he was staring up at a horror he could never have imagined— and it was now real.

He had time for one long scream before the dog's jaws darted onto his throat, tearing out a fist-sized, bloody chunk of flesh. The head snapped back, and the dog swallowed the meat whole, to then dive in for more; Rufus' shrieks of pain growing in volume. Blood geysered from the man's wound to spray the wall behind the bed crimson, and the dog's face was washed in scarlet as it dove in yet again, teeth gripping tendons and tearing, using its powerful neck muscles to work at the gaping wound continually.

By the time the dog was finished, Rufus' head had been severed from his shoulders, the jagged neck stump squirting blood in all directions, the top of the bed now a deep red as the liquid soon began to drip onto the floor. Rufus' arms twitched spastically for a few seconds before going limp, the legs kicking a staccato drumbeat into the mattress before stopping.

The dog chewed at the exposed stump, finally filling its empty belly, finally getting the food Rufus had denied it in life.

The dog fed for almost an hour, and by the time it was finished, the neck and parts of the shoulders were missing, as well as a large hole ripped in Rufus' torso, where the dog had fed on his moist organs, chewing on the heart and kidneys as if it was the finest veal money could buy.

The entire time, Rufus' head lay on his pillow, his eyes still open, as if he could see his body being consumed and was helpless to stop it.

Suddenly, the dog stopped feeding and its head snapped up. Its ears pricked to the side and the dog woofed twice. Swiveling on the bed, the dog jumped off and padded through the house, Rufus' corpse now forgotten.

The animal went to the back door and crawled through the hole again, woofing each time its ears would prick up. Unknown to human ears, a dog whistle had been blown, and the dog recognized the caller, having been trained when it was alive.

After pulling itself through the hole, and sustaining a few more tears to its flesh from wooden splinters, it hobbled around the house and to the front yard, where a woman in a large flowered hat waited for it.

Excited to see the woman, it began to move faster, its nub of a tail wiggling happily.

When the dog reached the woman, she knelt down on one knee, and with a handkerchief pulled from her purse, she quickly wrapped the bloody stump of its front leg.

"Look at you, you're a mess, you poor thing. Oh and look at your eye. Well, we can get that fixed up once I get you home."

She pattered her hip playfully and began to walk, the dog hobbling behind, looking as if it had just been in a hit and run.

"Once we get you home, we'll get you all cleaned up," Rufus' wife said as she paused, knelt down and clipped a leash onto the dog's collar, her hand caressing the talisman hanging from the dog's neck. "There you go, my baby, there's a leash law in this town and I wouldn't want to get a ticket."

The dog woofed once, as if it understood what she was saying.

The dog and its rightful owner walked away from the house, and as the woman reached the end of the driveway, she turned slowly and gazed back at Rufus' home, at the house of the man who had beat her, treated her worse than a slave, and she smiled widely.

"I win, you drunk bastard," she said softly.

Turning, she continued on, her loyal companion padding right beside her, its blood-coated muzzle trailing small red droplets of blood in its wake as it hobbled along at its master's side.

THE RISING

Hayden Williams.

It was a kind of spell that came over the land, something to do with those Southern lights, the aurora australis that hovered at times high over the ice of Antarctica and were visible in winter from the southern extremities of New Zealand's South Island. The penguins got edgy. At night you could hear the seals roaring for hours at the haloed moon, which for some reason became unusually bright. There were bergs breaking off that hidden continent regularly now, floating right up the east coast and not melting till they got as far as Christchurch. The whales were returning too, their backs breaking the surface near shore like bobbing black olives, like pupils dilating in a milk-green eye, as if even the ocean was becoming conscious of it, this sinister magic that approached.

Murray began to have nightmares. He dreamed of his long-dead working dogs, favourite old horses that died years ago, and relatives returning from the grave with warnings they seemed desperate to communicate. But silence was another quality of this insidious sorcery. The apparitions that filled his sleep were all mute. Their urgent signing eventually became furious – their bodies writhed and jacked, their eyes big like they were deep under water and drowning. That's what it was sort of like

– like being under water. Both the land and the sea were labouring under this alien force that weighed everywhere and filled everything with an urge to rise up above it, an urge to inhabit the air and breathe again. Others experienced similar nocturnal visions and were deeply shaken, but hardly anyone dared speak of it throughout the days. It was the community's 'elephant in the room'. And then, after the first meteor shower, it became the 'evil in the forest'.

Possum trappers and deer hunters began seeing these ancient creatures reconstituting themselves from the rot and mud that stinks under ferns. They'd come back from the dark interiors of the bush and tell their stories, sitting in shacks under storm lanterns, one eye on the door as they tried to get it straight without coming off as crazy. Sucking rolled cigarettes down to their brown burnt fingers, their stubbly necks moving in peristalsis as they chugged back whisky. Big men used to the cold, trembling like greyhounds. Their faces like the faces of timid abandoned children. The bravest listeners scoffed, swaggered with machismo, stocked up their jeeps, went off to investigate and never returned. There was a silence settled in with a pall of fog that hung about a metre from the earth. Occasionally it was broken by screams, and the unnatural blood-freezing cries of unknown animals.

Then people started actually seeing these things for themselves, right there in the street – giant flightless birds supposedly extinct for centuries, ripping open trash sacks and shoving their heads inside to feed. Giant moa, like over-grown lethal ostriches, splayed three-toed feet the size of tennis rackets. They stood high as stovepipes, broad backs like the backs of horses. They were supposed to be long dead, but here they were, herding through Murray's back yard. He could see the vertebrae tearing through the disintegrating skin. Their feathers clung in patches, dripping black ooze like murdered ink quills. Trails of filth dropped from the undersides of their bellies and gaps in their exposed ribs wherever they went. Their treacly bodies boiled, alive with maggots.

"This is impossible," said his wife, Martha, as together they watched some kind of long-forgotten, Gondwanaland marsupial drag itself along with the loop of its neck. The abomination – whatever this creature once was – now lost one of its eyes as it struggled along beneath their bedroom window. They locked all the doors and windows and in the typically laconic southern way said no more about it. They spent a sleepless night in bed, listening to the shuffling and groaning of unspeakable things moving through the silver of the moonlit fields of their farm beyond the drawn curtains.

There was no choice but to leave the sheep out in the top paddocks overnight. They bleated until dawn, could be heard high up, moving quickly across from one side of the hill to the other. They'd be frightened as hell; the lambs would miscarry or come out stillborn in spring. It seemed ridiculous, worrying about it. But farming was all Murray new and in this situation he was clinging to it. It was unbearable, not being able to understand what was going on and not being able to do anything. He couldn't even sleep. The dog, Bess, had been allowed inside and lay at the foot of their bed, whimpering and growling low all night. In the morning, Bess seemed as keen as her master to get out there and do something.

Heading up to the top fields, Murray pounded a fist against the roof of the truck's cab:

"Quiet down, Bess!" he roared, to no avail. Bess continued barking wildly as she chased back and fore along the truck's open bed behind. Probably she could smell or hear mountain bikers using the track that snaked through the bush-covered foothills, bordering the fence-line about forty yards to the right. Perhaps it was simply nothing more than that. Mountain bikers always drove her mad as a meat-axe, and normally Murray wouldn't have minded: he hated mountain bikers too – they rarely moved over to allow him to pass more easily, and they were always worrying sheep in the lower paddocks as they sped along the roads dressed in their bright ridiculous stretch-suits. So he would normally never have dissuaded Bess from barking at them. But now he was sure the guy on the radio was talking about farming in New Zealand's South Island. That was enough to get his interest. Then he realised they were talking about sheep and cattle stations in Eastern Fjordland, Southland and the Maniototo, which concerned him directly. A spokesman from the department of conservation was 'gravely concerned', and someone from the Ministry of Agriculture, Forestry and Farming was talking about mass culls. He had just used the word 'epidemic'. The plague of zombie creatures was causing mass panic and spreading some kind of virus as well.

The mud-spattered truck continued slowly up the steep rutted track that lead to the highest fields of his farm. The radio was drowned out by the noise of the creaking suspension as he crashed in and out of potholes, and the sound of Bess' insistent barking. Murray caught the tail end of the radio debate:

"But if the virus that seems to be spreading outwards from the centre of these attacks is indeed – as some experts have suggested – airborne . . ."

"As I said, we don't want to assume anything at this early stage . . ."

"*IF* it *IS* airborne, minister, then what use are road blocks going to be? What assurances can you give farmers that their livestock are going to be protected, and how will you compensate farmers like Terry McIntyre, whose entire herds have already been wiped out?"

"The government will look into compensation for affected farmers shortly, but at the present moment our priority has to be containing these creatures and bringing them under control. As I said, we have the best people working round the clock to determine what's going on and how this is happening. Until then we will be putting a freeze on all meat exports and expecting South Island farmers – especially those in the Fjordland and Central Otago areas – to cooperate by quarantining all animals including household pets."

The radio host thanked the minister for his time and began the next topic just as Murray reached the top of the ridge. Murray switched off the radio and let out a sigh. He'd heard of the McIntyres – they were a big wealthy family operating several large-scale farms in valleys less than two hundred kilometres away to the West. This was serious. He'd have to drive both his flocks down immediately and contain them. He'd split them into six different groups, he decided, and pen each group as far away from the others as possible. The heavy snows last winter had cost him, and as it was, he'd barely recovered from the summer's worth of drought the year before that. Over the past five years it had become a vicious circle, having to borrow more from the bank just to keep the farm from going under. If on top of all this weirdness a virus hit the area then he'd likely be finished.

Bess was still barking. The sun was up, the fog had cleared, and in the green valley below, the river was reflecting light like a bright kink of wire. He felt better up here. The air seemed fresher, less in the net of that mysterious gravity. Wee McCusker – the dwarf who owned the neighbouring farm – was out in his top field too. McCusker's sheep dotted the brown hills on the other side: Murray could see them moving down in a wide funnel, see the chrome of Mcusker's quad bike flash suddenly in the morning sun, and then the tiny black fleck of his dog moving back and fore at the opposite end of the field. The morning shadows were long and purple, the higher clouds turning orange as lower cloud – grey and rain-thick – began flowing in from the east. The way the valley changed colour and the way the light played across it was beautiful. It would be heartbreaking to have to leave.

Murray thumped the roof of the truck again:

"Quiet down, Bess!"

Cloud shadows ran across the fields on the other side, moving fast. Then the first ragged wisps of vapour began to hide the tussock grass and lichen-covered stones that surrounded him. There was a freakish gust of wind that rocked the truck. Bess was suddenly silent.

"Finally," he mumbled to himself. "She's stopped her yapping." He fished his cell phone out of the breast pocket of his fleece-lined tartan jacket. Someone had been trying to ring, and there was a text message waiting. It was from Martha. 'Come down at once or get to cover' was all it said. The message unnerved him. Martha wasn't the kind of woman to be insistent unless there was a real problem. What did she mean by 'get to cover'? She'd probably be looking up from the farmhouse below. Perhaps she could see some seriously bad weather moving in, or more of those . . . things.

The first wave of incoming rain-cloud cleared. In a gap of light, Murray watched a cloud shadow race along the face of the hills across the valley. He drummed his fingers on the steering wheel, but stopped – the cloud shadow began to wheel around, began to race back the way it had come. It must be a plane, he thought. But why couldn't he hear its engine? He hunched forward over the steering wheel and squinted to study the shadow's shape, but just then a second wave of rain-cloud rolled in, and the truck was swamped in cloud vapour.

He called out for Bess but there was no sound at all. Winding down his window, he stuck his head out and listened. At first there was nothing, not even the hiss of the wind in the tussock. Then he heard the first few drops of rain over the roof of the cab. A droplet landed in his hair. It felt warm. Murray called for Bess again and this time adjusted the rear-view mirror to look. The truck bed was empty, and beyond that there was nothing but grey-white vapour as thick as his morning porridge. He caught a glimpse of his own reflection and froze. Blood was slowly moving down his forehead. He touched it and saw it on his fingertip.

"What the – ?"

He listened again and this time heard something: the sound of someone running towards him. It was hard to determine direction but the footsteps were getting nearer. Murray saw the luminous yellow of the mountain-biker's stretch-suit before he heard the strained breathing and coughing. The mountain-biker emerged out of the mist from the direction of the bush to the right. His muscular legs were marble white and dripping with dark red blood. The mountain-biker – now, for some reason, a bike-less mountain-biker – was pressing his right hand flat against his left collarbone, like someone swearing allegiance. The hand was dark red too, and it covered a terrible wound that was spilling red down the man's chest. His chin was covered in blood as well, and his cycle helmet had somehow been split almost completely in half, a large section of it flapping lose at the back of his head. The man stopped abruptly when he saw the truck. His eyes – full of terror – locked with Murray's.

Murray watched, amazed, as the mountain-biker changed direction and started running towards the truck instead. At a distance of about thirty feet, Murray could see the blood pulse from the man's gasping mouth. At twenty feet he heard the bubbling and wheezing of what he now realised were supposed to be cries for help. Raised a Catholic in a very easy-going manner, Murray was surprised that the next thing he heard was the sound of his own voice reciting the Hail Mary. It seemed to be the only action he was capable of: mumbling this long-redundant prayer he'd been made to memorise all those years ago. Aside from that he couldn't even blink – couldn't take his eyes from the approaching stranger's agonised face, which suddenly looked up into the sky and cringed.

The mountain-biker halted his stumbling dash towards the truck with only about ten feet left to go. He stood stock still, his eyes shut tight and squeezing out tears. Murray was so transfixed by the sight of the wounded man that he hardly noticed how the cloud-mist began to swirl, fanned by powerful currents. The prayer stopped dead the moment Wee-man McCusker slammed into the left wheel-arch and coughed a lung-full of blood across the bonnet of the truck in a broad crimson stripe. Murray had the briefest glimpse of the giant talon relinquishing its grip of Wee-man's head, allowing the dwarf's stoved-in body to slide down the dented side of the truck.

Now Murray was moving. His heart spiked adrenaline through his entire body. At just five feet away, the mountain-biker crumpled, waving his one white hand like a flag of surrender as he began to pass out from blood loss. Murray shook as he wound up the driver window. He could hardly keep his hand still enough to turn the key and start the ignition. When he did, he revved the truck into life, slamming his boot down on the accelerator repeatedly, panicking when he realised he wasn't even moving. He remembered the hand-break and disengaged it. The truck bounced forward and stalled.

The cloud-mist cleared for an instant and he saw it – gliding on thermals high in the air above the valley, its broad wedge-shaped tail twitching as it turned abruptly for another run of attack. It was impossibly large: an eagle, black and white like a magpie, but with a wingspan of at least nine feet. It stuck out its red-crested head and began to speed forward, its talons drawn up to its body like raised landing gear on an aircraft. At fifty feet Murray saw its wings were tinged yellow-green nearer the tips. Gore falling from its belly made it look as though it was spraying crops. At thirty feet the truck restarted. At fifteen feet the eagle opened its beak and let out a single piercing screech that echoed down the valley. The next second Murray was screaming in reply and pressing his face into the vinyl of the passenger seat. He looked up in time to see the creature's monstrous talon punch out from its body as it hurtled over the truck: the windscreen puckered into the impact and popped, showering him with cubes of glass.

There was only the sound of the engine then. He sat up quickly and realised the truck was already moving, rolling slowly over the ridge and gathering momentum. He gave the accelerator a squeeze and pulled down hard on the steering wheel to swing it around. As soon as he was bumping down the track he gave it more gas and knocked it into second. He needed to get to the cover of the farmhouse as fast as possible, but somehow had the odd feeling that he was going the wrong way; that he needed to be heading upwards. Cold air rushing through the cab made his eyes water. In the rear-view mirror he saw the creature wheel as if one of its wingtips had momentarily been nailed to the sky. Then it was diving after him again.

Murray whimpered, pressed his foot down and moved into third. He saw the needle rise to fifty miles per hour but the creature was already upon him, folding its wings and dropping into the bed of the truck with a heavy slam, as though someone had just dumped an anvil in there. He heard the awful scrape and tap of its talons, looked directly into intelligent, compassionless eyes that were circled by tiny squirming white worms. It stabbed its head forward to smash through the cab's back window.

Murray screamed again as the creature easily sliced his left shoulder wide open with the hooked end of its beak. It was so quick and deep he felt no pain, and could hardly believe it when he looked down and saw bright red blood spraying from his severed brachial artery. The truck lurched to the right and jumped as it crashed into a bank at the edge of the track. The giant bird opened its wings and pounced up into the sky. He began to mumble the Hail Mary again, and by some miracle started the stalled engine once more. He got into fourth this time, and could at last see the farmhouse below as the vehicle rocked and threw him about. The passenger door was dripping, the window coated with his blood. Murray was quickly becoming dizzy but at least this time he was moving *away* from the horror: he could see the bird perusing him in the rear-view mirror, but was leaving it behind as he reached the relative safety of sixty, seventy, eighty miles per hour. He watched the needle and risked a little laugh of hope. Yet still there was that lurking instinct telling him to get up out of the valley, up into the sky's untainted air. He didn't see the gatepost in time and the right corner of the bonnet folded like a concertina.

Murray regained his senses and realised the truck had spun ninety degrees and stopped. Losing hope and energy, he swore before trying to start the engine yet again. He heard the call of the eagle behind him and another call answering it from further up the valley. Great: that meant there were two of these things. It was then he remembered the hunting rifle chained in its polished mahogany rack above the fireplace. The key to the padlock was on his key ring in the hip pocket of his jeans. When the engine fired into life he whooped with joy and understood that he now felt more alive than he ever had before. To die this way would not only be unfair – it would be completely absurd. Pride and grim determination were the only things fuelling his movements as he tugged on the wheel, pointed the truck at the glass patio doors of his lounge and squashed the accelerator against the now-sticky floor of the cab.

The front of the truck was too wide. Murray had forgotten to apply his seatbelt and was launched through the space where the windscreen had been. He crashed through the plate glass of the sliding door and landed on his back in the centre of the room. His tartan jacket was in ribbons now and there was a deep laceration across the front of his right thigh. He could see the gun on its rack. Raising his head, he saw the truck roll slowly back from the ruined side of the house, dragging the front bumper as it seemed to limp sadly away, shedding a hubcap. One of the eagles landed outside in the yard. The shadow of the second grew bigger on the ground until it too alighted. They both hopped across the lawn to investigate. He could smell their putrid flesh already. By the time they were cautiously sticking their decaying balding heads through the hole in the wall, Murray had dragged himself up to the level of the mantelpiece. I can at least save Martha, he thought, his fingers closing tight around the chain of the rack. But then he saw her. She was lying in a heap on the other side of the couch, thrown there by his impact, a cleaver-sized piece of glass stuck through her pale tender neck.

Murray opened his mouth and a primal roar came out. The two birds instinctively ducked their heads and retreated into the garden before carefully beginning their advance again. He gripped the chain and allowed himself to fall. The gun rack came away from the wall and landed on top of him; Murray landed on top of the overturned coffee table; there was a dreadful shredding noise – his sight momentarily fading and a pain-induced hissing in his ears.

It took a full three seconds for him to realise he was impaled on the coffee table's metal leg. Lying on his back, he looked down at the tubular iron shaft emerging from his right side. The wound seeped black like the truck's wrecked sump. He knew he'd probably pierced his liver and could never survive it on top of everything else. Snot bubbled from his nostrils as he wept out of pity for himself. He dug in his hip pocket and pulled out the key, fumbled and got the padlock open.

Murray recalled how beautiful the valley had looked from the top of the ridge just moments before any of this had occurred. Now he really was finished – but God would surely grant him the mercy of being able to end the lives of these monsters before it was time to leave his valley forever. He raised the rifle with a blood-flecked grin. The chain slid free of the trigger guard like a bright silver viper, and the two birds watched it fall as if mesmerised.

"Go to hell," Murray whispered, and squeezed the trigger. Nothing happened. In spite of all the years he'd been around rifles, this time he'd somehow managed to forget about shells, which were in the locked draw of the cabinet behind him.

Sharp talons stabbed into his legs and he gasped from the fresh new pain of it. A slimy beak darted forward and opened his steaming stomach; a second rummaged inside and Murray's head swam as it finally emerged again, pulling his entrails with it like a knotted string of pink-purple handkerchiefs. The stern, compassionless eyes were the last things he saw. The Ministry of Agriculture, Forestry and Farming inspectors found the bodies of Murray and his wife the following morning. They found Bess alive and well, her tail between her legs as she emerged from the crawlspace under the farmhouse and ran for the hills, for the last uncorrupted air of the mountains.

SWAT

Brian Pinkerton

Sergeant Koska held his breath, remaining perfectly still except for the movement of his eyes, which slid across their sockets, searching the dank living room with piercing intensity. He held out one arm, palm facing his four colleagues, signaling for them to stay motionless and on alert.

Koska could see the pale horror draped across their faces. It didn't matter that they were trained officers of the Louisiana State Police Special Weapons and Tactics team, an elite force equipped to perform high-risk operations beyond the capabilities of ordinary law enforcement. It offered no comfort that they were heavily armed with assault rifles, submachine guns and explosives.

The enemy they faced defied practical warfare methods and promised a swift and certain fate.

"We're doomed," muttered Jake, a SWAT agent of 16 years and the best sniper on the force.

Koska ignored the remark. As their leader, he needed to demonstrate courage, even if his own confidence was slipping. "We've secured every window and door," Koska said. "This house is sealed tighter than a drum."

"It won't help," responded Hank, a veteran of the first Gulf War and the team's specialist at dealing with barricaded gunmen. "They'll get in. You know they will."

"You told us we'd be fighting zombies," growled Anders, a six-foot-six African American of solid muscle, finely toned from his glory days playing college football at Tulane University. "Nobody prepared us for this. It's bullshit!"

"Shut up all of you!" shouted Tara, the toughest female SWAT member in the state of Louisiana. Her voice boomed off the walls and the four men stopped talking, returning the room to silence...

... except for the most terrifying sound of all.

A tiny, almost imperceptible zzt.

***

In the beginning, the assignment was entirely bizarre yet manageable: stop an outbreak of cannibalism that had overtaken a small, backwoods town. In a 24-hour period, the community of Clarkson, located on a flood plain between the Mississippi and Yazoo Rivers, had erupted into widespread violence. Ordinary citizens began attacking – biting – eating one another in random assaults. Once bitten, victims joined the ranks of their attackers, slipping into a semi-conscious "zombie" state, losing all rational behavior to a hunger for human flesh.

Clarkson's zombie population quickly grew and the state's SWAT force was flown to the scene with strict orders to rescue the uninfected and destroy the infected. Anyone bitten by a zombie was deemed dangerous and subject to immediate execution.

The National Guard sealed Clarkson's borders to prevent the disease from spreading to neighboring communities while SWAT operators infiltrated the town, going door-to-door to sort the living from the undead.

Survivors were whisked away in school buses. The less fortunate were put down permanently.

Koska marveled over the slowness and stupidity of the enemy. "its target practice," he declared, dropping the shuffling, slack-jawed zombies with ease with his M16. A bullet to the head finished them off and they made no effort to run or hide. In fact, the zombies barely put up a decent fight, even the bigger ones and the sneaky sonsofbitches who popped out of the shadows without warning. That's where the SWAT unit's training and weaponry came into play, years of drills simulating hostage rescues and counter-terrorism operations. The zombies were comparatively lame, like shooting fish in a barrel. Koska felt confident his squad would complete its mission without suffering a single casualty.

But then he received a special assignment that changed everything. As Koska's team made good progress, blasting through a leafy, residential street, dispatching close to two dozen zombies and rescuing nearly a hundred of the living, an urgent call crackled over the radio from Central Command.

A potential location for "Patient Zero" had been identified, a likely source for the zombie outbreak. Several townspeople spoke of a deranged family named Leery who lived in a decrepit southern mansion on the outskirts of town, tucked away in the swamps and bayous of the Mississippi Delta. The Leery family practiced voodoo, obsessed with finding a way to "call up the dead" through black magic and animal sacrifices. For years, the Leary's were dismissed as a hapless clan of mentally unfit, inbred hillbilly freaks. No one ever took them seriously...until now.

Bert, a long-haired cousin of the Leary's, had fled the mansion and told the sheriff's police a harrowing tale about witnessing the resurrection of a corpse. He claimed family members performed a voodoo ritual to bring a beloved uncle back to life. The endeavor proved successful with alarming side effects: the revived corpse displayed a total lack of memory, exhibited minimal brain activity, and manifested a fierce appetite for human flesh. The dead-alive uncle promptly began chomping on relatives, sending his victims into an equally zombified state. Cousin Bert escaped in his pick-up truck with the rest of the family literally nipping at his heels.

In the beginning, the sheriff's police howled with laughter at Bert's story and threatened to jail him for smoking funny cigarettes. However, the next day, when zombies staggered into town and began spreading an unthinkable plague, the laughter stopped.

Bert's story immediately gained credibility and he underwent intense interrogation by officials while SWAT troops stormed the town. Realizing the need to raid the Leery home, Central Command selected Koska's team for the mission. Koska received his marching orders: "Go inside that mansion, destroy every zombie you find and see if there are any survivors."

"No problem," Koska responded. After all, it was just another house to storm, a few more heads to plug with bullets. He gathered his platoon into an armored vehicle and headed for the deep reaches of the Louisiana marshlands.

Driving through the tall, wet grass, Koska could barely make out the fading roadways that twisted and turned toward their destination. The sun had started its descent and Koska did not want this house call to extend into nightfall. While his unit was well-equipped with flashlights and night goggles, he really didn't want to give the enemy a fighting – or biting – chance.

"Yo, see it!" cried Anders, pointing to a steeply pitched roof poking out of a dense thicket of oak trees. As the van advanced closer, the entire structure came into view across the windshield: a once-elegant Victorian mansion, church-like in appearance with arches, pointed windows and a long front porch populated with empty rocking chairs nodding in the breeze, as if they held ghosts.

Koska parked along the edge of a wild, sprawling garden. "Grab your weapons. We're going to see some action. We don't know how many ... could be a few, could be a whole nest of 'em."

"We have a greeter!" hollered Garth, the youngest and most trigger-happy member of Koska's unit. The spiky-haired blond hopped out of the van and dropped to one knee. He aimed his rifle at a slow-walking, whiskered man in a flannel shirt who staggered through the weeds. "Stop where you are and identify yourself!"

The whiskered man continued to approach the van with a vacant expression. Identifying zombies was no mystery – you just checked for the dead look in their eyes. This one stared right through them, indifferent to the gun pointed at his face.

Garth fired.

His target promptly crumpled to the grass as if someone had flipped an "off" switch in his back.

"Here comes Grandpa Zombie," announced Tara, and sure enough, a lumpy old man in a sleeveless t-shirt and vintage straw hat shuffled out of the house, arms extended, groping at nothing, sleepy-faced. "This one's mine."

She delivered a clean shot to the center of Grandpa Zombie's forehead and he tumbled down the porch steps to the red brick walkway.

"Let's go 'round back and check the exterior before we go in," said Koska.

"I get dibs on the next one," declared Anders.

They circled the mansion and discovered two zombie children in the backyard, mouths wet with blood from a recent feeding. Anders blasted them without remorse. The children's meal, a plump older woman with her innards exposed, sat propped on a bench in a broken down gazebo, staring at the SWAT agents with little interest. A bullet fired from Tara's rifle struck the woman between the eyes, a sudden red hole, and her body slumped sideways and eyelids drooped shut.

Finding no other zombies, Koska and his unit returned to the front of the mansion. Koska studied the grand, double-door entrance and sighed. "Let's do it."

The officers slammed open the doors and proceeded inside with caution, guns drawn. The floorboards creaked under the weight of their weapons and gear. Koska called out for survivors and no one shouted back. Instead, more zombies wandered into view, sporting blood-encrusted bite marks and colorless skin.

"Goodnight, dopey," said Garth, just prior to plugging a buck-toothed, middle-aged zombie in his balding head.

When a woman in a blood-stained apron staggered out of the kitchen, Hank called out, "I got it," and sent her right back in, blowing her brains across the front of the refrigerator.

"This is creepy," said Hank, staring down at the woman's body, dressed in a cheerful, flowery dress. "We just shot somebody's mom. Heck, this could've been one of our moms."

"Don't think about it," said Tara. "She was already dead. Her soul was gone, this is just the shell. We did her a favor."

"Can the chatter," said Koska. "Let's split up so we can get the hell out of here. Jake, Anders and Garth, take the upstairs. Tara and Hank, you come with me. We'll finish searching the ground floor."

Koska's trio moved across the first floor, kicking open doors with weapons in the ready position. In the library, they discovered a long-haired male with a shaggy beard and red teeth, sitting on an antique loveseat and chewing a severed arm pulled from a female torso that writhed limbless on the floor.

Koska shot them both.

"Holy shit, check this out!" exclaimed Hank, several steps down the corridor, standing in the doorway to the next room. Koska and Tara hurried to his side and looked into a large, pink-walled parlor.

"This must be where it all started," said Koska, taking in the scene.

The room held an elaborate voodoo temple with an altar populated with candle stubs, bottles of murky liquid, and collections of colored beads. Patterns of cornmeal dusted the wood floor. A narrow table in the center of the room held a collection of bells, rattles and small drums.

Rotted animal carcasses rested in heaps in front of the altar. Koska gagged. The sight for the eyes was bad enough, but the stink to the nostrils was overwhelming. The room's windows had been boarded up to keep out the daylight and any voyeurs.

"So this is it," said Tara."Voodoo Central."

"Let's burn this shit down," said Hank.

"No. We need to leave it," responded Koska. "It needs to be analyzed. That's not our job. We're here to wipe out the zombies and stop the infections. Let's keep moving."

A shot rang out in one of the rooms above them, followed by muffled shouts and a door slam.

Koska hurried to the foot of the staircase as Jake and Anders descended, followed by Garth, who was cursing and frantically slapping at his body.

"What the hell is it?" said Koska.

Garth reached the bottom of the steps, brushing himself off in shudders. "Goddamned mosquitoes!"

Tara broke out laughing. "Wimp!"

"Screw you," muttered Garth.

"It was disgusting," related Anders. "We opened the door to a bathroom off the master suite and there was this naked zombie sitting in the bathtub, taking a bath. The window was open and he was covered in mosquitoes. He didn't even flinch, probably been sitting like that for hours."

Jake said, "Garth shot him in the head and the mosquitoes jumped off the zombie and came after him."

"Insect bastards," said Garth, scratching his neck and face.

Jake continued, "We shut the door and got the hell out of there."

"You sure the zombie's dead?" asked Koska.

"Hell yes," said Garth, insulted by the notion he would miss such an easy target. "One bullet to the head and his bathwater became bloodwater." Garth continued to scratch all over his skin. "Damn fucking bugs!"

"You gonna be okay?" asked Koska. "We got a lot of equipment, but I don't think we have anything for bug bites."

"Suck it up, big boy," taunted Tara.

Garth shut his eyes. "Screw you. It's not funny... Seriously, I don't feel so good." He hugged himself. "Jesus, when'd it get so cold in here?"

Koska noted the red lumps all over Garth's face and hands and felt some pity. The Mississippi Delta, soaked with swampy bayous and stagnant water, was one of the most fertile breeding grounds in the country for mosquitoes. Garth would probably scratch himself raw in the hours to come.

As he noted the bug bites, Koska observed something else – a ghastly pallor overtaking Garth's complexion – and a foggy look in his eyes.

"You okay, Garth?" asked Koska.

Garth swooned. His hands dropped to his sides and the clawing fingers relaxed. He turned his head to stare at the hulking, fleshy Anders, who stood next to him.

"Why you lookin' at me like that?" said Anders.

Garth's lips curled back, showing teeth. His SWAT colleagues exchanged quick, alarmed looks and immediately reached the same conclusion.

Koska lifted his rifle. "Move back," he told the others. He aimed for Garth's head.

Garth looked into the barrel of the gun with a blank, dopey expression.

Koska felt sick to his stomach. In an instant, it all made horrible sense: If the zombie plague could spread through bites from the infected, why couldn't a mosquito, feeding off the blood of a victim, transfer the condition to a healthy human?

Garth took a step toward Koska, his jaw chomping at the air, hungry for...

Koska fired.

Garth dropped, dead. Permanently.

The rest of the SWAT troop stared down at his crumpled shape, in shock.

"Done in by a goddamned mosquito," muttered Hank.

Koska's gaze lifted from Garth to Anders and Jake.

"What about you two?"

"What about us?" said Jake.

"You were up in that bathroom."

"No, no, man..." said Anders, vigorously shaking his head. "Them bugs only got Garth. We were standing in the hallway. When he ran out, we shut the door. Them things never touched us. We're cool."

Tara whipped her head around, examining her surroundings. "There could be a lot more of them in this house... in this room!"

Anders made a move toward the front doors, sweat glistening on his face. "Jesus, we gotta get the hell out of here!"

"Stop!" called out Koska. "Not so fast. We're not going anywhere. We're safer in the house."

Anders halted and looked at him, dumbfounded. "Are you serious?"

Koska gestured across the room. "Take a look outside."

Anders turned to face the long, rectangular window that overlooked the backyard. Dense clouds of mosquitoes hovered above the ground, growing in size and strength. Black dots fed on the fallen zombie children, attacking exposed skin.

Tara said, "The sun's going down. This is their time."

Jake moved closer to the window. "It's like they're watching us."

"That's crazy," said Hank, but a growing legion of mosquitoes gathered at the glass, occasionally striking it with tiny clicks.

With a swift pull, Koska shut the window drapes. He turned to face the rest of his unit.

"Stay calm. First things first. We must secure this house. Close every door to every room. Shove something under the cracks. Make sure every window is shut tight, every fireplace flue. We'll meet back here in five minutes. Go!"

The mansion erupted with the sounds of rapid footsteps and slamming doors. Koska moved to the front entrance. The large doors appeared sealed tight. Instinctively, he flipped the lock, then chuckled at himself. Was he worried an army of mosquitoes could rotate a door handle?

Perhaps.

Regrouping in the living room five minutes later, the SWAT officers circled Koska as he radioed Operation Z's Central Command for assistance.

The radio offered no response. Instead they listened to the droning static until Jake covered his ears and erupted, "It sounds like a hundred mosquitoes. Shut it off!"

Koska snapped off the radio. "We're not getting a signal. Maybe we're out of range. Or maybe something's happened to..."

Zzt.

"Did you hear that?" said Hank.

"I sure hope that was more radio static," said Tara.

Zzt.

"Radio's off," said Koska. His eyes circled the room. "We have got ourselves a mosquito."

"Shit!" shouted Jake, spinning in a circle, waving his arms. "Find it! Kill it!"

Wham! Hank slammed the base of his rifle against the wall, startling everybody.

"Got it," he said, pulling the rifle back from a tiny black stain.

"Everybody stay quiet. Keep listening," said Koska. "There could be more."

Standing perfectly still, they glanced around the room, eyes big, ears on alert.

Zzt.

"I hear something..." said Jake.

"But I don't see it," said Tara.

"Shut up!" said Koska. "Keep listening!"

Zzt. Zzt.

Then Koska saw it – directly above them, skimming the ceiling, a tiny, floating black speck. "Look up!"

All eyes stayed on the bug as it circled in a slow descent, landing on the edge of a fat, upholstered chair.

Koska picked up an antique vase from a nearby table. He brought it down on the insect in one powerful, shattering blow.

"Got it?" said Hank.

"Got it," said Koska, breathing a sigh of relief, observing the mosquito's remains. Unfortunately, the remains left a small red stain, indicating a victim had already been claimed...

"Oh shit," said Koska under his breath.

"Aarrrgh!" roared Anders, arms outstretched, mouth opened wide, lunging for Tara. He grabbed her in a bear hug and thrust his teeth toward her neck. She desperately pushed his head away, screaming as he snapped his jaws like a mad dog.

Hank jumped on Anders' back, punching him, and the large man swirled around to swat him away with his big arms. Tara slipped free in the commotion and Koska had a split second to pull off a clean shot. He blasted a hole through Anders' temple and the big man toppled, completing a whirlwind transition from alive to undead to real dead in less than a minute.

"Damn, he was bit and we didn't even know it!" said Hank, rising from the floor.

Koska swung his gun from Anders to Jake, who stood, wide-eyed in terror, across the room.

"What about you?" Koska asked Jake.

"What – what about me?"

"You sure you don't have any bites?"

"Positive. I mean it. I'm clean!"

"Then why," asked Koska, "did I just see you scratching your face?"

"Scratch? Me? N-no..."

"You scratched under your left ear. You have an itch, don't you..."

"Please..." said Jake. "I'm fine..."

Hank walked over, examined Jake and frowned. "I see a little red bump. Right under your ear."

"It's not what it seems!" said Jake, panicked. "I got bad skin."

"You know what this means, don't you?" said Koska calmly, pointing the rifle at him.

"Shit..." said Tara, looking down at the ground. "Son of a bitch!"

"I'm a goner," said Jake in a small voice.

Koska slowly nodded his head.

Jake shut his eyes, resigned. He reached up... and scratched hard at the mosquito bite, relieved by the freedom to do so. The truth was out. "Okay... Get it over with..." He continued scratching.

Koska hesitated. He had known Jake for seven years. This wasn't going to be easy.

He had never killed a friend before.

Koska could see that Jake was trembling.

"Before we do this..." said Koska. "You want a drink? I got my good stuff."

Jake looked at him and made a small, crooked smile. "You got the SC?"

"It's part of my gear. Goes everywhere I go. You know that." Koska reached into his jacket, the secret pocket sewed on the inside, and pulled out a small flask of Southern Comfort, 100 proof. He reserved this private stash for those harrowing moments where he desperately needed to collect his nerves.

This was one of those times.

Koska consumed a quick, hard shot of the liquor. It burned. It felt good.

He stepped over to Jake.

"Open your mouth, I'll pour it in," he said. "I don't want your mouth to touch the flask. Germs. I'm sure you'll understand."

"Of course," said Jake. He tilted his head back, opened his mouth and shut his eyes.

Koska poured a steady trickle into Jake's mouth. Jake kept drinking until he couldn't keep up with the alcohol stream and coughed.

Koska pulled the flask back. Jake completed a swallow. "Thank you," he sputtered.

"Ready now?" said Koska.

"Ready," said Jake.

Koska placed the open flask on a nearby table, next to its cap. He brought the rifle into firing position. He aimed for the center of Jake's forehead.

"Goodbye Jake," said Tara.

"We love you, man," said Hank.

"I'm sorry, Jake," said Koska, and he knew there was no more time to waste...a foggy look had started to fill Jake's eyes. His skin was turning pale. He began to rock off balance. His lips moved, possibly saying, "Goodbye" and then Jake was gone, replaced by another zombie thing, disguised as Jake, but not him, not really...

Blam.

Jake dropped dead to the floor.

"Now it's just the three of us," said Hank.

"Those fucking bugs," said Tara between clenched teeth. "Those goddamned fucking bugs!"

"We have to stay cool," said Koska. "Any one of us could be next. Keep watching the room. We can't let a single mosquito to escape our sight."

Hank continued eyeballing the room. "This is making me a nervous wreck. I'm jumping at every little speck."

"It's getting darker in here," said Tara. "It'll be harder to spot them."

Koska stepped over to a thick candle resting on a buffet cabinet. He checked the drawers until he found a box of matches. "This will give us some light, plus they won't like the flame."

He lit the candle and its soft glow flickered against the living room walls. Outside, the sun melted into dusk. The mansion's remote location promised a night of total and utter darkness.

"That little flame isn't going to scare away anything," said Tara.

"Ssh!" said Hank. "I think I hear something."

The three of them froze.

After a long moment, Hank said, "Now I don't hear it."

"Maybe it's landed," said Koska.

Tara compulsively brushed her arms and face. "I'm not going to be done in by a freaking mosquito!"

"I think I see something..." said Hank, pointing across the room. "On the curtains."

"That's just a spot," said Koska, straining for a closer look.

"These goddamned shadows are playing tricks," growled Hank.

"Shut up! I hear something," said Tara. "Do you hear it?"

Hank listened hard and shook his head. He looked over at Koska.

Koska said, "No... wait... maybe... I hear a humming sound..."

Tara shrieked, "Son of a bitch, one just flew past my ear!" She grabbed a fireplace poker and started swinging it wildly. "Where are you? I'll kill you!"

Koska yelled, "On the lampshade!"

Tara hammered the poker against the lampshade, sending the lamp crashing to the floor.

"Is it dead?" asked Hank.

"Has to be," said Tara. "I hit it straight on. I don't miss." She bent over the lamp.

A tiny, mangled mosquito lay on the floor next to the lamp wreckage. "He's history," she said.

But then the mosquito somehow pulled itself together, straightening its bent limbs. In an instant, it jumped from the floor.

The three SWAT agents shouted in unison.

"It's a goddamned super mosquito!" said Hank. "The zombie blood... it rejuvenates them. These things won't be easy to kill."

"All the pesticide in the world might not stop them," said Koska, keeping his eyes on the lethal, fluttering speck.

"We can't beat them," said Hank, his voice wavering with resignation. "There are too many."

"Hell yes we can," growled Tara. Her eyes flashed wild, overcome by the madness of their predicament. "We'll kill every last one of them. I don't care if there are hundreds, millions, they're all DEAD!"

"I see one on the couch!" yelled Hank.

Tara whipped around and fired her machine gun at the mosquito. "Die you son of a bitch!"

"Tara, NO!" shouted Koska. Tara blasted the room with bullets, screaming profanity, crazed with panic. Koska ran to stop her, but it was too late. A spray of bullets punctured the drapes... shattering the glass behind them.

Then Tara froze, struck by the realization of what she had just done. The gun dropped to her side.

"Oh shi—" she started and before she could finish, a stream of mosquitoes emerged from behind the curtains. They collected into a single black cloud and attacked Tara's face.

Tara screamed, clawing at her eyes, ears, nose and mouth. They stung her repeatedly, dozens of tiny needles piercing her skin, invading every orifice.

Koska snatched the burning candle from the buffet. He flung it into the curtains and they erupted into flames. The billowing smoke disoriented the mosquitoes... at least for a moment.

Koska turned to Hank. "Quick, into the kitchen!"

"One sec." Hank held out his pistol, steadying his arm. With a single bullet, he shot Tara in the head and her screaming stopped.

Before racing into the kitchen, Koska grabbed his flask of Southern Comfort and capped it. He returned it to the pocket in the lining of his jacket. Priorities.

Once inside the kitchen, Hank and Koska slammed the doors and wedged dish towels to fill the cracks underneath. They tried to ignore the dead mother zombie in the apron, still sprawled on the floor.

Koska stared at Hank, searching for any faded look in his eyes. "You okay?"

"I'm cool. I'm good," said Hank. "You?"

"I'm clean. But we gotta get out of this house. Those things know we're in here. The smoke will only stop them for so long."

"Won't it be worse outside?"

"Yes, but if we can make it to the van, we'll be safe." Koska peered out a small window above the sink, focused on the armored vehicle parked a few hundred feet away. "Inside the van, we can get to our gas masks. We'll put them on to protect our faces. We can get our gloves. There won't be an inch of exposed skin."

Hank asked, "But how do we get to the van without getting chewed up?"

Black clouds hovered in the front yard, legions of mosquitoes thirsty for their next blood fix. Koska could see Grandpa Zombie face down on the red brick walkway, covered in insects, like a second skin. He turned back to look at the kitchen doors, where wisps of smoke trickled from the edges.

"If we stay here, we'll be cooked alive," said Koska.

"And if we go out there, we'll be eaten alive," responded Hank.

Koska continued to watch the smoke. It gave him an idea. "Not necessarily..." he said.

Koska reached down to his SWAT utility belt and extracted a small cylinder. "I have two flash-burn grenades. This is what I used on that barricaded wife killer in Baton Rouge, remember? They don't make a big explosion, but they simulate one to create a lot of confusion and disorient the enemy. They produce a lot of smoke..."

"...to hold off the mosquitoes," said Hank.

"Precisely."

"It's worth a try." He could hear the crackling flames in the living room. "We don't have much time."

"Then say a prayer," said Koska, gripping a grenade in each hand. "Because here we go."

Koska kicked open the kitchen door with a swift thrust of his boot. He plunged forward into the fiery living room, immediately spotting swirling clouds of black specks – ashes or bugs? No time to figure it out.

"Keep moving!" he bellowed at Hank, who followed behind.

They made it to the front doors and Koska pulled them open.

Sure enough, the front yard was dense with mosquito swarms creating a single, steady hum like a monstrous machine. Before the insects could pursue the fresh prey, Koska lobbed the first grenade. It lit up the yard with a loud bang, spewing billows of smoke.

Koska ran into the haze, keeping his eyes focused on the van on the other side. He could hear mosquitoes buzzing near his face, hopefully too dazed to attack.

Koska tossed the second grenade and again the yard illuminated for a quick blink of daylight before going dark and thickening with smoke. Koska could hear Hank coughing behind him.

Almost there.

Koska fell on the door handle, yanked it and jumped into the van at the same time Hank entered from the passenger side.

They slammed their doors and immediately scrambled for the gloves and gas masks.

Koska tightened his mask as tight as he could without cutting off his circulation. He heard his own panting amplified in his ears. He tugged the gloves as high up on the wrists as they could go.

Safe at last.

He looked at Hank. Hank also wore gloves and a gas mask, covered from head to toe. He gave Koska a thumbs up.

Koska returned the thumbs up, grinning. He turned to look back at the mansion.

The fire was spreading fast and several windows along the ground floor glowed orange. The front yard remained a hazy fog of smoke. Angry black specks zigged and zagged in the air, circling the van.

Koska watched the mosquitoes skip across the windshield, separated from their food, watching through the glass, hungry.

"The vents are closed, everything's sealed tight," said Koska. "They're not getting in." He finally felt a moment of triumph over these savage insects. He stuck his middle finger out at them.

"Screw you, zombie mosquitoes!" he called out and the comment was so absurd, so hopelessly crazy, that he had to laugh.

Hank joined him in the laughter. Once they got going, the two of them couldn't stop. They laughed like lunatics, rocking in their seats, clutching their sides, overcome with relief and delirious from the sheer absurdity of it all. The van filled with their raucous laughter...

...and then Koska abruptly stopped.

He stared in horror at his partner.

Hank realized something was wrong and sobered up, returning the stare. "What is it? What is it?"

Koska's eyes observed a small, dancing mosquito caught on the inside of Hank's gas mask. Before Koska could reach out and rip the mask off, the mosquito landed on the bridge of Hank's nose.

Hank jerked his head back, feeling a tiny jolt of pain, and in an instant, all was lost and both men knew it.

Hank's eyes filled with tears.

Koska reached for his gun.

Hank begged, "Don't do it." He brought out his own pistol. "I'll do it."

Hank climbed out of the van, shut the door, and planted his boots into the swampy Louisiana bayou. He placed the pistol to his temple and shut his eyes. Clouds of mosquitoes swirled around him, searching for an entry.

Koska turned the ignition and the engine roared. He thrust the van forward. He did not look back.

As he sped away from the burning southern mansion, flames licking the sky, he heard a single gunshot.

Koska wept throughout the drive back into town.

***

Koska arrived at Operation Z's Command Center representing the sole survivor of his unit. His tale of deadly swamp mosquitoes confirmed the military's worst fears: the entire town of Clarkson would have to be destroyed. Total annihilation was the only way to ensure the removal of every living organism that might carry the zombie plague.

After the uninfected townspeople had been rescued, the SWAT force pulled out and the military moved in. They were equipped with a single mission: to devastate everything within the town's boundaries and eradicate all forms of life.

The resulting explosions and fires could be seen for many miles. Clarkson was wiped off the map, replaced by a sterile, desolate dead zone of scorched earth. The nation mourned the tragedy at the same time it hailed a victory: all signs indicated that the zombie outbreak had been stopped and the plague contained.

For his courageous entry into the zombie den where it all started, Koska received special honors and recognition. He shunned the publicity the best he could out of respect for his fallen comrades. He did not return media calls.

But then an offer arrived that Koska could not refuse. As the country celebrated the swift and efficient containment of the zombie outbreak, a prominent visitor flew to the scene to personally thank the hardworking troops: the President of the United States.

The President's press secretary arranged for the media to cover the event. Koska was invited to meet the President as a representative of the state's SWAT force, while other individuals were selected on behalf of the army, air force and National Guard.

Although exhausted, Koska agreed to attend. After all, who could turn down a personal thank you from the President? Once the event concluded, Koska planned to close out his term of duty and return home to his wife and kids, whom he hadn't seen since the beginning of the zombie outbreak. He missed them terribly. He needed a return to normalcy.

The President's handlers arrived in advance to outline the protocol for the visit: Don't speak to the President unless spoken to; no autograph requests; no photographers or video aside from the authorized media attendees; and shake the President's hand only if offered.

As the momentous occasion approached, Koska grew nervous thinking about what he would say to the President, surrounded by television cameras capturing the event for a global audience. For Koska, it was the capper on the most intense week of his life and a full realization of the magnitude of the crisis.

Special occasions required special measures. Koska planned to bring a secret companion to the event – a friend with the initials SC.

The flask fit securely into the interior pocket of his sport coat and promised just what he needed to settle his nerves before the big meet and greet.

On the day of the President's visit, Koska joined six other high-ranking representatives of the victory over the zombies. They gathered in a small room in a municipal building in a town outside of Clarkson that served as home base for Operation Z's Central Command.

"The President will be here in five minutes," announced a short, brisk woman on his staff.

Koska exchanged nervous smiles with the others in his group, including the gray-haired army general who coordinated the bombing of Clarkson. While the camera crews scrambled into place, Koska took a quick step toward the wall, pretending to examine a series of framed pictures of old southern generals. With his heart thumping and back turned, he pulled out the flask and uncapped it, prepared to take a quick and calming swig.

However, as Koska removed the cap from the flask, a tiny mosquito emerged, buzzed past his ear and disappeared into the room.

"Holy--!" said Koska, stunned.

And then the realization hit him. This was the first time he had opened the flask since sharing a drink with Jake in the Leery mansion... Jake's final drink before receiving a bullet to the head.

In the madness, a mosquito must have entered the flask before Koska returned the cap.

Panicked, Koska threw aside the flask and began hunting for the escaped mosquito. He caught a glimpse of the black speck dancing across the room but then it disappeared in a sudden flash of camera lights.

"The President is here!"

Koska scrambled into place, his designated spot, standing between the army general and a National Guardsman.

The President of the United States entered the room. He stood tall, confident and immaculately dressed. He made a small speech about heroes and bravery and conquering an unspeakable enemy that threatened the country.

Then he moved down the receiving line, praising the "brave and noble combatants," shaking hands, clasping shoulders, exchanging pleasantries as video cameras and still photographers captured his gratitude for the masses.

When the President reached Koska, he smiled warmly and extended his hand. "Thank you for everything you have done for the American people," he said.

Koska reached out to accept the handshake. But then the President abruptly withdrew his hand and brought it up to his face to smack himself on the left cheek.

The president's smile vanished and he grimaced.

"Ow."

THE END

www.severedpress.com

AUTHORS

TIM CURRAN lives in Michigan and is the author of the novels Skin Medicine, Hive, Dead Sea, Resurrection, The Devil Next Door, and Biohazard. Upcoming projects include the novella The Corpse King, from Cemetery Dance, Hive 2 from Elder Signs Press, and Bone Marrow Stew, a short story collection from Tasmaniac Publications. His short stories have appeared in such magazines as City Slab, Flesh&Blood, Book of Dark Wisdom, and Inhuman, as well as anthologies such as Dead Bait, Shivers IV, High Seas Cthulhu, and, Vile Things. Find him on the web at www.corpseking.com

TED WENSKUS is a freelance writer and lives in Rochester, NY. He earned his M.A. in English literature from the State University of New York School at Brockport, writing his graduate thesis on the two-hundred-year evolution of vampire fiction. He has had several short plays produced throughout New York, as well as a short film, and is currently working on numerous projects including his first novel.

ERIC DIMBLEBY lives in the backwoods of Maine with his wife and newborn son. He works as an IT Director for a non-profit company, but spends his evenings writing short stories and novels. He is hard at work on his fourth novel, while editing and submitting his previous novels to publishers. He is not a hunter like the main character of this story. In fact, he is a vegetarian and animal lover.

WILLIAM WOOD lives with his wife and children in the mountains of Virginia in an old farmhouse turned backwards to the road. He's a lucky guy. Mostly the good kind. His short fiction can be found in titles from Living Dead Press, House of Horror, Black Matrix Publishing and Lame Goat Press and is forthcoming from Library of the Living Dead and Northern Frights Publishing. He sometimes sleeps instead of writing.

WAYNE GOODCHILD'S work appears all over the place, but most recently in issue 3 of Jodi Lee's New Bedlam project. He has also got a number of stories set to appear in various anthologies from Library of the Living Dead / Library of Horror Press. He hates creepy-crawlies, despite spending his early life in Australia, where the insects are big enough to pay rent. theycallmepotato.blogspot.com has the full skinny on this mildly astounding individual!

CARL BARKER'S work has previously appeared in *Midnight Street* and *Estronomicon*. His novella, *Chancery Lane*, is also available from *Newsstand Books*. He currently resides in the North of England and writes whenever he gets the chance. For more information about his fiction please visit his website, www.holeinthepage.co.uk.

RYAN THOMAS works as an editor in San Diego, California. You can usually find him in the bars on the weekends playing with his band, The Buzzbombs. When he is not writing or rocking out, he is at home with his cat, Elvis, watching really bad B-movies. His novels include The Summer I Died, Ratings Game, and Hissers. His shorts stories and novellas have appeared in numerous markets such as Twisted Cat Tales, Undead 2 & 3, Undead: Headshot Quartet, Vault of Punk Horror, Hallow's Eve, Elements of the Apocalypse, Dead Science, Nanobison, Space Squid and many more. Visit him online at www.ryancthomas.com

J. GILLIAM MARTIN died in 2008, and is now the personal scribe of the devil Himself. 2010 will be the year of Hell's literature, including many published shorts and his first novel, "The Preposterous Baron Grill" from Severed Press. His current project, Hippies vs Zombies, can be read at **SadKraken.Blogspot.com**. He burns in Hell with his wife, abominable beagle, and demonic chihuahua.

ANTHONY WEDD was born in Ceduna in South Australia in 1971. He spent time in a variety of country towns across South Australia as a child before studying Physics at Flinders University in Adelaide. After brief stints as a computer programmer and an applied physicist, he became a meteorologist in 1999 and moved to Brisbane, where he still resides. He has been a devoted fan of horror fiction since adolescence and would cite Ramsey Campbell as his favourite author in the genre. In his spare time, he enjoys writing and long drives in the outback at night.

ANTHONY GIANGREGORIO is the author and editor of more than 40 novels, almost all of them about zombies. His work has appeared in Dead Science by Coscomentertainment, Dead Worlds: Undead Stories Volumes 1-6, and Wolves of War by Library of the Living Dead Press. He also has stories in End of Days: An Apocalyptic Anthology Vol. 1 -3, the Book of the Dead series Vol. 1-4 by LDP, and two

anthologies with Pill Hill Press. He is also the creator of the popular action/zombie series titled Deadwater.
Check out his website at www.undeadpress.com.

HAYDEN WILLIAMS is a Welsh-New Zealand writer whose poetry, essays, articles and short fiction have appeared in a variety of publications. His story 'The Old Man and the Puddle' was recently published in The Severed Press anthology 'Dead Bait'. He has an interest in Jungian psychology and is at a total loss as to what to do with his life next besides writing.

BRIAN PINKERTON'S novels include the thrillers Abducted and Vengeance for Leisure Books. His other books include Killer's Diary and Killing the Boss. His short story "Lower Wacker Blues" appears in the crime anthology Chicago Blues. Brian's screenplays have finished in the top 100 of Project Greenlight and top two percent of the Nicholl Fellowship of the Academy of Motion Picture Arts and Sciences. His cyberhome is www.brianpinkerton.com

Breinigsville, PA USA
15 November 2010
249382BV00001B/11/P

9 780980 606591